SMALL HOURS

Also by Bobby Palmer

Isaac and the Egg

BOBBY PALMER

SMALL HOURS

REVIEW

First published in Great Britain in 2024 by
Headline Review
An imprint of Headline Publishing Group

1

Cataloguing in Publication Data is available from the British Library

Hardback ISBN 978 1 0354 0265 6
Trade paperback ISBN 978 1 0354 0264 9

Typeset in Adobe Caslon by CC Book Production

Printed and bound in Great Britain by Clays Ltd, Elcograf S.p.A.

Headline's policy is to use papers that are natural, renewable and recyclable products and made from wood grown in well-managed forests and other controlled sources. The logging and manufacturing processes are expected to conform to the environmental regulations of the country of origin.

HEADLINE PUBLISHING GROUP
An Hachette UK Company
Carmelite House
50 Victoria Embankment
London EC4Y 0DZ

www.headline.co.uk
www.hachette.co.uk

For my parents

'My father, who had derived such happiness from his childhood, found in me the companion with whom he could return there.'

Christopher Milne, *The Enchanted Places*

'Some people talk to animals. Not many listen though. That's the problem.'

A. A. Milne, *Winnie-the-Pooh*

Forest floor.

Between trees, under rain

and over puddles, trees, more trees.

There. Over there. Spectacles, dropped in the dirt.

The fox stops, noses them, looks around for their owner.

Humans love to be lost. The fox's eyes shine like coins found.

The fox runs now. It runs and runs, the water running off its back.

This is it, the fox realises. Cold rain on my fur, warm earth beneath my paws.

I exist, thinks the running fox. I live, I've existed, and I am happy to have done so.

It runs and it runs, until: a bright flash, a loud bang. Lightning? The fox stops.

The sky falls in sheets and the ground has become a flat, slick mirror.

The fox does not move. It is waiting for something, for someone.

A man steps from between the trees. Wild, wide eyes.

Hair like beansprouts. Soaking wet, caked in mud.

He shields his eyes. He squints.

Looking for something? Yes.

For you.

part one
CITY

one

'Sorry, I think I'm hearing things.'

Jack hadn't been paying attention. In his defence, there was a squirrel jumping from branch to branch in the tree outside the window of the meeting room.

'No, you aren't hearing things.'

Jack allowed his vision to blur, the acrobatic squirrel becoming an indistinct smudge of fur, yanked this way and that like a puppet on a string. His eyes refocused, taking in the two men opposite. The man on the left's brow was furrowed, the man on the right's mouth tightly pursed. I wasn't ignoring you, Jack wanted to say. There was a squirrel.

'Sold,' he said, instead. He turned the word over in his mouth. It had a bad aftertaste. 'Wait. Sold?'

Across the glass-topped table, Hugh looked at Hugo. Hugo looked at Hugh. Hugh laced his fingers before him on the

5

tabletop. Visible through the glass, one of Hugo's chino-clad knees began to jiggle. Jack looked from Hugh to Hugo, Hugo to Hugh. To most people, they'd be indistinguishable. But up close, Hugh's hair was mousy brown, Hugo's a dirty blond. Hugh tended to smirk, while Hugo preferred a sneer. They both stared at him with inscrutable expressions now, as if they might break character at any moment and admit it was all a joke. Jack was the first to break eye contact, looking down at his legs. His own knee was jiggling now, no matter how hard he tried to stop it.

'Yes,' said Hugh.

'The company is being sold,' said Hugo.

Not 'We're selling the company', as that would suggest some agency on their behalf. And to come to a decision like that at an agency like this, they would have had to tell their third-in-command. Jack handled the money side of things. And though Hugh and Hugo had begun to take more of an interest in the company accounts of late, asking him to produce extensive financial records for mysterious third parties, Jack had been stretched so thin that he hadn't had the time to question their motives. He'd been silently optimistic, hoping that there might be new backers on the horizon. He'd been obliging, as per usual. He rarely asked questions.

Jack's eyes flicked over the mug in front of him, the company logo on the side, the black coffee sitting untouched. He wondered if it would seem strange to take his first sip now. He wondered if it had already gone cold. He wondered if he was so sweaty because, on a warm day like this, he'd opted for smart wool trousers and a button-down shirt. He'd known he had an important meeting this morning, but he hadn't expected it to be about this. Jack clenched his fists, unclenched them, set his palms flat on the tabletop. He moved them again, transferring them to his lap, leaving a sweaty smear on the glass. He looked up at Hugh and Hugo, avoiding the brown envelope that lay on the table between them.

'Sold to whom?'

The pair shared a glance.

'Multiple buyers,' one said.

'Sold off, really,' added the other.

'Stripped for parts.'

'Gutted.' A pause. 'Like a fish.'

Jack didn't know what to say. He tended to avoid conflict, so he wouldn't say what he wanted to say, which was: how could you? And how am I only now hearing about it? Instead, he stole a quick look at the envelope. It was thin. A redundancy pay-off would be thicker. Wouldn't it? Working things out was Jack's forte. And Jack had worked out, a while ago, that he could make himself into someone indispensable. He never took time off. He worked harder than anyone else. Redundancies happened to other people, people less integral to the operation, people who didn't want it as much as he did. Even as his bosses' spending became ever more erratic and the company found itself in ever-choppier waters, Jack had assumed that he could fix things. He'd thought that he alone could turn this ship around. He hadn't considered that Hugh and Hugo might have been making their own plans behind his back. Now their lifeboat was disappearing into the distance, and here he was, clinging to a glass tabletop to keep from drowning. There were beads of sweat forming on Jack's hairline. He was beginning to think it wasn't just his clothes. He was beginning to think he'd made a miscalculation.

'So, we keep going?' Jack said, though his voice betrayed him. 'With new backing?'

Silence.

'We're actually going to be stepping back,' Hugh said, eventually, reluctantly.

'Stepping back?' Jack blinked at one of them, then the other. 'What about me?'

'That's the great thing,' Hugo said. 'The world's your oyster.'

Hugo and Hugh both looked down at the envelope. They both looked back up at Jack. In perfect unison, they frowned. The effect was unnerving. There was a sound from outside the meeting room, and Jack glanced over his shoulder, as if expecting to see someone holding up a placard with instructions. *Frown.* But, no. Just two of his colleagues, weeping. Jack watched as one of them put his arms around the other, gently manoeuvring her out of the way of two removal men shimmying past, carrying the coffee machine. He'd imagined offering to mentor these two, both junior to him, next year. He'd hoped that he'd be good at it. He'd hoped that he'd have more time. Jack had barely ever spoken to them, beyond weekly team meetings and hurried budget reports. He'd never been a shoulder to cry on.

Jack's eyes returned to Hugh and Hugo. He wanted to say, surely there's something we can do to fix this. Surely at least *I* can stay.

'We all wanted to make it work,' said Hugo.

'We're all gutted,' said Hugh, sliding the envelope slowly across the table.

'Gutted,' Jack murmured. 'Like a fish.'

His eyes went to the window again, but the squirrel was gone. He felt the sharp corner of the envelope pressing against his solar plexus. He took it, slid it under the table, let it sit unopened on his lap.

'We're going to the pub in a bit,' said Hugo.

'For a swiftie,' said Hugh.

'Or four.'

'The parting glass.'

Jack knew it would be odd to open the envelope right now, just as he knew it would be odd to drink his coffee, now definitely cold. He knew he couldn't grab both Hugh and Hugo by the collars of their clean shirts and slam their heads into the thick glass below, though the twitching of his hands made him feel like he just might. Bile rose in his throat. His vision was edged with black clouds, with sparkling lights. He needed to be somewhere, anywhere, else. Abruptly, he pushed back his chair and stood up. The metal legs clanged against the glass wall of the meeting room. Jack gulped, holding tightly on to the envelope as if they might try to take it back. Tell them what you really think, he thought.

'Thank you,' was what he said, forcing his mouth into a smile.

'No,' they both replied, smiles unforced. 'Thank *you*.'

The glass door of the meeting room wobbled pathetically as Jack closed it behind him. The door of the office building was quieter, the click of it shutting behind him barely audible over the howling sirens and tutting bicycle spokes, the beep-beep-beep of a reversing truck, the hyena-like laughter of a passer-by on the phone. And the hollow sound of Jack's own, thudding heartbeat, which now filled his ears at such a deafening volume that he felt as if it might knock him off his feet. Jack found himself, lost, on the pavement. For the first time in over a decade, he didn't have a clue what came next.

————

To Jack Penwick's logical brain, his career had been like a computer game. Everything was laid out in levels to be completed, with high scores to be achieved if he only worked hard enough. Jack was a numbers guy, and nothing had ever added up so easily. For the best part of the last fifteen years, he had progressed diligently from stage to stage. In his late teens, while his schoolmates deferred university places and planned gap years, he landed work experience in the city with their uncles and godfathers. He got himself on a good course at a good university, scored an even better placement in his third year, beat out competition for the best graduate scheme going when graduation came around. Finance felt like a calling, the ultimate equation to be solved. But as the numbers grew bigger, the levels got harder. And as the hours got longer, the friendly faces became fewer and further between. If it became more difficult to come up for air, to look around and wonder what he actually wanted – and if this was actually it – then that email from Hugh a couple of years ago came at just the right moment to stick a plaster over the opening wound. Jack and Hugh had known each other since university. Now, with Hugh's contacts and the financial backing of his friend Hugo's father, they were starting their own business. They shook his hand. They offered him equity. They showed him the numbers, and the numbers looked good. When they told him that the company was going to be a unicorn, Jack had swallowed it hook, line and sinker. Like a fish.

Jack now sat beneath a tree, on a bench on the common, unsure exactly how he'd ended up there. Leaving the office had been like stumbling, bloodied, from a battlefield, P45s billowing out of printers and shreds of sensitive documents raining from roaring shredders. He remembered, of course, that he'd been on the pavement outside his office, then on a bus. He'd disembarked at his usual stop, taken the usual, direct route home across the common. But his memory of these events – and the mechanics of how they'd led here, to this particular bench – were hazy. He supposed he'd needed a rest. He supposed there wasn't much point going any further. Jack had no one to come home to, no one to tell. And the spacious two-floor flat which had once been a towering monument to his sizeable earnings already seemed like a gaping void into which he was throwing an income he no longer had.

It was game over. How had Jack not seen this coming? And even if he'd had an inkling, how had he not been smart enough to stop it? He'd thought of himself as a startup Svengali, a Doctor Dolittle for the age of digital disruptors. He might not have been the boss, but he'd thought he had a handle on things. He'd at least assumed there would be more conversations before that one, the final one. He reflected on the open-plan loft office that had cost four times what the company could afford, the ingoings and outgoings that were uneven, even to him, the guy who was supposed to make it all add up. Hugh and Hugo never listened. They fobbed him off with the same things they said to all the app developers, to the event organisers, to the angel investors with deep pockets and short attention spans. Don't focus on the numbers. Focus on the feeling.

Jack didn't feel good. From the glances he was getting, he looked even worse. His hair had become lank in the heat, his exhausted eyes ringed by welts of purple. His face was stuck in a grimace, though that wasn't just a today problem. Jack had spent £4,000 having his teeth whitened and straightened a couple of years ago, and for what? Smiling still didn't come naturally. He massaged his jaw, catching the concerned eye of a woman pushing a toddler in a pushchair. Jack looked down at the box he was clutching. It had been the only empty container left in the almost-empty office, one last humiliation on his way out. A huge, gold-ribbon-wrapped gift box, now filled with the sparse remnants of his former life. A notebook, a laptop, a vape pen. One phone charger, one vape charger, one laptop charger. One charging case, containing one pair of wireless headphones. One small desk plant, proven to boost office productivity. One small bottle of CBD drops, proven to reduce work stress. The woman with the pushchair was smiling now. She probably thought it was his birthday.

Jack scowled, then opened the box and took out his vape, which he inhaled from as if it were an oxygen supply. As steam billowed from his nostrils, he surveyed his surroundings. The lunchtime sunbathers with their picnic blankets had moved on, leaving only a few stragglers. A couple of teenagers were snogging on the next bench along. A greyhound zipped back and forth across the dry grass, chasing squirrels it never managed to catch. Jack thought of the brown envelope in the box, of what might be inside. He didn't know what he'd do without a job. He didn't know how he'd cope, who he should call. His family had never understood the importance of his work, and he'd never been much good at maintaining friendships. Above his head, a pair of bright green parakeets leapt from a branch and took flight over the common. Jack thought about crying. He'd never been much good at that, either.

Jack's shoulders were rigid, his upper lip stiff as ever. But as he sat on the bench and stared out across a hazy expanse of yellowing grass, he felt something begin to give. It started with a jiggle in his left leg, then a slight twitch in his right eyelid. Then, pain, both physical and metaphysical. He clenched his fists, clenched his jaw, rocked slightly back and then slightly forth. He wondered if it might be a migraine. He'd been plagued by them all his adult life. It felt like there was always one hiding in his peripheral vision, crouching just out of sight behind his eyes. They seemed to creep up on him from nowhere. He could pinpoint all of the triggers: screens, stress, screens, too much socialising, too many screens. Was it normal to always feel this tired? To be thirty-three years old and exhausted in every bone in one's body, at every hour of every day? Creatine was a plaster, caffeine a crutch. And though Jack kept himself going with six black coffees a day, he was really surviving on adrenaline alone. When a migraine did finally break against the walls of his brain, all he could do was crawl to his bedroom, close the blinds and ride the crashing wave with his head under a pillow.

He wanted to crawl there now, back to his bed, and envelope himself in darkness. He closed his eyes, tried to shut out the ever-familiar nausea and that excruciating pain that seemed to slice like a cleaver through his cranium. This time, there was a noise attached to the pain. Something tinny. Not the wheeze of distant traffic or the squeal of playing children, but a scratch, a scrape, a high-pitched, hollow moan. Like the sound of an old radio, tuning in.

Jack rubbed his eyes, then the back of his taut neck. He thought of his empty bed, in his flat on the other side of the common. He thought of Hugh and Hugo, back in the office on the other side of a glass table. And as he sat there on the bench, plagued by that awful sound scraping itself along the back wall of his skull, the still-functioning part of Jack's brain beat against the confines of his throbbing head. He held on to his seat as if he were battling seasickness, tried to find a fixed point on the horizon. To focus on something, anything.

There, in the distance. Something moving, slowly, across the grass. Jack steadied his breathing, felt some of the tension dissipate. It was a dog, he thought. But then, it didn't seem to have an owner. And it wasn't moving like any dog he'd seen before. His heartbeat picked up again. The dog-like creature was limping, loping. Jack leaned forward, frowning. There were two black dots behind it, jumping about, not leaving it alone. With his eyes almost closed, the creature looked like a lit match, a tiny sun with two black planets in its orbit. With his eyes wide open, it looked like what it really was.

A fox. An injured fox. A half-dead fox, stalked by crows.

two

Did you know?
On Alderney, the hedgehogs are blonde.

If he stood in a particular clearing in a wild, old place and he
opened his eyes, he'd see this.

Through the clearing he'd see the trees, and through the
trees he'd see the woods.

Through the woods he'd see the bracken, and through the
bracken a hedge which turns into a slope which turns into a
garden.

And there's a type of shrew that only occurs
on the Isles of Scilly.

The lesser white-toothed shrew, it's called.

Looking further still, he'd see what the garden holds. A disused shed, a peeling set of patio furniture, the rotting husk of a half-built treehouse.

Beyond the patio furniture, a building. The lower half mossy brick, the upper half weathered white clapboard.

It's the only shrew that lives on a beach.
Imagine that.

Tiles tumble from the roof, ivy creeps up from the ground.

The woods seem hungry to swallow the house up.

The forest wants it back.

One unassuming little ancestor sneaks on to a boat.
Causes a genetic schism.

He'd look, keep looking. A window in the brickwork, the frame painted apple green years ago, then left to the elements.

Through the latticed panes a woman would stare, a half-empty mug in her hand.

Seated at the table behind her, there he'd be.

Now you've got blonde hedgehogs.
And your shrews fall asleep to the sound of the sea.

Looking at nothing and thinking of nothing more, his palms flat on the table, his marmalade-on-toast untouched in front of him.

He'd turn to his wife, look as if he might be about to say something. He'd look beyond her, instead.

His eyes would find the window. Through it he'd stare.

Isn't the world wonderful?

He'd stare through the glass, stare further, through the garden. He'd stare through the bracken and the woods and the trees. He'd stare into the wild.

Something would be staring back.

three

'Hello?'

Jack had dialled the number automatically, right after he'd automatically crossed the common to reach the fox. He'd stood up from the bench, pointed and looked around him, but there'd been nobody to confirm what he was seeing. Just him, a fox, and a hundred yards between them. So, although Jack Penwick wouldn't have thought he was the sort of person who'd rush to rescue an injured animal, rush he did. He told himself he just needed a closer look. To make a calculation. Now he stood here, the fox swaying in front of him. Jack was swaying, too. He'd made the call without thinking. Someone from an animal-rescue charity was asking questions on the other end of the line.

Hello there. Can I start by taking your name, please?

Around the fox's ears and down its scruff, bright orange fur

19

blazed like the head of a comet. By its bony shoulders the fire dwindled. Somewhere around the fox's midriff it sputtered out entirely. The fox was almost bald on its lower back, its dry skin crackling like dying ashes in a grate, its tail and skinny hind legs curled like paper thrown on to a hearth. The animal had its head bowed towards the earth, scarcely registering Jack's proximity. Its snout drooped, its eyes with it. It limped forwards a couple of steps, tottered, its twisted legs barely able to touch the ground. It was those legs which the hungry crows tried to peck, each jab only narrowly missing. Jack had always been squeamish, couldn't abide the sight of blood. But even as he averted his eyes from the fox, his conscience surprised him by putting its foot down. When we see an animal in pain, it said, we don't just look the other way.

'Jack. My name is Jack.'

The fox tilted its head slightly, as if listening. Slowly, its body followed. It lolled to one side, caught itself, quivered with the effort. Foxes were a familiar sight around here. Jack sometimes fed them loaf crusts or end-of-night fried chicken, when he was sure that no one else was looking. But to see one in broad daylight, so brazenly out and about, felt jarring. It was so *orange*. Jack blinked rapidly. His eyes were dry. His head was hurting again, the pain now lodged just behind his brow.

'I've found a fox.'

A fox?

'An injured fox.'

The radio-tuning sound was back, too. It whirred in and out of Jack's brain, as if someone was turning a dial at the base of his skull. The cawing of the crows below sounded like someone

20

dragging open a heavy door on creaking hinges. It sounded like laughter. Jack was hit by a wave of nauseous confusion. Why was he out here? Why wasn't he in the office? He looked from the crows to the swaying fox, aware that the voice on the other end of the phone was still asking questions, aware that he was somehow managing to answer them.

What's wrong with the fox?

Where to start? It looked like its back half was already dead, waiting for the front half to catch up. The crows may as well have been tying napkins around their necks.

'It's . . .'

The fur diminished the further down the fox it got. It made its orange head look so large, its purple body so small. Its tail was as bald as a rat's, its shoulders mottled grey and hunched like a hyena's. The white apron beneath its throat was limp and dirty, its black ears drooping, its eyes screwed shut. The fox kept trying to sit, but its hind legs seemed so painful that it winced every time its rump brushed the ground. There was a railway running along the edge of the common, to the left, the direction from which the fox had limped. Perhaps it been caught on the tracks.

'It looks burnt.'

Although, no. Its skin wasn't scorched, its fur far from singed. It wasn't so much baked as blistered. Peering closer, Jack could see that the fox was covered in sores, travelling up its bony legs and jutting ribs and along the ridges of its hairless spine. It looked like it had scratched off half of its fur.

'Fleas,' said Jack. 'No. Mange.'

That's how they'd describe it on TV. Mangy. A mangy animal.

Mange?

'It looks pretty mangy to me.'

Jack suddenly felt unclean. He took an almost-involuntary step back, the fox's head moving ever so slightly with him.

Where exactly are you?

Taking his eyes off the fox, Jack scanned the common, the slope down to the railway, the line of trees on the opposite side. Beyond that, the busy road. Beyond that, a scattering of cafés and shops. Beyond even that, his street, his apartment. He suddenly felt exposed. What if one of his neighbours saw him, skiving from work, stuck between a dying fox and some carrion crows? Would they wonder why he was out here, in the middle of the day? Jack refused to consider the fact that no one would recognise him, that none of his neighbours even knew what he looked like.

'I'm on the common,' he said. 'In the middle of the common.'

He squinted, gave a road name. Squinted harder, searching for another. He could hear the operator's fingers clacking on a keyboard.

And is it moving?

'The common?'

The fox.

The creature had grown still, save for the odd shudder and the occasional twitch.

'No.'

And does it stay still if you approach it?

'Approach it?'

Yes, approach it.

'I haven't tried.'

The fox had raised its head slightly. Jack avoided its gaze.

I'm going to need you to approach the fox, said the operator. *If it's able to run away, there's no use getting someone out to try and help it.*

'What if it bites?'

It shouldn't bite.

'Shouldn't?'

You could use a broom.

'I don't have a broom,' said Jack. 'I'm on the common.'

A pause on the other end of the line. *You could use a branch.*

'I don't have a—' Jack's eyes, still downcast, alighted on something lying on the grass. 'OK, I have a branch.'

As Jack crouched to pick up an unwieldy stick left behind by a long-gone dog, he could feel the fox's eyes on him, burning into him. One hand firmly on the branch, Jack looked up. The fox was doing its best to watch him, though it couldn't quite raise its head high enough. Its eyes were somehow more orange than the fur around them, so bright that they blazed against the dirty, greying fur along its snout. There was something livid about them, as if its head was being squeezed by some unseen force, as if the effort with which it was staring at Jack might cause its eyeballs to pop right out of its skull. *Help me*, those eyes seemed to say. *I need your help.*

'It's going to be alright,' Jack said, in a voice which didn't sound like his.

And, despite everything, he almost believed what he said. He suddenly felt calmer than he had all day. The radio tuning had stopped, as had the throbbing pain in his forehead. In a world that was completely silent, a world that contained only himself and the fox, Jack held up his hand like a lion tamer, palm facing the wild beast. With the branch held like a spear in the other, he approached. The fox just watched him. Jack thrust the branch forwards, scaring away the crows. The fox didn't flinch. Even when Jack waved the stick directly under the animal's snout, even when he was so close that he could have reached out and stroked its matted fur, the animal didn't move an inch.

'It's not running away.'

Even when you get close to it?

'Even when I get close to it.'

And is it contained?

'Contained?'

As in, could it run away if it wanted to?

'It's not going to . . . Shit.'

The fox was running away. With surprising agility, the creature darted around Jack, limping through the line of trees and across the path to the edge of the road. Jack followed it, swearing and tripping on the discarded branch as he went.

'Stop that fox!'

On the street, the fox was already causing problems. It had rushed out in front of a bike, which had screeched to a halt. The bearded, Lycra-clad rider was half-heartedly attempting to obey Jack's order, using his bike wheel to block the fox's escape across the road. This only made the fox more desperate. It peered through the spokes of the wheel like the bars of a cage, its hackles raised, its neck twitching this way and that, its ugly, hairless tail flicking about like a fresh-caught eel. The fox feinted one way, throwing the cyclist off balance, and quickly fled in the other direction. Jack gave chase, dashing across the road in the wake of a bin lorry, through a heavy fog of exhaust and a hot flurry of newspaper scraps. He extended his palms and mouthed rushed apologies at the drivers. Horns beeped, tyres screeched. Post vans and courier scooters clipped by, none of them flattening the fox, some of them very nearly flattening Jack.

Are you still with the fox?

'Hold on,' Jack said, to the operator. 'Hold on,' he said, to the fox.

Exhausted after its bid for freedom, the fox was now limping slowly along the pavement, using only one of its shrivelled back legs for support. Jack, out of breath, followed. The chase had taken it out of him, too. The fox rounded a corner. Jack rounded the corner as well. Seeing no sign of the fox, he felt more panic than relief. Then, a flicker of movement beneath a parked car. Legs. Two strong and blackish orange, two weak and purplish grey. Jack peeked underneath a gleaming Jaguar and spotted the fox, sequestered in the driveway of an imposing townhouse. The animal looked closer than ever to collapsing, desperately trying to sit down, but standing for all the agony. It looked like it was going to fall asleep on its feet. Jack knelt on the pavement, closed his eyes, raised the phone to his ear again.

'The fox is contained.'

Where?

'Driveway.'

Jack was panting, sweating, furiously taking stock of the fox's potential escape routes. One narrow gap between the car and the house, one narrow gap between the car and the brick wall on the other side. It was trapped. Jack shook his head, gathered himself up, stretched out his lower back. He gave the operator the street name, the house number, gulping in air between sentences.

OK, we're going to get someone out to you. Don't go anywhere.

As if he had somewhere to go. The clicking of spokes getting louder alerted Jack to the approaching cyclist, walking his bike down the road. Jack averted his gaze, plotted his own escape route. His flat was only two streets along. He could simply leave. Yet one glance back at the fox, its forehead grazing the brick wall, its snout grazing the concrete driveway, told him he had to stay. He put his phone back in his pocket, checked the time on his smart watch. The afternoon was melting away, but he had no one else to spend it with.

'Did we get him?' said the cyclist.

Jack shifted uncomfortably, kept his eyes on the watch. 'They're sending someone out,' he said.

The cyclist craned over the car bonnet to get a glimpse of the fox. 'Poor little guy.'

Jack didn't look up. Neither did the fox. The owner of the house twitched her curtains at the two young men loitering next to her Jag.

'You really don't need to worry,' said Jack, eventually, to the cyclist. 'I can manage this on my own.'

The cyclist, for a moment, looked hurt. Then he shrugged. 'If you say so.'

Spokes clicked away. The curtains twitched once more, then fell still. Jack and the fox were once again alone. For a moment, Jack stood, staring at his watch. He checked the window of the house, saw no further sign of movement. He looked up the street, then down it. No passers-by. He frowned. Then he pulled a plastic ice-cream tub from a nearby recycling bin, filling it with water from the tap on the side of the house. He squeezed down the gap between the shiny car and the brick wall, placing the makeshift bowl in front of the thirsty-looking fox.

'There you go,' he said softly. 'Drink up.'

Jack returned to his spot on the pavement, his back to the car and the fox behind it. The crows from before had settled on the fence to his right, still cawing and eyeing the fox hungrily. Jack regarded them with disdain, then glanced over his shoulder at the two quivering points of ears just visible behind the car. Jack's phone was buzzing in his pocket, but he ignored it. He just closed his eyes and waited. His head was empty. He was almost dozing. Then a van door was opening, and someone was asking him questions again.

'Jack?' the man said. 'You called about a fox?'

Jack nodded, went to speak, but the fox man had already gone round to the back of the van and opened the doors.

'What might be wrong with it?'

The fox man didn't answer at first, simply kept rummaging through the contents of his van. Then he brushed past Jack, assumed an ungainly crouch on the pavement and peered around the side of the car. Jack stood awkwardly by the van, unsure whether to follow or leave.

'Sarcoptic mange,' said the fox man, after a while. 'It'll make them tear their own skin off.'

Jack glanced in the direction of the fox, screwed up his face, scratched his forearm. 'What will you do with it?'

The fox man turned to Jack now, his expression softening a little. 'Take him to the vet, see if they can treat him,' he said. 'Then, who knows? He's got his whole life ahead of him.'

Jack looked back at the space behind the car. The 'if' hadn't gone unnoticed.

'He seems pretty old,' Jack said.

'Old beyond his years, maybe,' said the fox man. 'He's about two, three at a push.'

Then the fox man was gone, crashing about in the back of his van once more. The fox remained frozen, its eyes almost closed, its forepaws firmly planted on the ground, one twisted back leg hovering above the concrete. It didn't seem to have touched the water.

'Right, then.'

Jack turned to the sight of the fox man pulling on an outlandishly long pair of thick, red gloves, then depositing a rusted white metal cage on the pavement. He rubbed his hands together, the muffled rasp of dirty suede.

'Let's get him.'

Instinctively, Jack stepped back as the fox man squeezed his burly body down the narrow gap between the car and the wall. The fox disappeared from view. The fox man did, too. For a moment, there was nothing. The crows didn't even caw. Then the fox man emerged holding the fox. One hand cupped the filthy white fur of its chest, the other held the cracked and hairless rump in such a solid grip that the gloved fingers seemed as if they might break the fragile skin.

Jack raised a hand to intervene, but stopped himself. The fox's teeth were bared and it wriggled slightly, but it didn't put up much of a fight. It didn't seem lucid enough. Carefully, holding the fox up high as if he were wading through deep water, the fox man advanced on the open cage. He placed the fox in it, removed a latch, closed the lid. Jack released his breath, which he hadn't realised he'd been holding. He unclenched his fists, which he hadn't realised he'd been clenching. Behind the white bars, the fox appeared passive once again, head bowed, eyes closed.

'All done,' said the fox man, lifting the cage as if it weighed nothing and placing it in the back of the van.

The whole thing seemed to be over before it had even begun. And now that the fox was out of sight, Jack could feel his nerves jangling again, that same dull ache rising behind his eyes. Jack turned back to the fox man, but he was busy writing in a notebook, and Jack didn't have the energy for small talk, anyway. So he decided to check on the fox instead, creeping over to the back of the van, the doors of which were still open. Checking that the fox man wasn't watching, Jack leaned in and placed one hand on the bars of the cage. The fox barely twitched.

'Good luck,' Jack whispered, then felt stupid. 'I mean, I'm sorry.'

Jack shook his head, sighed. He looked back down the street, wondered what he'd do after this. Then, as he heard the fox man coming over to shut the doors, he looked back down at the fox. Instinctively, a sharp intake of breath. Jack took his hand off the bars. The fox hadn't moved, not really. It still stood on one injured back leg, the other twisted around it, still supporting its weight on tired forepaws. But though its back was still arched and its shoulders still hunched and its body still ravaged, it had managed to raise its head and look through the bars. It was looking right at him. Inches away from his face, the fox's golden stare burned into him with a melting intensity. Its pupils were like black holes, the irises around them blazing like twin suns.

They were eyes which held Jack's, eyes which bored into Jack's skull, eyes which sent a shock down Jack's spine and ignited every nerve in his nervous system. Eyes which told Jack that it knew, the fox knew, it knew, it knew, it knew, and if it knew, perhaps Jack wasn't on his own. Jack stared back, unblinking, unbreathing. He placed his hand, once again, on the bars of the cage. And the fox, which hadn't once looked down, bared its fangs and licked its cracked, black lips. Then it spoke.

Thank you, said the fox.

Before Jack could react, the van doors were slammed shut in front of him and the fox was gone. The fox man was saying his goodbyes, then he was gone, too. And through it all Jack was left standing, slack-jawed and alone, swaying on his own unstable legs with all sense of sense and sanity crashing down around him. In his pocket, his phone started ringing again, and Jack wasn't sure his shaking fingers or his trembling larynx would be able to take the call. How was work? His stomach lurched. He'd lost his job. Why does your voice sound like that? His legs began to tingle, the tendons in his forearms twitching. He'd met a fox on the common. A fox that could speak. The van was already halfway down the street, slowing to let an approaching car past. Jack pulled out his phone, but only in the hope that the fox man might be calling because he'd forgotten something, that he might be about to turn back. He hadn't. It wasn't him. And it wasn't any of the usual suspects, not his mates nor his now-ex-bosses, though the two groups weren't exactly mutually exclusive.

'Charlotte?'

His sister never called. She wasn't a caller.

'Jack,' came Charlotte's voice on the other end of the line. 'It's Mum.'

Jack was distracted. The van was disappearing into the distance in a puff of white smoke, and the fox behind its doors was already faltering in his memory like a figment of his imagination or a half-remembered dream. Jack couldn't bring the fox's voice to mind, though he could hear his own voice, in the meeting room, thanking Hugh and Hugo for the opportunity of having the whole life he'd built flattened into something which could fit into a thin, brown envelope on a thick, glass tabletop. He twitched at the memory, felt like there were fleas in his hair, ticks on his skin.

'Mum?' he said. His voice was as distant as an echo. 'What about Mum?'

Jack conjured an image of his mother, standing at the bottom of an old oak tree. Smiling, eyes crinkling in the sunlight, the legs of her dungarees rolled up to stop them getting soaked with river water. Then his father stepped into the way, blocking out the sun. He loomed, and as he loomed, he cast a shadow which obscured Jack's mother, obscured everything. Jack squinted after the van, but it was long gone. He turned around. At the top of the street, the common had emptied out, the road just as busy but, somehow, silent. It was like the sound of the traffic had been switched off, as if all of that was happening in one place, and this was another. Jack was left standing on an empty road near an empty common, two streets away from an empty flat, listening to the disembodied voice of his sister on the other end of the line.

'She's gone,' said Charlotte.

And suddenly, a talking fox didn't seem so absurd after all.

31

The fox knows many things,

but the hedgehog knows one important thing.

Who said that? What's the thing?

The hedgehog wonders, from the bracken,

as it leaves the forest and crosses the lawn,

soundlessly   arriving   lightly   treading

snuffling   and   sniffling   trundling

returning to the forest, to the undergrowth,

just as a young man opens the garden gate.

Who is he? What does he want?

The fox lurks in the shadows, licking its lips,

but the hedgehog is too preoccupied to notice.

trundling sniffling and snuffling

> *reaching the patio with a puff of relief.*
>
> *Every crossing, road or lawn, is a risk.*
>
> *The hedgehog's reward: a bowl of cat food,*
>
> *left out especially. No cat lives here.*
>
> *If it did, the hedgehog wouldn't come,*

treading lightly arriving soundlessly

part two

COUNTRY

four

Anyone who saw the garden might have assumed the house was abandoned. The shed seemed disused, the patio furniture peeling, the half-built treehouse little more than a rotting husk. The bird feeder had no diners, the bee hotel no guests. Even the rain had stopped visiting. An early summer drought had pushed the local council towards a hosepipe ban, and the lawn towards an uninviting shade of bleached brown. Blades of grass curled like talons, thirsty leaves scraping against brittle branches. The air was heavy with dust, skewed with the shimmer of humidity that comes on a thick day under a dense canopy. Through this haze, he arrived. The man who was going nowhere.

Jack hesitated at the garden gate, staring up at a wonky old house which squatted like a troll on top of a lumpy hill. Removing his hand from the gate, he pushed a few black strands of unwashed hair from his forehead, rubbed cheeks which were grey with tiredness and greasy with stress. He surreptitiously sniffed one armpit. The train from the city to the nearest town had been stuffy, and the lack of air conditioning on the bus from there to the village had only compounded his sour smell. What was waiting for Jack, on the other side of this gate? Once upon a time it would have been his mother, who'd have picked him up from the train station or at least have been standing on the porch, drying her hands on a tea towel and shaking her head at the fact that he'd arrived a day and a half later than promised. Or perhaps he'd be welcomed by Patti Smith, their old cat, senile and near-blind and reclining like a grumpy monarch behind one of the lattice windows. His mum wasn't there. Patti was long gone, too, along with all the rabbits, guinea pigs, hamsters and goldfish who'd once resided within these walls. Even the house seemed to be diminishing, like a pop-up page in a children's book being very slowly closed. A battered sign hanging from the lopsided gatepost welcomed him to Mole End, because there was no one else to do so.

A rustle in the undergrowth, followed by a hedgehog, to accompany the sound. It trundled awkwardly away from the house and across the grass, uncomfortably exposed, doing that thing that hedgehogs do when they lift their spiny skirts and tiptoe on skinny legs. The tips of its spikes weren't a uniform brown, but speckled, grey and white and gold, like the static on a television. Jack watched the hedgehog traverse the lawn and disappear into the hedgerow at the edge of the garden, swallowed up by the darkness between the looming trees. Jack's mind went with it, down the slope, through the hedge, into the bracken and straight into the same foxhole it had kept disappearing down over the last few days. Jack had enough to worry about, with his mum, with his lack of a job. But eventually, all thoughts found their way back to the fox.

Thank you.

Jack Penwick was a man who took things at face value. If a fox spoke to him, it meant that the fox could speak. What was the alternative? Hallucination? A full-blown detachment from reality? Jack had too much on his plate to go insane. Remembering his humiliating dismissal made him despondent, depressed. Over a decade of hard work, and he was back where he started, more tired than he'd ever been, about to enter a house which wouldn't exactly greet him with open arms. Where was his mum when he needed her? Where was his mum, full stop? Jack shook a heavy head, attached to a body which felt even heavier. He barely had the energy to open the gate. *Thank you*, the fox in the cage had said, its eyes burning and its voice charged with electricity. Jack hadn't said anything. He'd just watched in stunned silence as the doors of the van had been closed and the fox had been taken away.

'There you are.'

The front door was open. Jack had a welcome party after all, though Charlotte's arms were crossed. His kid sister wore an oversized hoodie, her mouth pursed in a small pout that made her look like a sulky child. Yet she looked older than however old she was supposed to be now. Twenty-one? Twenty-two? She looked wearier than he remembered, too, as if she was making a supreme effort to hold the door open. Jack was usually the serious one, Charlotte usually cracking jokes at his expense. And while he'd expected her to be spiky, Jack was taken aback by quite how sullen she seemed. He tried to snap into big-brother mode, wondered if he should offer some words of comfort.

'Here I am,' he said, eventually, attempting a hug, but bottling it at the last minute.

Charlotte recoiled from him, kept her arms crossed. The heavy door stayed where it was. So did the scowl. She was half in shadow, but Jack could still see that her dirty-blonde hair was unwashed, piled up on her head in a messy bun. The whites of her enormous eyes were ringed with red, but the irises were as brown as ever. He'd compared them to chocolate buttons, once, in a poem he'd been forced to write in an English class. Pick someone you love, the teacher had said, and he'd chosen his baby sister. All of his classmates had laughed at him. He didn't wear his heart on his sleeve any more.

'What happened, then?' he said.

Jack was trying to make an effort, to let her know he was listening. He already knew what had happened, because she'd told him on the phone. Charlotte had come downstairs on Thursday morning, and their mum hadn't been there. Not in the house, not in the garden. Their dad hadn't noticed, hadn't seemed to care. But Charlotte was worried. Their mother's walking boots were missing, as was her anorak. She wasn't responding to texts, wasn't answering her phone. It was like she'd vanished into thin air. When lunchtime came and went and their mum was still missing, Charlotte called Jack. Now here Jack was, increasingly aware of the weight of the weekend bag strung over his left shoulder.

'I already told you what happened.'

She'd called him on Thursday. Now it was Saturday. The fact that he'd taken two days to get here hovered between them like a cloud of midges. Charlotte would be even less impressed if she knew that he hadn't spent the Friday working, as he'd told her, but had instead been holed up in his flat in a strange sort of paralysis, oscillating between an enormous, intangible feeling of failure, and smaller, stranger thoughts of a fox and the fact that it had spoken. Now that he stood on the steps of his childhood home, being looked down on by a little sister who'd clearly needed him, it was embarrassing for Jack to recall those wasted couple of days on his sofa. An actual cloud of midges hovered briefly between them. Jack used his free arm to wipe the sweat from his brow, avoiding Charlotte's piercing glare. Did she know? Charlotte had always been smart, perhaps even smarter than him, the sort of person who liked foreign films and books in translation, who quoted the kind of learned philosophers that never cropped up in the TED Talks which Jack had a tendency to watch. And yet, if Charlotte was as smart as he'd always thought she was, why was she still working in the local pub, having dead-end conversations with the same dead-eyed villagers? Why was she still here?

'Do you still think it's a misunderstanding?'

Charlotte had said that, on the phone. Jack had used it, inside his own head, as justification for staying where he was. Now, looking at her, he wasn't so sure.

'Well,' Charlotte said. She swallowed. 'There's still been nothing.'

Jack wanted to be surprised, but wasn't. Their mum hadn't been returning his calls, either.

'So, you've called the police?' Jack asked.

Charlotte hesitated. Now she was the one avoiding eye contact, picking awkwardly at one sleeve of her hoodie.

Jack shook his head. 'You haven't, have you?'

She caught his eyes again, looking even more angry than before. 'I was waiting for you.'

'And what about him?' Jack said, staring hard into the hallway, his jaw set. 'Has he done anything to help?'

With a sort of flinch, Charlotte glanced over her shoulder. Jack followed her gaze into the shadowy hallway behind her.

'Of course he hasn't helped,' Charlotte said, in a small voice.

Her anger made sense now. Jack tapped out a distress signal with one foot, rubbed his knotted chest with the heel of his palm.

'Where is he?'

Charlotte tilted her head towards the kitchen. Then she bit her lip and dipped back into the shadows. Jack delayed for as long as he could before following her into the hallway. His sister hesitated before disappearing up the stairs, every wooden step creaking its indifference. Inside, nothing had changed. The same broken umbrellas in the same stand, the same old raincoats on the same hooks, bar the one that was conspicuously empty. The terracotta tiles on the floor were just as chipped, the wood on the banister just as scuffed and splintered. This place. The first time Jack had invited friends for a sleepover, they'd been perplexed by the need to wear thick socks and woollen jumpers because of the draughts, flummoxed when

Jack told them they'd need to wash with a handheld shower in a roll-top bath in the single bathroom. He'd stopped inviting friends over a long time ago. He'd stopped coming back, not long after that. He was always busy, with work. He'd thought he was indispensable, that the company would have crumbled around him had he ever left the city for a holiday. If Jack took even a long weekend, he was worried that Hugh or Hugo might make a withering remark about his absence, or that he'd be usurped by one of his underlings during his short time away.

Jack sighed, peered up the stairs. Willing Charlotte to come back down, to not leave him on his own. Most of the picture frames on the staircase hung at wonky angles. One of them was missing entirely, leaving a lighter square of unblemished wall where it had previously been. The light coming through the mottled window at the top of the staircase was dusty and unfiltered. Jack suppressed an urge to sneeze, to blow his nose, to go and wash his clammy hands. He stuffed them into his pockets, then wiped them on his jeans, glancing around, avoiding the kitchen door. On the console table in the hallway were a number of family photos, some of them in black and white, all of them taken by his ever-artful mother. In this one, he was hoisting Charlotte on to his shoulders, knee-deep in the old river, smiling with a comical gap between his two front teeth. In that one, the rest of the family were grouped together, all laughing. Jack was nowhere to be seen.

He took off his trainers, carefully placing them in between some stiff old galoshes and a threadbare pair of walking sandals. He imagined a space where his mum's boots might have been. They were one of the only things she'd seemingly taken with her. Where had she taken them? Jack tried to remember the last time they'd spoken, but came up short. He knew that if he opened his phone, all of the messages between them would be from her, a one-sided avalanche of grey boxes filled with unanswered questions. Now Jack looked at her garden wellies on the floor, so small and so empty, and felt a chill at odds with the warm air still rolling through the open front door.

As Jack shivered, the kitchen made a ghostly sound. A shifting body, a clearing throat. Jack straightened up, felt his hackles rise. He cocked his head to the spectral creak of a seat. He rubbed the back of his neck, then turned and, finally, headed towards the kitchen, where he paused in the doorway, gripping the frame as if the only way he'd be able to enter the kitchen was by propelling himself in by force. He exhaled, took a couple of steps forward. The countertops were strewn with tea towels and soil-speckled vegetables, the daylight filtering through the dusty window obscured by a medley of low-hanging bronze pots. He thought of cooking in this kitchen with his mother, thought how much easier this would all be if he was coming home to her. His eyes lingered on the pans, on the countertops, on the window. Then, when he could no longer avoid it, he turned and faced the source of the sound.

A heavy old dining table, with a half-eaten slice of marmalade-on-toast upon it. Beyond the table, long windows, the overgrown garden behind them and the dense forest beyond. And between that table and that forest, a man, his jumper littered with crumbs. The man sat and stared out of the opposite window with wild, wide eyes, behind a pair of thick, greasy and perfectly circular spectacles. His beansprout hair spiralled off in all directions, his waxy cheeks as pale as parsnips.

The man realised he had company. He stopped chewing. He swallowed. There was a long pause, in which he silently pushed his thick spectacles up his nose. He stared at Jack, and Jack stared at him. Then the man's face broke into a smile, a smile so welcoming that Jack almost felt the compulsion to smile back.

'Hello,' said Jack's dad, with all the warmth in the world. 'Who are you?'

five

Hello.
Who are you?
And where was I?

Gerry sometimes felt as if his brain were a river, and he was
hurtling down it, clinging to a branch.

He never much liked deep water. He preferred his wide,
open spaces on dry land. There was nothing wide or open
about the space around him now. A better metaphor for his
mind would be a caged animal.

Or maybe his thoughts were the animal, his mind the cage,
a cage getting smaller and smaller and smaller, a cage which

felt as if it would only stop shrinking when it had squeezed out every single one of those thoughts.

An empty cage.

> That's it. Hedgehogs.
> On the Isle of Scilly. Or, no.
> The lesser white-toothed shrew.

If time used to be a stream, running in a generally straight line towards one thing – the river, then the ocean, which Gerry supposed was a pleasant metaphor for death – then the stream had been dammed.

Now time was a lake, and Gerry was struggling to stay afloat in the middle of it. His memories were like water, impossible to keep hold of. There was no order to them, as he kicked and flailed and tried to keep his head above the surface.

No past, no present. Nothing ahead of him, but nothing behind, either. His closest memories were simply the ones within his grasp.

Like Johnny. Like the alder tree in his childhood garden. Like the barn owl that kept calling him, from the woods.

> A sad sound.
> A shriek that says, *Oh-o-o-o-o,*
> *that I never had been bor-r-r-n!*

His wife didn't like the sound, but Gerry had been mesmerised. I hear you, he had wanted to say. Or perhaps he'd wanted to scream back.

It was oddly comforting, for a shriek. Perhaps that's why Gerry had followed the sound.

Here are some facts about owls.
If an owl has orange eyes, it hunts in the day.
An owl's face is a disc so it can channel sound
towards its ears.

The barn owl in the forest wasn't looking to make friends.

It stayed hidden when Gerry found himself alone and uncertain in the middle of the woods.

Gerry thought they could be kindred spirits, the owl and him. Both of them were endangered. Both of them were alone in this, each in their own way.

If a barn owl shrieks in the forest,
but doesn't want to say hello,
who is there to hear it?

His wife wasn't happy when he came home, the moon still hanging above Mole End, haunting the house like a spectre.

The police weren't happy, either, or the doctors. Where were you? his wife had said. Isn't it obvious? I was at the oak, with the owl.

No one took Gerry seriously any more. He constantly had the feeling that he was being made fun of. He felt more ashamed, more often, more than anything else.

When he couldn't get out of his bedroom because he couldn't tell the difference between a wardrobe and a door, his worst fear wasn't being trapped. It was being found out.

So he hid things, hid that he did things. The barn owl still shrieked just before dawn, but Gerry had learned his lesson. Gerry, who never had much to say anyway, would listen from a distance.

Who is Gerry,
if he isn't
who he was?

The thing is, most of the time, Gerry very much felt like himself. He'd never been talkative, never been much in touch with other human beings.

He'd never acted in the way that people expected other people to act. Most of the time, he remembered everything, and he remembered that he sometimes didn't remember things, and that people expected him not to remember anything.

But other times, times like now, he'd find himself forgetting. He'd find himself sitting at his own dining table, without a clue where or how he was.

Wait. Where was I?
In a strange house. At a strange table.
With a strange young man staring back at me.

The young man entered and stared at Gerry like he'd seen a ghost. What he was doing in Gerry's kitchen was anyone's guess.

There used to be a boy who looked just like him, living in the empty room upstairs. A confusing little boy. Was it Johnny?

The birds in the forest call for him to come and join them. The mice in the walls are whispering things only he can hear.

Gerry was losing the sense of what was real and what was imagined.

Right. That's right. The boy who used to live here was Gerry's son. But he'd gone away a long time ago. This couldn't be him.

'Hello,' Gerry had said to the angry young man in his kitchen. 'Who are you?'

And while you're at it,
Who am I?

six

'Who are you?'

Jack had been so taken aback that he hadn't known how to respond. He'd mumbled an explanation. He might even have apologised. Then he'd left the room.

Jack knew, of course, that something was going on with his dad. But the pair of them had always been a mismatch, like two pieces of Lego which would never fit together. Jack's father had never had been interested in giving him the time of day, so days had turned into years with no contact between them. They'd been so estranged for so long that the specifics of his dad's condition had simply passed him by. Standing in the hallway, on the other side of the kitchen door, questioning whether his father no longer knew who he was, Jack felt furious for being kept out of the loop.

Had his sister been keeping this from him? Why hadn't his mother said just how serious things had become? Jack couldn't believe it. They were both always here, and he wasn't. Surely they had a duty to tell him that things had got to this point. It was embarrassing to be uninformed. It was infuriating to have been focusing on other things, when perhaps he should have been focusing on this. Jack thought about storming upstairs, about confronting Charlotte. But he stayed put, racking his brains instead for the last time he'd asked his sister for an update, for the last time he'd shut his mum down when she'd tried to talk about Dad. He remembered one short conversation, when he had been out for a celebratory drink after the company had closed a particularly sink-or-swim deal.

'Do you understand what I'm saying?' his mum had said, on the other end of the line.

Jack had nodded, jostled by passers-by, his finger crammed into his other ear to facilitate his hearing. Yes, he did, he'd replied, when he realised his mum couldn't hear his nod. He thought he did. But he'd been thinking of other things, already, by the time he'd rejoined that perfect semicircle of brown shoes back on the pavement outside the pub. What difference would it make, if Jack and his dad hadn't spoken in years, anyway? Being forgotten by your own father was the second most painful thing in the world. The first was him never having known you in the first place.

mange in foxes

Now Jack was sitting at his boxy old computer, in the dark, typing things into the search bar. He'd retreated to his bedroom on the pretence of having some work to catch up on, and had taken a plate of food with him. He'd sat, chewing a limp sandwich, having already given up looking for jobs on a website where the listings all blurred into one before his eyes. The whole room was smaller than the en suite in his flat, the desk and bookshelves crowded with plastic participation trophies and patched-up teddy bears. Jack had fiddled with the old Roberts radio, but couldn't tune it to anything. The Wi-Fi operated like it was powered by steam. Jack stared at the dim screen, dimly aware of the contents of his bag spilling on to the bed behind him. A sorry reminder of what he'd lost. Not just his mother, not just his job, but the contents of a gold-ribbon-wrapped gift box which he'd left unattended on a bench while he went in pursuit of an injured fox. When he'd returned, it had gone. He guessed he'd never find out what was in that brown envelope.

The police had said they'd look into it. They said they'd look into his missing mother, too, when he called them earlier. He wasn't holding out much hope. He'd gone round in circles, being asked to explain several times that, though it seemed like his mum had been planning an escape, though she was clearly equipped and in her right mind, this whole thing was entirely out of character. Charlotte had whispered that he didn't know her character, but Jack had shushed her. Their mum was in her sixties. Wasn't she too old to be running away? He didn't want to tell his sister how worried he was, because he didn't want to lose face. His fears, so far, had ranged from a secret second family to a short trip and a long fall, down a well or a crevasse or something similarly steep and hazardous. She liked to hike. She used to talk fondly of adventures gone by. If the most likely scenario was that she'd run away, had taken her hiking boots and hiked into obscurity, that only worried him more. Because what was she fleeing from, and why hadn't she told her children where she was going?

The police said they'd look into it. He'd hung up, feeling more hopeless than before. The irony wasn't lost on him that, in coming back to Mole End, she'd been the one person that he'd wanted to see. He wanted to ask her what was going on with his father, why she'd kept the gravity of the situation from him. He wanted her to stroke his hair like she used to, when she told him that he'd got himself in a tizz. He wanted her to tell him that everything was going to be alright. Instead, Jack sat alone in his bedroom, listening to the sound of cutlery clinking on plates downstairs, typing queries into a search box and staring zombie-like at the answers.

what is sarcoptic mange

Canine scabies. Mites which make foxes gnaw at their own flesh. Jack read about how mange used to be a West Country thing, how it thrived in the warm climate of the Gulf Stream. Parasites die in the cold, but winters aren't as cold any more. Since the seventies, mange had been travelling north as the weather grew warmer year by year, leaving a host of dead foxes in its wake. Spreading up the country like, well, mange itself. Scottish foxes had previously never encountered it. Now it was killing them en masse.

do foxes survive mange

Rarely on their own. Most die in six months, without treatment, sometimes even with. And if mange didn't get them, cars did. With morbid fascination, Jack read about how road accidents kill 100,000 foxes a year, how the ones that don't die suffer concussions and fractured legs, torn-off tails and broken teeth. What are the odds? he thought. How often are ill and injured foxes put down? And would the fox I met not have been put down if I'd acted sooner? Jack bit his lip, his thumb hovering over the keyboard.

can foxes talk

He didn't even wait for an answer, but closed the browser and shut down the computer.

Jack had done a lot of this sort of thing, on his sofa in the city, the day after the incident on the common. A lot of searching. An injured adult fox will always be released as close as possible to where it was found, he'd learned. Foxes are difficult to domesticate, because they'll dig up your carpets and piss all over your walls. Go upstairs at night and they'll scream until the morning; open your back door in the morning and they'll run away and never look back. Thoughts like this had been keeping Jack awake at night since then. Here, now, he turned off the light and lay in a bed which had been too small for him even as a teenager. Jack breathed in through his nose and out through his mouth as he listened to the death rattle of the window frame, creaking with every shift in the breeze.

He'd always found Mole End creepy after dark. Even on hot nights like this, it was somehow always cold. The pipes whistled, the walls murmured to themselves. And the woods beyond the window, though he couldn't see them, seemed to lie in wait, watching. They always had. Behind his eyelids, he conjured childhood visions of animal eyes in the undergrowth, of an endless expanse of twisted roots and hidden hollows where one could get lost for days. He remembered the cold sweat of suddenly finding himself alone out there, his mother disappearing momentarily between the trees. In his mind's eye, he saw his father, too, emerging from the shadowy woods before sunrise. And he saw himself, watching from his bedroom window, ducking out of sight so as not to be seen.

Tonight, back in his old bed, Jack still sensed a whisper of something watching from the shadows. He heard the hint of a creak on the stairs. He screwed his eyes tighter shut. Far off in the night, a haunting shriek. His dad would know what it was. His dad's eyes wouldn't be closed. Jack grunted, hugged his arms around himself, turned away from the window. Then he rolled over again, picked up his phone and plugged in the cable of his spare headphones. He opened a sleep app, put on some sleep sounds. Noises of the forest. Songs of the whales. When he eventually did drop off, Jack tumbled into one of those vivid dreams where it felt as if he'd been awake the whole time, save for a barrage of nonsensical images which would later seem unreal. Flaming eyes. Icy ravines. His mother, lost in the woods. The house, consumed by the earth. And a great oak tree, stretched out like a fallen giant, its front door blown off its hinges and the books from its cavernous library scattered in the mud.

Morning came. Jack only knew he'd been asleep because, where previously it had been dark, it was now light. He could tell even through closed eyelids. He sighed, then shifted himself in bed, careful not to wake the sleeping cat on his chest. Patti liked to do this, to sneak in and steal your warmth during the night, but she gave off heat like an electric blanket in return. Jack's head felt heavy, his mouth claggy. He placed a lazy hand on Patti's stomach as he swam to the surface of sleep, felt the cat's slow breathing against his sternum and her soft, slightly matted fur between his fingers. Like a static shock, that same old sound of radio tuning began to whine inside Jack's ears. His shoulders tensed, his fingers clenched. Even the sounds from his sleep app couldn't drown it out. Except his headphones were silent. Eyes still closed, grumbling sleepily, Jack felt between his fingers the frayed point in the wire where Patti had chewed it in two. His only headphones. Now Jack growled, and in his habitually irritated state on waking he finally felt his mind kick into gear. Something was bugging him, something far more pressing than the chewed-through cord of his headphones, something which his brain was only just grasping as it shook off the shackles of sleep.

Patti couldn't be lying on top of him, because Patti had died years ago. And with that, Jack's whole body spasmed. All at once, he gasped, opened his eyes, retracted his hand and choked on the last vestige of spittle in his mouth. A fox was sitting on his stomach. A fox, which was staring at him with eyes that burned like cinders.

'Shit!' Jack shouted, and rolled off the bed.

The fox, having been using Jack as its own bed, rolled with him. The duvet in its novelty cover erupted into the air like a parachute, two scrambling creatures thudding to the floor beneath it. Jack found himself face down on the faded carpet, trying his best to kick his way out of the fallen duvet and assume a convincing stance of self-defence. The fox, alarmed but much more agile, squeaked and leapt into the air before landing deftly on all four paws, on the other side of the room. Free from the duvet, clad in only his boxers, Jack scrabbled backwards and placed his bare shoulders against the cold wall. His heart was racing. His eyes refused to blink. The fox, which had positioned itself against the opposite wall, arched its back and snarled defiantly at Jack. Jack clawed at the carpet, pressing himself against the wall.

A momentary stand-off. Then, when it seemed to have deemed Jack incapable of further movement, the fox's countenance changed. It relaxed. Its black paws kneaded the carpet, then it sat comfortably on its hind legs. And somehow, either with the fangs that gleamed under its tight black lips or the eyes that glowed over its bright orange snout, it smiled.

Hello, said the fox, in that same voice that seemed to crackle with electricity. *I hope I'm not intruding.*

A fox is born beneath a tumble-down shed in somebody's back garden. It is the last cub in a litter of five, and it is hungry.

Hungry for regurgitated meat. Hungry for the mice and worms its mother brings home. Hungry for the world beyond that home, beyond this shed, beyond that fence. Hungry for the world beyond.

So, the fox ventures further, in search of living deliberately. A lone fox learns to hunt down dirty pigeons, day-end doughnuts left in bin bags, fried chicken bones discarded in polystyrene boxes on pavements.

A lone fox comes to love its life in the city. A lone fox learns to shun that which will cause it harm.

The fox's brother meets the business end of a bus, his corpse scooped up by a street cleaner with a shovel and deposited in a bin. Laid to rest in a grave of used newspapers and cigarette butts.

The city is an insatiable beast. More people, more wheels, more accidents waiting to happen. More ways to die, but much more to live on.

And isn't that the point of life? To live?

A fox which was born beneath a tumble-down shed in somebody's back garden becomes lord of the common.

It feasts on the delights of the bus-stop bin. It hunts on the high street and its tributaries. It sleeps in the dirt between the grass and the railway line. Never worried about going hungry, always somewhat wary.

The fox gets to know that the yew tree in the overcrowded cemetery is a veritable buffet, its crevices crawling with bugs, the graves beneath it a smörgåsbord of sticky red berries.

It gets to know the see-saw song of the great tit, the simple chirp of the sparrow, the lazy puff of the wood pigeon, and the differing taste of their delicate meat.

The fox starts to see patterns in things. Fellow foxes and ambulance sirens scream together in winter, a cold and howling chorus. There's no pleasure like the brittle crunch of a frozen park underfoot, but warmth and rain brings worms to the surface.

There's a lot beneath the surface. After a while, the fox begins to look at that railway bridge and see not a bridge, but a damp arch with a small nook in which a family of pipistrelle bats have just come out of hibernation.

It begins to look at that skyscraper and see not a skyscraper, but the eyrie it has been turned into by a peregrine falcon, the sharp precipice treated in the same way as the raptor would treat any cliff, anywhere.

The fox begins to look, and it begins to see. This place is its wild. This place is all it needs.

For a while, the fox simply lives. Yet while it doesn't know exactly when the pain began, at some point it starts to hurt.

Soon, it hurts all over, all at once.

The fox becomes ill. It becomes disoriented. By the time it realises it has no one to turn to, the fox is plagued by an itch so uncomfortable it would seem a blessing to simply roll over and die.

The fox can't remember its own decline, nor the downward slope which leads it into the middle of the common, in the middle of the day, broken skin hissing in the afternoon sun.

The smell of rust, the sound of engines. Crows cawing behind, traffic roaring ahead. I'm going to die, thinks the fox. I'm going to die. The fox knows it is going to die.

The fox is impossibly thirsty. The fox knows its fate. If the pain is going to end, make the end be quick.

A pale man approaches from the other side of the common. Blue eyes glow in dark sockets. He holds a scythe in his hand. This is death, the fox thinks. I have met my maker.

But the pale man is just a man, and the scythe is just a branch, and the man waves it in the fox's direction as he speaks to a disembodied voice.

Jack, he says, my name is Jack. It's going to be alright.

More humans arrive. The fox tries its best to flee. The fox finds itself trapped between metal, concrete and brick. It cannot slake its thirst. It cannot find its way back to the common. It cannot wriggle free, when it is wrenched from the earth and placed inside a rusty cage.

But even in the belly of a grumbling metal monster, those eyes, which are, if not exactly kind, then cool, or calm, tell the fox what the man doesn't need to say again. It's going to be alright.

Thank you, says the fox.

And the man understands. He understands! Imagine that. The man understands.

Van doors close. A cold cage soothes tender skin. In the darkness, the fox drifts off to the irony of being understood, after uttering the very last words it will ever say.

Doors open. The fox awakens, in the afterlife, bathed in the light of a cool and shining place.

Imagine this: the fox is alive. The fox is free from pain. And the fox thinks of only one thing, of that pair of eyes.

So, that next night, the fox escapes from a cage, escapes from a building. Untangles itself from IV drips and wires. Chews through a wire fence and crawls through ivy.

On weak legs, the fox finds itself in a forest. Guilty for not thanking the humans who saved its life. Aware that those humans weren't Jack, that they wouldn't understand the words.

Jack.

This single name propels the fox deep into the woods, the moon lurking like a threat overhead, the dry ground rustling beneath its paws as if a thousand dangers are skittering about beneath the surface.

Out here, the smells are different to those of the city, stacked on top of one another like some vast new promise, like layers in a living sandwich or the tiers of a living cake.

Sap upon pine upon fern upon stalk upon flower upon beetle upon soil upon silt upon worm upon the bodies of quivering creatures.

Everything is out here. Everything but Jack.

Without a trail to latch on to, the fox sniffs around for a name. It follows its nose. Towards a common, which was in a city, which was in a place nothing like this. Not much to go on. But next-to-nothing is enough.

Time shifts. The fox finds Jack. And Jack. And Jack and Jack and Jack.

In the villages it reaches, old men named Jack spray it with garden hoses and young boys named Jack feed it crisps and sandwich crusts beneath picnic tables.

The day is long. The fox follows its path to dozens of Jacks, but never the Jack it needs.

No matter. Life is a new adventure. And in every new place, the fox only feels more thankful for this extra day, and for the man who'd made it possible.

Jack.

The afternoon limps on, slower than the morning. The fox's paw pads are cracked, its still-healing body almost as sore as before.

The fox doesn't give up. It listens to the wind, follows a feeling. By dusk, it finds its way to an oak. Within that hollow oak, an owl. The owl looks towards a scent, one which leads out of the woods and into the bracken.

The fox finds itself in a hedge and, in that hedge, a hedgehog, reeling from the destruction of its home, a copse which had become another field for a nearby farmer's crops.

The hedgehog will not act afraid. Not of the fox, nor the man.

The man? Yes. The one in the garden. The one with the sleek black head of a raven and the stark white face of a barn owl.

Jack.

Beyond the hedge and the hedgehog, a slope that leads up to a garden. The fox waits until night has fallen, then slips in the back door while the humans are asleep.

It tiptoes through the empty kitchen, climbs carefully up the creaking stairs. Follows the scent along the landing, towards the room at the end.

The fox hoped to make its introduction sooner. The fox wanted to say: here I am. It's going to be alright.

But it's been a long journey, and the fox is tired. The fox falls asleep, and is woken by Jack, waking.

Once the chaos has subsided, the fox makes its introduction.

Hello, it says. I hope I'm not intruding.

seven

Is it not a bit drastic to be calling the police?
says the first voice. The second one huffs.
No, it says. She's missing.

The mood in the house had changed since the angry young
man turned up.

Or maybe it had changed before that, when Gerry and his
daughter had arrived downstairs to find their family one
member short.

She's not 'missing', voice one says.
She took her crampons. And a sleeping bag.
The second voice ignores her, interrupts.
Regardless of whether she—

Gerry stood in the hallway, outside the kitchen door,
listening to an argument taking place upstairs.

He had a mug of tea in his hand, but he wasn't drinking it.
He was concentrating on the conversation.

A sleeping mat. A tent.
His daughter is the one interrupting now.
Gerry can tell that she's losing her patience.
Regardless of whether she wants to be found or not—
the second voice continues, interrupting right back.

From a distance, from the bottom of an echoey staircase, it
was hard for Gerry to keep up with the conversation, to work
out what it was about.

Gerry focused, instead, on the concentration of the liquid in
his mug. He was trying to work out if he'd boiled the kettle
before brewing his tea.

The camping stove! says his daughter.
Regardless, she's still missing, says his—

Wait. Who's missing?

Gerry frowned at his tea, then bit his lip as he looked up the
staircase, at the blank space where a picture frame used to
hang.

He ordered his thoughts, searching the dusty corners of his mind for evidence. He hadn't seen his wife in a while. Were they talking about her?

Down here, right here, was the spot where her boots were supposed to be. They weren't there. Her anorak was gone, too.

Aren't you supposed to wait twenty-four hours?
says his daughter.
You're not supposed to wait at all, comes the reply.

Was it like her to leave without warning? Had Gerry done something to drive her away?

His memory wasn't what it used to be. He often felt guilty for things that might not have happened.

He worried about things that might not come to pass, but he supposed that everyone did that. The anxious young man upstairs certainly seemed to.

If she's gone, Gerry wanted to say, you shouldn't worry about her. We used to be adventurers. We never needed screens to navigate uncharted territories.

I'm not sure—
And it's been forty-eight.

And yet, how could Gerry not worry? He didn't have a clue where his wife was. And those distant voices were discussing the police.

Gerry sipped his tea, if only for an excuse to gulp. From the spindly click of a rotary phone, Gerry could tell that a dial was being turned, that the call was being made.

From the creak of a chair, the creak of a floorboard, Gerry could tell that Charlotte sat swivelling at her desk, and that the young man was standing rigidly by the side table outside her door, where the phone was kept.

Hi, I'd like to report a missing person, says the young man. Yes. Thanks. Yes, I'll hold, says the young man.

The young man shifted. The floorboards told Gerry as much.

The young man's tone changed. Intuition was enough to inform Gerry that he was now addressing Charlotte, not the phone.

Does Dad know that Mum's gone? says the young man. You don't think he knows more than he knows? he adds.

Gerry stood silently in the hallway, wondering what he was supposed to know.

If there's something I'm supposed to know, he wanted to say, to this young man, to the stranger upstairs, please let me know it.

Because I don't know what I'm supposed to know.

> Charlotte is saying something,
> but Gerry is already on his way.
> Right out of the kitchen
> and into his garden.

There was no time to worry when there was chard to be checked on, runner bean shoots to be trimmed.

There was no need to worry his daughter. If he told his daughter that he was worried, she'd only worry more.

> An unwelcome change,
> to be saying this about her mother.
> We're worried about you.

Worry slows things down. Fear speeds things up. Caught somewhere in the middle, Gerry's day proceeded at the pace of any other.

He spent his afternoon trying to solve the current crisis, in his head. He spent dinner telling Charlotte facts about snub-nosed monkeys and star-nosed moles, hoping to cheer her up. She was clearly just as worried as him.

The angry young man was avoiding them. He ate his dinner alone. But Gerry knew some things. He knew that the angry young man was worried, too.

What did his wife used to say, about their son?
He's just acting out.
That must be nice, Gerry thinks. I only know how to act in.

Gerry lay in bed that night, alone, and even the creaking of the house and the shrieking of the woods couldn't comfort him.

He rolled over, but he had no one to turn to. He was worried about his wife, but he wouldn't say a thing.

eight

Foxes aren't supposed to speak. Jack knew this. That's why, when the animal first spoke, for the second time, he recoiled so hard that he banged his head against the bedroom wall. He'd doubled over, swearing and cradling his smarting skull, but the energetic fox didn't seem inclined to stop and check on him. It kept speaking, its words tumbling out into the space between them. So Jack stopped swearing and started listening, sitting on the bedroom floor and struggling to blink.

I used to be a lone fox, said the fox.

Jack tried pinching himself and rubbing his eyes to make the pacing, talking fox go away. It didn't. Double vision became triple, before settling down again. Three foxes became two, became one. In the morning light creeping in beneath the curtain, the fox's orange coat seemed to glow, its dark-pricked ears and sandy-coloured whiskers fluttering as it told Jack its story.

Jack could reach out and touch it. Jack did reach out and touch it. It was really there. And despite its effervescent energy, Jack knew it was the fox he'd met on the common. Its fur, lustrous at the front, had been shaved comedically short on the back legs and tail, like a dog whose groomer had abandoned the appointment halfway through. The sores were gone, but the marks of cannulas and swabs were still faintly visible. Could it have healed so quickly?

'You seem better,' Jack said. I'm talking to a fox, he thought.

I am!

'I thought you were dead.' And the fox, he thought. It's talking back.

I'm not!

The white bib of fur beneath the fox's chin, which had been yellowing and greasy before, was dazzlingly clean and blindingly white. The fox bared its pointed teeth and grinned. Jack knew that, just as squirrels bury nuts, foxes bury the half-eaten corpses of their prey. He came to his senses. He looked for an escape route, realised the fox stood between himself and the only door in the room.

'This isn't happening,' Jack said, then began to chant it, like a mantra. 'This isn't happening, this isn't happening.'

The fox cocked its own head, looked momentarily concerned. There was a twitch of one rusty ear, a ripple in that bib of bright white fur. Jack watched the fox from behind hands which cupped the lower half of his face, as if he thought he might vomit into them.

'This can't be happening.'

Oh, but it is!

'This isn't real.'

It's real! And it's fantastic!

Unable to contain itself, the fox was now jumping around. It bounded about beneath the desk, darted up on to the bed and back off again. Jack tried not to watch it, tried to focus on breathing.

'What is happening?'

It's wonderful! said the fox, giddily trotting about in small circles like a dressage horse. *To be alive! To be reunited!*

'You can't speak,' Jack said, his chest still heaving, gravelly saliva coating the inside of his cheeks. He slammed his head back against the wall again, closed his eyes. 'You can't be here.'

With this, the fox closed its eyes, yelped, fell to the floor with all four paws rigid in the air. No sooner had it hit the ground than it rolled over, returned to a seated position, hopped up, sat again. Jack glanced at the bedroom door, scratched his forearms, looked back at the fox. His mouth tasted stale. He felt dehydrated. He wanted to be out of this small, stifling room.

'Why are you here?'

It was a valid question. The fox had told him how, not why. Now it sat on its hind legs, kneading its forepaws, snout ticking this way and that, as it considered its answer.

I realised something as I lay in the back of that van, it said, suddenly sombre.

'And what was that?' Jack replied, his eyes closed.

Lone foxes die alone.

A short silence, in which Jack couldn't find the words with which to answer. The fox stared, expectantly. Dust settled in the light between them.

'Jack?'

Jack had been so slack-jawed by this point, so convinced that the whole surreal scene was happening in his sleep, that the tap at his bedroom door almost knocked him through the wall behind him. He banged his head again, clutched it and bit his lip, then opened one eye as if still expecting to have woken up and found the fox not there. The fox was still there. Its hackles were raised, its orange eyes trained in alarm at the door.

'Yes?' said Jack, coughing, scrabbling around for yesterday's clothes.

'Who are you talking to?' said Charlotte, from the other side of the door. 'Is it Mum?'

'It's—' he said, pulling on his tracksuit bottoms. 'Not Mum.' He yanked his T-shirt over his head. 'But it's important.'

He looked at the fox. The fox looked at the door, then back at him, not once blinking its orange eyes.

'Are you working?' Charlotte said. 'It's the weekend.'

Jack sat on the side of the bed, pulling on his socks. The fox jumped up on to the bed, too. It seemed surprised by the springiness of the mattress, and pushed down firmly again with its forepaws. Then again, then again.

'No, it's—' said Jack.

Boing! said the fox. *Boing! Boing!*

It was bouncing up and down now. Jack finished putting on his socks, gritting his teeth.

'I'm—'

Boing!

'It's—'

Boing!

'It's a friend,' Jack said.

Charlotte considered this from the landing. 'You have friends?'

Boing!

'Shut up,' Jack said, to the fox. 'Shut up,' he said, louder, to Charlotte.

'Whatever,' Charlotte said, before disappearing out of earshot.

Jack was left alone with the fox, which had stopped bouncing and was now staring at him with inquisitive eyes. Averting his gaze, Jack turned towards the window. Outside, birds chirping. Downstairs, a kettle being filled and then clunked into place on the stove.

Who was that?

Jack didn't answer. The fox, undeterred, sat down next to him. Its fur brushed against Jack's arm, causing him to bristle. Jack rubbed his eyes, kept his hands over them, breathing slowly. The fox was still there. He could feel it, waiting patiently beside him, staring up at the side of his head.

You saved my life, the fox said, simply. *That makes us friends.*

Jack clasped his hands together, looked at the ceiling, exhaled. 'That's not going to work,' he said. 'I think it's best we say our goodbyes. I've got a lot to do.'

The fox didn't seem disappointed. It didn't show any sign of leaving, either.

Goodbyes always come too early, it said slowly, as if reading to a toddler. Its warm eyes were fixed on Jack. *Better to never say goodbye at all.*

Jack knitted his brows. He was unnerved by the fox's self-help manner of speaking, as if it were a motivational poster on four legs. It spoke like any number of the business gurus whose front-facing videos Jack used to watch on a loop, dead-eyed former monks and Californian tech CEOs who spoke with a seize-the-day optimism as they revealed the keys to happiness and financial success. Jack searched for some sense of irony in the fox's blazing eyes, but couldn't find it. There were bigger issues at hand.

'I've got a—' Jack began, wringing his hands, speaking quietly, like a boy trying to wriggle out of detention. 'Family emergency.'

Oh no, said the fox.

'Oh yes,' said Jack, disarmed by its genuine concern. 'And I've got to attend to it, right now.'

The fox didn't take the hint.

'So I'll be going downstairs.'

Great, said the fox. *I'll come, too.*

Jack had considered locking the fox in his bedroom, but he was worried about the damage it might do to the furniture, the germs it might leave on his bed. He'd let it follow, instead, reasoning that he had more pressing matters to attend to. He did his best to ignore the cloud of restless orange which loitered in his peripheral vision. Questions battered him as he scoped out the empty kitchen, wanting only to make himself two slices of toast. *Is this your favourite room? Is that your favourite food? What's your favourite thing to do, and shall we do it now?* It's sleep deprivation, Jack told himself. It's pressure. It's stress. But the fox wouldn't let up, still chattering, so Jack shut it out more literally. He tempted it into the garden with a third piece of toast, then locked the back door behind it.

Back in the kitchen, Jack sighed, rubbed the tight spot at the nape of his neck, scanned the countertop for anything that might make up for his lack of sleep the night before. Chia seeds, hemp powder, supplements of any kind. All he saw was an open jar of marmalade, which he tutted at, then closed and returned to its rightful place. Every jar of jam and preserve in the cupboard was homemade, the handwritten label on each one illustrated with funky little drawings of the type of fruit inside. Jack pictured his mum, painstakingly crafting the labels for each fresh batch. He pictured his dad, slurping marmalade off his paws like a bear in a picture book. Then he closed the cupboard and picked up a Post-it note, stuck to the counter beneath where the open jar had been.

SUNDAY CROSSWORD HARDER

Had his dad intended it as an observation (that the Sunday crossword was harder), or a warning (to his family, that it was harder)? Perhaps it was some sort of experiment: tracking the crosswords day by day, week by week, to see if their level of difficulty changed. Jack chewed the inside of his cheek. He knew it was none of the above. Every cupboard in the kitchen was diligently labelled, though these labels had no illustrations. The notes were everywhere, notes stuck on top of more notes, a cascading avalanche of multi-coloured notes, all scrawled in his dad's meandering handwriting. They were about as easy to ignore as the fox jumping up and down outside the kitchen windows, trying to get Jack's attention.

'Charlotte!'

By the time Jack had crumpled the note into a tight ball and dropped it in the kitchen bin, Charlotte had answered his call, arriving impatiently in the doorway. Arms crossed, like normal. One eyebrow raised, as per usual.

'What?'

When Jack explained that he'd like a family meeting, Charlotte rolled her eyes and said that she'd get their dad. When Jack explained that they didn't need their dad, Charlotte snapped that it wasn't a family meeting, then. When Charlotte explained that a family meeting required the whole family, she didn't follow up with what they both must have been thinking. That one-quarter of that family was still missing, and that the dread was mounting with every hour in which she stayed gone.

'Right,' said Jack, once they were assembled, standing at the head of the dining table like a founder presenting a pitch deck to would-be investors. 'If the police aren't going to help, we'll have to find Mum ourselves.'

What Jack didn't say was, it wasn't his responsibility to fix this family. He hadn't lived here for a long time, and it had been even longer since he'd felt like he belonged in this house. All Jack wanted was a way out of this place, a way back to his real life in the city. Mole End made him uncomfortable. The woods creeped him out. But someone needed to take action, and the busier he kept himself, the easier it would be to pretend that he was far away from here and none of this was happening. No unemployment. No missing mum. No talking fox.

His dad and his sister stared up at him from the dining table. Behind them, outside the window, the fox was still jumping up and down. It made eye contact with Jack at the high point of each jump, jerking its head towards the back door.

'Thoughts?' Jack said, ignoring the fox, addressing only his sister. 'Ideas?'

Charlotte stared coldly at him, with the casual disdain of a teenager in detention. Their dad, on the other side of the table, was now staring into the middle distance. His uncombed hair floated above him, shock-white, and as buoyant as if he'd massaged a balloon on his scratchy sweater then rubbed it all over his head. It was the opposite of Jack's own hair, which was tamed with pomade and already shrinking back into a widow's peak, no matter how much caffeine shampoo he used. Jack cleared his throat. His dad's fingernails were filthy, Jack observed with mild revulsion. He looked away when his dad caught him looking.

'I've been gardening,' his dad said, to Charlotte.

Charlotte smiled and squeezed his hand. Jack stared at the back door, wondered how his dad had got in since Jack had locked it. The fox, following Jack's gaze, started nodding vigorously at the door, jumping with increased frequency.

'I was digging a carrot trench,' his dad continued, still addressing Charlotte.

Jack shook his head, directing his sister towards the Post-it notes stuck all over the cupboards. 'Should he be gardening?'

'Why not?' Charlotte said. If she'd been chewing gum, Jack imagined she'd have chosen this exact moment to pop a bubble.

'Please,' Jack said, rubbing his forehead. 'Where's Mum? Where might she have gone?'

Charlotte was teetering backwards on her chair, picking off

flecks of black nail polish and flicking them on to the tabletop. Their dad, meanwhile, had fished out a small pile of pistachios from somewhere and was daintily unshelling them with his own dirty fingernails.

'Charlotte,' Jack said, screwing up his face, casting a glance at the sink and the hand soap beside it. 'Can you tell him not to do that when I'm trying to—'

'Dad,' Charlotte cut in. 'Can I have one?'

Jack was getting increasingly vexed. He fidgeted on the spot, watching his dad attempt to toss a pistachio into his laughing daughter's mouth.

'Look,' said Jack, as a pistachio shell bounced off his chest. 'Can we just—' he tried again, before another pistachio shell hit him square in the face.

His dad was stifling a yawn. His sister was teeing up another pistachio shell, this time to be flicked. And the fox, getting more and more frustrated, was bouncing higher and higher outside the window, as if there were a miniature trampoline hidden out of sight.

Jack! It shouted, as it bounced. *Jack! Jack!*

'That's it,' Jack said, raising his voice, both in pitch and in volume.

Charlotte dropped the pistachio shell. The fox stopped jumping. And his dad, who'd been halfway through turning to look out of the window, finally faced him.

'I feel like I'm the only one taking this seriously,' Jack said.

There was a long silence. Jack's dad looked at Charlotte, then looked out of the window, at the blank space where the fox had been. Charlotte, still facing Jack, opened her mouth slightly. She shook her head, pushed her tongue against her bottom lip.

'What aren't you getting?' she said. 'She left us,' she continued, quieter. She followed her dad's gaze out of the window, away from Jack. 'It must run in the family.'

Jack was about to say: I didn't leave you, when the doorbell rang. Then he was about to say: I had a reason to leave, but the doorbell rang again. In the end, he said nothing at all, leaving the kitchen in a huff, crossing over to the front door and wrenching it open with a little more force than was necessary. The postman stood on the front step, grunting hello, riffling through a sheaf of letters. Jack could see, over the postman's shoulder, the fox sitting dejected by the front gate, as still as a garden ornament. The postman handed Jack an assortment of post. A brochure for a retirement home. A leaflet for a conservatory company. A flyer about the sinister intentions of a candidate for the local council.

And a postcard. From their mum.

nine

Autumn. Two people meet in an orchard. It's early, and the dawn light seems rusty, not yet awake, as it yawns and filters through a canopy of orange and brown. Leaves rustling above. Leaves laying a carpet below. Upon that carpet, shiny red apples, the sort you'd see glistening in a fairy tale. Over those apples, an upturned bucket, and upon that bucket, a woman taking a breather, taking a bite from one.

She barely heard the man approach, despite his heavy boots, despite the fact that there was no one else at work in this specific row of trees. His footsteps were soft. His voice was gentle. He'd have needed to raise it to be heard over the crunch of the apple. He didn't raise it. It didn't seem in his nature.

'Sorry?' Hazel said, still chewing, wiping her mouth. Decorum had never been her strong suit.

'I said,' he said, a little lilt of somewhere else in his voice. 'I don't think you're supposed to eat them.'

The trees waved in the wind as if wagging their fingers. An apple fell to the ground between them, like a gauntlet thrown down.

'If they don't want me to eat them,' said Hazel, already baring her fangs for another bite, 'they'll have to pay me more.'

The man looked at her for a moment, quietly contemplating. Her eyeliner was thick and black, her boots shiny and black-laced and stitched with yellow, hardly designed for apple picking. She had freckles across her cheeks. And her hair, which had until recently been gelled into points, was bushy and untamed, the same shade of jet black, enveloping her head like a storm cloud. His own hair better matched the setting, another shade of rust, a conker-brown cascade which fell almost to his shoulders. Pretty hair, she thought. He was wearing sturdy trousers, a thick flannel shirt, a tattered wax jacket with a book poking out of one pocket. From where she was sitting, it looked well thumbed. The man adjusted the thin, gold frames of his glasses, scratched his beard. Hazel liked this beard, one which had clearly taken some growing. It was so thick that the man almost seemed to have no mouth, until he started to smile, and a row of crooked but surprisingly white teeth appeared. The smile turned into a grin, which turned into a gentle laugh. He bent down and picked up an apple of his own, which he then polished on his sleeve. He bit into the apple, its juice running into the beard that Hazel already liked.

'I hear you,' he said.

Above them, from a telephone wire, a swallow took flight. Hazel didn't notice. She'd never had much time for birds, though she'd soon make time, would soon come to see them as he did. In his other pocket was a pair of binoculars, but Hazel didn't know that yet.

Before that, before binoculars, before birds, Hazel was thinking about the odds. Of being lost, of loping between part-time jobs at pubs and festivals and family farms like an itinerant worker of old, of ending up at this particular orchard with its bunk-beds and its buckets like the one she was currently sitting on. The odds of having saved just about enough to leave this wretched country behind for good. To leave behind a country which sneered at strikers in the north and battered rioters in the south, a country which dragged free-thinkers like her from beanfields and beat them with clubs. The odds of a country like this being in the rear-view mirror, and then, at the last minute, this beard appearing. And this man, with it.

'I'd offer you a seat, but it's a small bucket.'

He enjoyed that one. The smile, and its teeth, reappeared. And if he'd been looking at the swallow, not Hazel, he might just have turned the conversation towards it. He might have remarked that it was late in the year for it to be sticking around. Fly, my pretty, Hazel might have replied. Don't you have somewhere else to be? Migration is a strange and slow-moving process, and if this swallow hadn't yet undertaken its journey to the other end of the earth, there must have been something unseen which was keeping her here, suspended in the air above this particular orchard on this particularly balmy autumn day. Down there, on top of a bucket and under an apple tree, Hazel had been ready for a migration of her own. Little did she know, from a carpet of apples and a flurry of rusted leaves and a reddish beard belonging to a stranger, she'd already started gathering that with which she'd build her own nest.

ten

You're sure it's from her?
It says, right here.
Mum.

Gerry was struggling to keep up with yet another heated conversation. Something about a postcard, something about a mum.

Had Charlotte's mother been in touch? Had she told them why she'd left? Gerry knew that his own mother was long dead, and had an inkling that his daughter's mother was long gone.

He was lucid enough to wonder where she was, although he did find it hard to remember the last time he'd actually seen her.

She says she's in Alderney.
She says there's something she needed to do.
Where the fuck is Alderney?

Before the postcard arrived, Gerry had been gardening. Then he'd been called to the table, under the pretence that he was about to have his lunch.

Had his daughter said anything about lunch? When he sat down at the table, there was no food to be seen.

The young man was angry again. He reminded Gerry of his son, same fussy temper. But Gerry's son was all grown up.

I am hungry
and lunch is not served.
Hence why I carry pistachios
in my pocket.

The top of the young man's white ears were turning red. That was another similarity he had with Gerry's son.

Gerry's son never liked it when people misbehaved. He hated it when people didn't follow the rules. Gerry was once an anarchist. His son would have been as bad an anarchist as Gerry was a dad.

The doorbell rang, and Gerry found himself alone for a

moment. Charlotte came back in, and look! She'd brought Johnny with her. Or, no, not Johnny. Someone who looked just like him.

They were talking about a postcard. Gerry tried to hide his disappointment.

                              Where is Alderney?
                    That's what everyone's asking.
                              They should ask him.

Gerry knew that, on Alderney, the hedgehogs were blonde. He also knew exactly where Alderney was.

And yet, if he tried to tell them where it was, they'd look back at him with annoyance or condescending sympathy as if either of them could point to Alderney on a map.

This was happening more often. People taking things he did and said and turning them into symptoms. Forgetting to eat. Misplacing his glasses. Still not knowing how to work a mobile phone.

I've always done those things, he wanted to say. I've always been me.

                       Say something, Gerry thinks.
                    Is it from your mum? Gerry says.

93

A pause in the conversation. The young man, who wasn't
Johnny, really did look familiar.

He looked awkward, too, averting his eyes and fiddling
with the postcard. Who's this? Gerry wanted to say, but his
daughter was already speaking.

Don't worry, Dad. She patted his arm, couldn't hide the pity
in her expression. Gerry tried to copy their mannerisms.

His daughter's concerned eyes.
The young man's downturned mouth.

The conversation continued without Gerry's input.
Nowadays, he worried that people wouldn't talk to
him unless he said something of substance.

He'd never had much to say. He'd never much liked talking.
But he'd rather force himself to speak than fade into the
background.

The thing that frightened Gerry the most was being lost.

So, he says things like:
Have you seen your mother?
And his daughter says things like:
Don't worry, she'll be back soon.

That morning, even the crossword had seemed to mock

Gerry. As if it was making a point of testing his memory. As if they'd made it harder just to spite him.

Could they do that? It was worth investigating. He'd written a note, just as the doctor had told him to, but he couldn't remember where the note had gone or what the note had said.

I told you, says his daughter.
If she was missing, she wouldn't send postcards.
You were the one who told me she was missing!
The young man pauses, shakes his head.
I can't believe she'd just leave.

The young man was frustrated, yes, but it was Gerry's daughter who was angry now.

Gerry knew his daughter. What annoyed her, and who had the power to hurt her. Beneath all that anger, it wasn't hard to see the hurt.

I can't believe she'd just run away, the young man says.
Can't you? his daughter replies. It's what you do.

In the silence that followed, the young man transformed before Gerry's eyes. His mouth closed tightly, as if it were painful, holding in all of those things he wanted to say.

The young man turned angry, back into an angry young

man. And Gerry, who'd been transforming, too, of late, saw the angry young man become Johnny.

Johnny had also been angry. Johnny had also been young. Tie around the collar around the veins upon his neck, the weight of his entire world upon his shoulders.

Live in the real world! said Johnny, to Gerry.
Johnny? says Gerry, to the angry young man.
What? says the angry young man, to Gerry.
What? says Gerry, to all of it.

At least they'd stopped arguing. Instead, they were both looking at him.

He was looking at the floor.

Come on, Dad, says his daughter.
Let's dig that carrot trench.

And Gerry wanted to hug her, but he didn't. He simply told her it was a good idea and left the shadow of Johnny in the kitchen.

In the garden, while his daughter fetched the shovels, Gerry had a moment to clear his head. The woods had always felt like reason to him, so he stared into them, reasoning.

If his wife were here, she'd understand. She'd know how
to make their daughter happier, the angry young man less
afraid.

> I can't do it
> without you.

He'd been nervous, the first time they'd gone for a drink, the
two of them together in a dark-carpeted pub with a too-hot
fire.

He'd said all the wrong things. And yet, she'd known exactly
what he'd meant. She always had.

I'll marry you, one day, he'd thought. She took some
convincing, but one day, he had.

> Now Gerry stares into the woods, looking for reason,
> wondering if he's driven his wife away.
> Padding paws offer no answer.

The sound that Gerry turned to was, in his assumption, the
sound of his daughter returning from the shed.

But his daughter was still gone. In her place was a fox,
standing silently on the patio at the side of the house.

For a moment, the fox looked at Gerry, and Gerry looked at
the fox, and Gerry thought he remembered something, or

perhaps knew something, some fact, suggested by the fox's presence.

Then the fox scampered away, towards the back door, and the fact become hard to grasp, and reason became harder to come by, and the fox soon felt like some part of a wider puzzle which Gerry couldn't solve without his wife.

You're not in Alderney.
We both know you wouldn't run away,
and only make it that far.

Gerry was sure that the postcard was meant for him. That he was expected to understand.

You're sending me a message, he wanted to write back, to a return address which didn't exist. But I don't know what it is.

I'm too far gone for puzzles, he'd write. I don't know how to do this by myself.

No, you're not in Alderney.
Hazel, where are you?

eleven

A woman stares into a pair of binoculars, though she doesn't exactly know how to work them. They feel heavier than expected, the lenses worn and foggy through overuse. It is barely morning, the sky tinged with violet, bruised by bluish clouds. Only something nocturnal could see clearly, out here. The woman frowns, tries anyway, squinting through the lenses. She's skilled with a film camera, but binoculars are alien to her. She's about to give up when another pair of hands, a man's, reach around her shoulders and steady them for her. The man turns a dial between the lenses, then adjusts a lever above the dial. Suddenly, it's like a fog has lifted. Suddenly, the woman can see clearly.

'Do you see it?'

Who was Hazel, before she met Gerry in that orchard? She'd often felt as if she'd been born on one stormy morning at sea, though she must have been five years old, perhaps older, by the time she found herself on the boat in question. In her memory, the sound of that particular morning coursed through her like a rhythm. Or perhaps it had been the rhythm which beat itself out like a sound, the slosh of milk in a pail, the slop of an overflowing bucket being carried, heavy-handed, down a country lane. Little Hazel could almost have been lulled to sleep by the waves, the way they rocked her to and fro as she crouched, hidden, in a makeshift cradle, rusty crab cages on one side and buckets of hastily patched wire netting on the other. Do not allow yourself to be lulled, she thought. Hazel wouldn't let the creeping tendrils of tiredness sabotage her great adventure. She heard heavy footsteps across the deck, a smoker's cough, male laughter. She made herself smaller, kept her breath held despite knowing they'd never hear it over the sound of the sea, that giant bucket. The water smacked against the side of the boat she was pressed against, as if patting her on the back. She'd done it. She'd really done it. Then the footsteps became louder, the tarp was torn from over her head, and the gentle rolling of a genial ocean revealed itself for what it actually was. A violent storm, bearing down upon her.

Why had she always remembered that day as stormy? She knew that, if she dug up the shipping forecasts, they'd have proclaimed the weather moderate, or slight. But Hazel was a born romantic, and her memories were romanticised accordingly. Baiting anaemic-looking crabs with bacon rinds and trapping them in claustrophobic buckets seemed, in her head, an idyllic exploit worthy of an Enid Blyton book. Her father, the fisherman, became a roving adventurer, a bastion of moustachioed masculinity, a Hemingway hero who was only at home on the high seas.

Was her father really a sallow-faced drunk who was barely ever there? Was it in fact calm that morning, devoid of thunder? Her dad was a lot of things, but he wasn't irresponsible. At least, not when it came to his boat, the only child he actually bothered to take care of. The sea hadn't really been stormy. She'd just been small. She still remembered his face as it had loomed over her when he discovered she'd stowed away, the bulging vein in his forehead, the redness in those ever-glassy eyes. He'd said that she'd wasted his morning, that she was a waste of space, that she never listened.

'You can't just do whatever you want all the time,' he'd said. Why not? He could.

Who was Hazel before that orchard? She'd played synths in a band as a teenager. Butcher's Dozen, they were called. She'd shaved her head once, pierced her ears with safety pins more times than she could count. She'd spent her entire adolescence doing whatever she'd wanted, simply because she'd been told not to by a man who stank of kippers and tobacco and spent all of her book money on cheap Scotch. She much preferred her eccentric aunt in the city, with whom she'd moved in as an idealistic art school graduate. With that aunt's encouragement, she'd planned to conquer Camden Market, then Carnaby Street, then the world, with nothing more than a battered sketchbook, a broken sewing machine and a mindset more wide-eyed than her cynical manner suggested. But she wasn't her aunt. She wasn't cut out for city living, unprepared for the cut-and-thrust of it. She'd always preferred wearing the clothes she made to hawking them, and her short temper and customer-is-always-wrong attitude didn't endear her to snooty shops or self-important shoppers.

Hazel was a born romantic. She'd always loved hearing stories of her aunt's flamboyant life, cigarettes in elegant holders and crystal coupes overflowing with champagne, an ever-revolving door of beautiful strangers and thrilling liasons. Hazel had long fantasised about a life just as hedonistic, but a bit more her: smouldering joints to accompany that champagne, ear-splitting music which never stopped, strangers who were even more beautiful for their tongue piercings and neck tattoos. The city was hers for the taking. And yet, Hazel had no money. She was tired, all the time. The music got louder, the days longer, and she found herself out of her depth. The grind was something she hadn't accounted for, and it wasn't long before it ground her down. For all her romantic ideas, Hazel could only take a few years of the rat race before she jumped ship.

Who was Hazel before that orchard? That's what she was trying to find out as she backpacked towards her mid-twenties between festivals and communes, bartending gigs and seasonal stints picking whatever she was told to by whichever farmer paid promptly, in cash. She was saving to travel. She was desperate to see more of it, all of it. Since that morning at sea, since long before that morning, she'd been in love with the natural world, and fierce about protecting it. No more fish guts, no more baited crabs. Her first job had been in a cat shelter, her first suspension on account of freeing all the frogs earmarked for dissection from the school science lab. She was still in college when she started attending protests and sabotaging hunts.

Her guerrilla expertise ranged from homemade tinctures which would throw off hounds, to the perfect method of going limp if apprehended by hard-hatted policemen outside a centre that tested on beagles.

What lay beyond that orchard, for Hazel? She wasn't exactly sure. If she was soul-searching, all she knew was that she'd find what she was searching for somewhere very far away. Managing habitats for the endangered wildcats of Clashindarroch Forest in Aberdeenshire, perhaps. Or even further. Rescuing sea turtles from flotillas of plastic in the Indian Ocean, or hunting down elephant poachers on the South African savannah. Right now, she couldn't see very far ahead. Her vision had been blocked by a man with wire-framed glasses and shoulder-length hair, a rust-brown beard and a well-worn jacket with a well-thumbed book sticking out of its pocket. *The Pocket Guide to British Birds*. He'd said he was putting the title to the test. Because, you know, it was in his pocket. And if that joke seemed awkward, it was nothing compared to the quality of his conversation at a pub table in the nearest village that Friday night, after she'd taken the initiative and asked him out on a date.

'Is it hot in here?' he said, fanning the bottom of his thick corduroy shirt. 'It feels too hot in here.'

In his defence, they were sitting in front of a roaring fire. But the fact that this question came just after he'd returned from the toilets, face recently splashed with cold water, and just before he knocked a brimming pint of brown ale over the table and the shrieking barmaid, suggested that something else was at play. He was nervous. He spoke too quietly for the noisy surroundings, stuttered when he tried to speak up. When he tried to compliment Hazel on her hairstyle and ended up comparing it to the mane of a Highland cow, it sent her into peals of laughter which turned him even redder than he had been already. And by the time he'd confessed that he rarely came to pubs, that he'd always felt more at home outside than in, he was already shaking his head and glancing at the door, clearly confident that he'd blown it.

His glasses were fogging up. The stuffy old locals wouldn't stop staring at her Highland hair, so tall and so dramatically cascading from an immaculately gelled point over her forehead. Hazel didn't notice anyone else. She sat fascinated, like a zoologist discovering a new animal for the very first time. None of the other men she'd been out with had listened to her, truly listened to her, when she'd talked about her dad, about the sea, about how angry the old man could get after the drink took hold. No one else could have got that information out of her in the first year of a relationship, let alone on a first date. She felt embarrassed, equally out of her element, though she was far better at hiding it. Was she oversharing? Or had she finally found someone with whom she wanted to share?

Hazel smiled, took Gerry's hand. He seemed surprised, but he didn't pull away.

'Where would you rather be?' she said.

Which is how they ended up standing on the crest of an open field, semi-submerged in a weedy hedgerow, still awake somewhere between last orders and the sun coming up. That bruised sky. That violet light. Other guys took Hazel to sticky bars and stinking nightclubs. Gerry brought her here, to this dark and yet luminous place, and handed her his most treasured possession: a beaten-up pair of binoculars.

'Look there,' he said, and his voice sounded different to how it had just a couple of hours before. She'd found his habitat. 'Owl.'

And she looked, and he helped, and she saw. It sat on a fence post, like an extension of the wood. A creature made of bark, a creature of another time, its small movements accompanied by the imagined creak of something wooden, something old. When its shining black eyes turned in her direction, she felt something like fear. She supposed it was awe.

At the pub, she'd been provocative.

'Birds?' she'd said, taking a sip of Guinness. 'I love animals, but looking for birds seems a bit boring.'

He'd flushed, yes, but he'd replied with an unexpected confidence. 'Then you're not looking in the right places.'

When that owl looked at Hazel – or, she supposed, at something else, something behind her, it couldn't care less about her existence – she understood what he'd meant. And she felt, as she had been feeling for a while, a sense that what she'd been seeking with the punks and the crusties wasn't the kind of freedom she truly craved. She wanted something more profound, something not counter to culture but beyond it, something beyond everything. Her life before had been defined by noise. Now she was away from it, she'd never felt more alive.

'It's so quiet,' she said, unable to hide the wonder on her face.

'Oh, I wouldn't say that.'

Gerry closed his eyes. So Hazel followed suit, closing hers, too. And he was right. She'd barely registered the dawn chorus. Or, if she had, she'd always thought of it as something subtle, something soft and peaceful. But here in this field with her eyes closed, the sound of the birds wasn't small, like the birds themselves. It was enormous, like the entire sky. Hundreds of voices crying out, though for what, she didn't yet know. The man next to her, the man she hardly knew, the one whose body she now nestled into, would have been able to pick any voice from that throng and identify it. He'd tell her the difference between a chaffinch and a jay, a wren and a nightjar, a blackcap and a black-capped chickadee. But there'd be time for that. For now, she was content to let the crescendo of chirps and tweets and hoots and caws roll over her. There was so much she hadn't noticed.

twelve

Charlotte had always said there was a magic to Mole End, and Jack had always rolled his eyes. But by the third day of being back, he finally knew what she meant: the place was cursed. He'd woken, this morning, and for a moment he'd forgotten about the fox. But his delusion wasn't a twenty-four-hour thing, like food poisoning. When the fox had found its way into the house once again and started scrabbling at his bedroom door, Jack knew it wasn't a dream because he hadn't been able to sleep. When it had eventually pushed its way inside and hopped up to lie across his belly, Jack had been too busy thinking about the postcard to protest. This morning, when he checked that the fox was still there, he once again felt fur between his fingers. Jack didn't have the energy to scream or throw himself on to the carpet.

The postcard had changed things. On the face of it, their

mother had abandoned them on purpose. On the back of the card, she'd written that she was sorry, that she was so thankful for Charlotte, that she hoped she'd see them again, one day. Dramatic stuff. Now Jack stood in the kitchen, staring at the message again, trying to find some clues beneath the surface of that fading blue ink. The postcard had brought with it a strange sense of déjà vu, as if this wasn't the first time he'd been here, trying to work out where Alderney was. There was no return address. Her phone was still off.

Charlotte was upstairs, his dad outside. And the fox was sitting by Jack's ankles, prodding his leg over and over again with its moist black nose.

What's the issue? the fox had asked when Jack first picked up the postcard.

'My mum's gone AWOL,' Jack had replied, distractedly, forgetting that the fox didn't exist.

The fox had paused, cocked its head, flicked its ear. *What's a wol?*

Though Charlotte had always said there was a magic to Mole End, Jack had never believed her. As a grown-up, he favoured his cold, hard facts to her crystals and horoscopes. She had a flair for the dramatic, could be put in a funk for days on account of a pessimistic palm reading, had refused to engage with Jack's ex-girlfriend in the city on account of her 'bad aura'. Though he'd never admit it to her, Jack had found the woods beyond the house terrifying as a child, had lain in bed night after night with the feeling that things were out there, and that those things were out to get him. Charlotte had always been the opposite of him. She'd talked cheerily of imaginary friends and monstrous things that went bump in the night, even built little twig-and-moss cottages for sprites on the threshold of the forest. Jack always made it clear that he was too sensible to believe in fairy stories. While other children might have imagined otherworldly creatures scurrying about behind this house's irregular walls or beneath its creaking floorboards, theirs was the kind of imagination that Jack simply didn't have. He'd always found it hard to give his attention to things which weren't there.

What are we going to do today?

Jack ignored the fox, again, but wondered what he'd do, today. In the city, when he was feeling harangued, cornered or under assault, he'd go running or spend his time cooking. Both required focus. Both were best done alone, and in silence. Both were Jack's way of meditating, and so he'd do both, today. What do we seek in the country? A retreat. Hugh and Hugo would always head to the countryside when things got a bit much. A renovated cottage on a sprawling estate. Clay pigeon shooting and cold-water swimming. Private chefs and small-batch whisky. They were probably somewhere, out there now, resting and recuperating.

Where are we going? said the fox, as it followed Jack down the front path and out of the front gate.

It kept pace with him as he ran, around the corner and down the steep lane and on to the straight road that led into the village. As Jack pounded the pavement, his pulse pounding with it, the fox stuck by his side, tirelessly repeating the same question. The weather was muggy. Jack was already sweating, but desperate to wring some enjoyment out of the experience. He'd always wanted to run barefoot, or at least get a pair of those running shoes which looked like human feet, a hole for each toe. He didn't have the money for new trainers, so he ran in a pair of beaten-up old running shoes, clenching his jaw, driving each step into the ground as if he were trying to push it away. He descended, and his route descended with him, into pastoral parody. One warning which said 'HEDGEHOG CROSSING AREA', another which said 'TOADS ON THE ROAD AT NIGHT'. A wonky black-and-white road sign close to toppling over, one arm pointing downwards, the other up. A derelict old farm building with an undulating crack in its roof, the missing tiles giving it the impression of an enormous gap-toothed grin. All the while, the fox dipped in and out of sight behind the trees, squeaking like a dog toy all the while.

Wait for me! Wait for me! Wait for me!

The fox was clearly reticent about encountering people. By the time they reached the outskirts of the village, it became more inclined to skulk in alleyways or hide behind bins than nip at his heels as it had on country lanes. Despite the deadening heat and the worsening drought, the triangle of grass on which the war memorial stood was still AstroTurf green, the old folk congregating outside the pub where Charlotte worked still dressed in woollen suits and itchy-looking cardigans. Only small hints betrayed the fact that the village was changing, looking to appease Jack's old friends in the city who'd started moving out to places like this. The village shop had gone zero-waste. Electric car charging points had sprung up along the road, next to signs outside the village's other pub, advertising Negroni happy hours and Bottomless Mimosa brunches. The greengrocer's was the only shop which remained relatively unchanged, apart from the cardboard Sellotaped to the insides of the windows. Even on a day like this, looking at it was enough to give Jack goosebumps.

Last year, his dad had closed down the greengrocer's. According to Jack's mum, he'd been finding it a bit much. She said that she was too old to take over, that Charlotte was too young. Besides, his sister was apparently content with the job that she already had. What about Jack? Charlotte and their mum must have thought that the idea of him coming back and taking the reins was laughable. His dad had never had any real staff to speak of, so the place had been shuttered. It had sat dormant since then, his dad stubbornly refusing to sell. When Jack had asked Charlotte about it, she'd been uninterested, her mind on other things. She'd told him, yesterday, that the doctor had suggested that their dad sign some forms. That if it came to it, his family could make certain decisions for him. Legal ones, financial ones. Unsurprisingly, Jack's dad refused to do that, too. Jack would have been able to sort the place out, on the family's behalf. He knew a guy who specialised in office real estate. He could picture it now, as a glass-fronted co-working space, an out-of-the-city retreat for laptop-toting digital nomads. And yet, the picture in his mind, and the thought of making the call to make it happen, filled him with a deep and squirming kind of malaise.

'Hey,' Jack said suddenly, to the fox, which was crouching at the end of the alleyway beside the shop. Jack crouched, too. 'I need your help.'

My help? said the fox, eyes glittering.

'My dad used to own this place,' Jack said, gesturing at the greengrocer's. 'I need to see what state it's in.'

What state it's in? the fox repeated, dreamily, looking up at the blank wall.

'But I don't have any keys,' said Jack, theatrically frowning, theatrically patting his pockets.

No keys, said the fox, eyes darting back and forth, mind racing. *No keys! No problem! Leave it with me.*

And the fox was off, down the alleyway, snuffling up and down the perimeter of the property, pointing its snout upwards towards any possible entrance. Jack watched, pretending to stretch his hamstrings, massaging his bad ankle. Jack knew foxes were sneaky. But weren't they supposed to be wily, too? Tricking the fox had felt like plucking low-hanging fruit.

Walking alone back to the road, Jack didn't feel good. He felt empty, and as he looked behind him at the empty greengrocer's, he felt emptier. On the other side of those boarded-up windows, when Jack was little, his dad had shelled raw peas and fed them to him. A rare memory of the pair of them, just them, together. Jack in shorts, spindly legs swinging from the countertop, all the doors and windows flung open to counter the summer heat. The peas had tasted sweet, strangely cold. The adult Jack wasn't one for sentiment. He got that from his father, a man who, instead of affection, had given him an encyclopaedic knowledge of mushrooms. That's why the recollection of the peas unnerved him. Usually, when he thought of his dad, he found it hard to bring memories to mind. If questioned on this, Jack might have pointed to the fact that his dad was always too distracted to play with him and his toys, and would only stoop to spend days with him if they sat silently with fishing rods or a pair of binoculars. He might have mentioned that his dad had never once come to any of his football games, or his cricket matches, or anything at all where one might hope one's father might be. He might have said, I don't know about your dad, but the one time mine was supposed to pick me up, I spent my evening, alone, in the car park.

It had always been in his father's nature to be stiff and unloving. It was always in Jack's to counter his rejection with avoidance. His dad had quietly disapproved of his chosen course of study, and had made that disapproval loud with a conspicuously empty seat at his university graduation ceremony. For the entirety of Jack's adult life, his dad had decided to be absent. For the audacity of wanting more for himself, of wanting out of this place, Jack had been made to feel like an outsider. Black sheep. White Fang. For Jack, distance turned into disdain. There was one moment which felt pivotal to him, a painful scene which had played out in the corridor of his student flat on the very day he'd moved to that red-brick university his father would never deign to visit. It had since replayed in Jack's mind, more times than he'd care to admit. One of Jack's new flatmates, saying goodbye to her parents in the corridor of their hall of residence Her father, hugging her, saying 'I love you.' And Jack, standing dumbstruck and alone with a cardboard box filled with his possessions, thinking: my dad would never do that, never say that. My dad never has.

Jack hadn't realised that he'd stopped moving, that he was

rooted to the spot at the end of the alleyway. He cricked his neck, clenched and unclenched his fingers, glanced in the direction of the fox he thought he'd just got rid of. It was currently trying to climb a wheelie bin beneath a fire escape. It jumped up, but couldn't get high enough, bouncing off the bin with the sound of a hollow drum. Back in the dirt, it scrabbled, shook itself off, then got back on its feet, un-deterred. It jumped again, missed again, bounced again. And though Jack would have liked to convince himself that he couldn't feel anything for something which he still suspected wasn't really there, he couldn't help but swallow hard and notice a tight knot of something close to guilt unravelling in his stomach. This wasn't a migraine. It was the other thing, the thing he didn't tell anyone about, the waves of panic which left him doubled up and unable to breathe. He'd tried to stave them off with a stable job. Running, cooking, those were meant to be reliable fallbacks. Why was he still feeling like this?

The fox had finally succeeded. Now, with considerably more grace than before, it hopped on to the fire escape, climbed a few rungs and slipped into the shop through an open vent. At the moment just before it was gone, Jack thought about calling out, but he was dizzy, and he was focusing on trying to breathe. He couldn't see the fox any more. Where was the fox? Jack closed his eyes, breathed through his nose, breathed out of his mouth. There was something else, apart from the peas, boring its way into his brain. The back legs of the fox, quivering as it slipped through the vent, had called to mind a rabbit. Frail back legs trapped by twisted metal. Stuck firm, trying desperately to escape. Jack stood still, urged his mind to stop. He begged, silently, for it to stop.

———

Back in the kitchen at Mole End, Jack acted like nothing had happened. He'd put all thoughts of the village firmly out of his mind. He'd done the same with the desperate climb back, when his chest had been so tight he'd had to stop and lean against a tree in order to ensure he kept breathing. He'd put on a brave face for the shopkeepers, had returned replete with brown paper bags filled with ingredients from the deli, the butcher and the village shop. He had not returned with the fox.

'What are you making?' said Charlotte, from the doorway.

Jack ignored her. Cooking was a solo endeavour. When Jack was in the kitchen, his mind couldn't be further from missing mothers and tricked foxes, from crippling migraines and unexpected panic attacks. The safety of being held within a recipe, the surety of repetitive motions, the smoothing chop and snap and sizzle. The silence. Back in the city, Jack lived on his own. Even before he lost his job, the evenings could get very long without an extravagant meal-for-one to prepare. The patience, the prep, was his own form of meditation. He had his own special knife, this one that he'd brought with him from the city in its leather carrying case. It was hand-forged, high-carbon, imported from Japan.

'Earth to dickhead.'

'What?' Jack said, impatiently, his eyes trained on the blade. The knife was as sharp as it was expensive.

'What are you making?'

Jack looked at the asparagus, now extricated from its brown paper bag and rubber bands, rolling around in ruthlessly sliced discs. He'd shelled the peas, zested the lemon. He turned to his sister. He remembered a purple streak in her hair, last time they'd seen each other, back in the city. It was gone now. And how long had she been taller than him? Jack's neck was tight after his episode in the village, his legs aching from his run. He used to work them harder than other parts of his body, simply because he was self-conscious about them. He hated that his lean, gymnast's physique had once been described as 'elfin', as much as he hated the idea that his angular face was 'impish' or that the six feet in height he claimed was actually closer to five foot nine. As for his legs, he'd always felt he lacked muscle in his lower half, always felt he looked like he'd skipped leg day, always felt people in the gym were watching and sniggering when he tried to stretch his hamstrings and couldn't touch his toes. Jack checked the recipe. *Trim off the woody stalks.* He blocked the pieces of asparagus which were trying to escape the chopping board, crossed the kitchen and scraped the offcuts into the bin.

'Pasta,' he said.

Charlotte made a sound of approval or disapproval. It was always hard to tell with her. As she played around on her phone, Jack unwrapped a greasy parcel of meat, made several more incisions. He sliced pieces into smaller pieces, throwing them into a mixture of butter and oil to render the fat. Using this pan, that wooden spoon, felt sacrilegious, like toying with a dead person's precious belongings. This kitchen was his mother's domain, and spending time in it only served to remind Jack that she wasn't here. She'd taught him to cook in this very room. Peeling carrots and parboiling potatoes after a long walk on a Sunday morning, or weekday afternoons spent standing at this stove, perched patiently on a footstool, stirring a bubbling cauldron of jam. His dad would play the hunter-gatherer role, traipsing his muddy boots into the kitchen, silently piling his fresh-dug produce on the countertop behind them. My caveman, his mother would call him. Young Jack wouldn't turn to see his dad's reaction, but he would take time to mime being sick.

Charlotte was off her phone. Her arms were crossed. 'Is that pork?'

Jack had been staring at his mother's knife marks, years of them etched into the wooden chopping board beneath his fingers. Now he followed Charlotte's chewed fingernail to where it was pointing, the pan within which the butter was already beginning to brown. Jack grimaced, turned down the heat.

'Guanciale,' he said, picking out some burnt bits.

'And is that pork?'

Jack looked at her impatiently. 'Cured pork cheek, actually.'

'Cured pork cheek, actually,' mimicked Charlotte, her voice high and clipped. Then her face went serious again. 'That's not vegetarian.'

'I know, thank you,' he said, shaking his head. 'I won't put any in Dad's portion.'

She continued to watch. Jack could feel her eyes on him.

'What?' he said, turning from the pan, wooden spoon in hand.

'I'm vegetarian, too.'

Jack stared at her for a while. She stared back.

'You could have said,' he said.

Charlotte shrugged. 'No one asks me anything.'

Jack sighed, put down his mum's wooden spoon. He gripped the counter, contemplating the spoon and the mother who wasn't here to use it. He knew what this was really about.

'Look,' he said, as calmly as possible. 'I'm just as angry as you.'

Charlotte laughed drily. 'You aren't.'

There was a long pause, in which Jack thought it probably best to agree with her. 'I am,' he said, quietly, because he couldn't help himself.

Charlotte's expression darkened. 'Believe me,' she said, voice like acid. 'You aren't.'

Before either of them could say anything more, the doorbell rang. Jack stood huffing. Charlotte huffed off. Over the sizzling fat and the hiss of the kettle, Jack's mind boiled over. Well-salted pasta water is the secret to an unctuous sauce, proper carbonara uses egg yolks instead of cream, his mother had upped and left and taken a ferry to Alderney and wasn't planning on returning any time soon. He leaned with his back against the counter, staring out of the long windows at the shape of his dad, standing at the end of the garden, half-hidden by the encroaching forest. Jack almost wondered what his father was thinking. Then Charlotte reappeared in the doorway, something in her hands. He could see from here that the card was just as whimsically retro as the last one, as if it had travelled decades as well as miles. On the front was a picture of a wooden bench and a grassy knoll, overlooking a lake at the foot of a range of enormous, snow-capped mountains.

The oil in the pan spat like a caged animal. Their mum was getting further away.

thirteen

A woman sits in the back of a van, its doors flung wide open on to an open hillside. She's drinking coffee out of a tin mug, and wondering if she's the coldest she's ever been in her life. The valley is verdant, only the tops of the mountains spread before them covered in with snow. They chose the time of year carefully, content to be chilly, but not to catch their deaths. Now they sit in the back of that van and stare out over this view and the woman, whose breath collects in clouds, has the distinct impression that she's looking not at a view in real life, but at a painting. It couldn't be more perfect, she thinks, until it is. The creature moves with total freedom, and with the curiosity of something that has never had that freedom curtailed. It watches them for a while, its horns as enormous as elephant tusks, so large and sweeping that they seem as if their weight should be pulling it backwards, off this rock and all the way down that slope. A chill runs down her spine. The wild beast snorts in greeting, its own white cloud forming an empty speech bubble in front of its mouth.

'Ibex,' says Hazel. Of course, he already knew that.

The young man she'd met in that orchard was, it turned out, a few years older than her. And though it would take months for her to find a way beneath that shy, introverted exterior, an excavation of Gerry Penwick always yielded surprises. He was full of stories, of plotting uproarious student demonstrations by candlelight in pub attics like Guy Fawkes, of chaining himself to a tree to protest about a new railway and having his nose broken for the trouble. Hazel had noticed it was a little wonky, but she was a sucker for imperfection. Gerry was a quiet revolutionary, a peaceful protestor with utopian ideas about using no money, about eating no meat, about living without cars or clothes or walls or roofs. He had calloused hands, knew how to work hard while expounding the benefits of hardly working. When he finally started speaking, really speaking, she never wanted him to stop. It was like hypnosis, always soft, always slow. In the forty years to come, he'd only once raise his voice. And the fact that he only ever spoke so expansively to her felt like a privilege, like he was a secret only she knew. Hazel couldn't imagine Gerry facing down a livid battalion of red-jacketed toffs on horseback, nor whipping a crowd of mass trespassers into a frenzy. And yet, she knew exactly how he'd done these things, so immersed was he in his quiet passions that it was impossible not to be swept along with him. She'd listen to him talk for hours. About the medicinal properties of psychedelic mushrooms. About the relative merits of reintroducing

beavers to British waterways. About the precedent set by the
heroes who marched on Kinder Scout ninety years ago to
establish the right to roam.

'Are you trying to get me to join a cult?' she'd asked, early on.

'I don't have the charisma for that,' he'd said. 'You're the only
one who doesn't fall asleep when I'm speaking.'

Since that evening in front of the pub fire and those early
hours behind the binoculars, she'd become a bona fide twitcher,
so they'd bonded as twitchers tended to bond. That is, on the
wing, accompanying each other from this adventure to that.
Hazel was the thrust of the pair, the get-up-and-go, and she
enjoyed embarrassing Gerry by forcing him to dance with her
at a ceilidh, or by picking fights with policemen who shoved
him with plastic shields at peaceful protests. He rarely swore.
She had a mouth like a fishwife, being the daughter of one.
They were opposites, and they attracted. And though he was the
knowledge on birds, he was hopelessly ignorant on everything
else. He'd never heard of Black Flag, or the Misfits, Minor
Threat or Bad Religion. When they watched the Berlin Wall
fall, on a tiny television in a Scottish island inn, she'd cheered
with the crowd while he'd basically just shrugged. Most aspects
of the human world seemed to simply pass him by.

'Have you heard of the hedgehog carousel?'

He'd asked her that, once, in the back of their van. It was a
peculiar mating ritual in which two courting hedgehogs would
circle each other, as if enacting a dance. Their own carousel
began in that orchard, and it followed its own series of dance-
like steps in the months that followed. After a few dates, they
ended up back in her bunk-bed at the farm, not as clandestinely

as the drunken pair of them might have believed. Of course, back then, neither of them knew that they'd be living together – in a campervan, yes, but still together – before the year was out. They moved fast, as far as humans were concerned. But by the time that second pair of campervan keys were cut, the lone swallow which had flown over their heads that day in the orchard had already joined a roosting flock of thousands, thousands of miles away.

Hazel and Gerry both knew that they were destined for things bigger than buckets and apple trees. Theirs would be a big love, the kind that crossed borders. Kazakhstan. The Khyber Pass. They'd live the life of migrating birds. On roofs, under stars. In the months that followed their first encounter, in pubs and on hikes and at friends' weddings, they raved excitedly to each other about following Darwin's route to the Galapagos Islands in search of blue-footed boobies, or settling under the South African sun between saddle-billed storks and southern ground hornbills. In their heads, these plans weren't fanciful. Yet for years, they found themselves grounded, unable to admit that it was money which stopped them from taking flight. Planes were expensive, as was petrol. They made do and mended. Gerry foraged for half of their food, grew the rest where he could. Hazel put her practical skills to good use, tooling up the van with a nearly new engine and a fairly old set of fairy lights. They had small adventures, all the while planning the big one. Hazel was often frustrated. Gerry was always, somehow, optimistic. He dreamed big, with a big smile on his face. Yet while Gerry would have happily hoped for the best and set off without a penny to their names, Hazel surprised them both by being sensible. If they wanted the adventure of a lifetime, first they'd need a safety net.

One year in. Living in the van, taking it on the ferry from Guernsey to Alderney. Oystercatchers and razorbills, and a jar filled with petty cash which was hidden in the glove compartment and rattled as they drove. Above the rattling, the ever-present hum of laughter. Two years together. A pilgrimage to the Isles of Scilly. The van broken into. A new jar started. Renting a small-town apartment which they both described as temporary, Hazel working at a newsagent's and Gerry driving forklifts laden with fruit and veg bound for supermarkets. Hazel's first attempts at home-baked bread. A running joke about Gerry being an insurance hazard in the kitchen. Three years. Trips to Tresco and Bryher and St Martin's and St Agnes, destinations which were fast becoming traditions for them, and for a van which was by now made up of so many replacement parts that Gerry had taken to calling it their Ship of Theseus. Everywhere they went, they bought postcards. But the only people they'd want to write to were each other, so the postcards stayed with them. Unwritten souvenirs. Blank memories. They spotted puffins on the Isle of May. A year later, they searched for sea eagles on Mull. One of the largest living birds of prey, from one of the oldest genera of living birds. Something huge and historical, something bigger, in spirit, than the both of them. Right here, within their grasp. Hazel never did spot one. She stood on a cliff having waited for hours with nothing but a Thermos of tea, watching waves which frothed like the champagne foam she'd once imagined would coat her life in the city. She'd always considered herself a glass-half-full person. More than half-full. In her mind, she'd always pictured her glass filling up and up and up until it would overflow with a cascade of foam, like that champagne, like those waves.

What are we waiting for? she'd thought.

'What are we waiting for?' she'd shouted, as she turned to Gerry, as the waves crashed and the sea spray erupted dramatically behind her.

Gerry's close-cropped beard revealed that same smile, those same uneven teeth, that same long hair buffeted across his face by the wind. 'You read my mind.'

So, Hazel and Gerry headed south for their great migration. They emptied the jar and filled the van with supplies, riding the Ship of Theseus from Newhaven to Dieppe, heading towards the Der-Chantecoq lake, along with thousands and thousands of cranes. A pit-stop near Dijon, another near Lausanne, wild camping all the while. All pointing towards this, the Alps, a tin mug of coffee and a vista like a painting and a curious ibex which neither of them would soon forget. Eyes like pits of fire smouldering in the desert, horns like the weapons of a Viking god. Wild enough to chill the blood in your veins, but tame enough that you could stay close, watching. She had her camera with her, but she couldn't bring herself to capture this on film. Some things are better kept in your mind's eye. Some moments are so peaceful, so pure and undisturbed, that it's inevitable they'll be followed by chaos.

They could have stayed there for ever, on that hilltop, with that ibex. But they had to leave. How were they supposed to know what would happen at the bottom of those mountains, in that tunnel, that very next morning? Everything was about to change, but Hazel and Gerry didn't know that yet. For now, they were just enjoying the view.

A fox exists on the edge of things, and so it makes no distinction between that and this. City and country. Village and forest. Human and beast.

And yet, this fox does not know what to make of this man. Jack, the human who so selflessly saved its life, but now seems horrified to have the fox here, alive, on his bedroom floor.

Jack, who had spoken to the fox, and heard the fox speak back, and yet now says nothing, encouraging the fox into the garden and then locking the door behind it.

Perhaps it was an accident. Perhaps Jack is having a bad day.

The fox stands beneath the back window, watched by a shrew too small and a hedgehog too spiky to offer it a leg-up. So, it jumps. And at the apex of each jump, it sees something different in the kitchen.

Jump.

Jack, holding court, the audience at the dining table distinctly uninterested.

Jump.

A girl, pelting Jack with pistachio shells. Jack, trying his best to ignore her.

Jump.

A white-faced, white-haired man. His wild, wide eyes turning the fox's way.

The fox lands, presses its body against the ground. Then it shuffles away, unsure of itself, afraid of being discovered by humans it doesn't know whether to trust.

On the front path, the fox watches a man in a red cap hand something to Jack. On the patio, the fox watches the older man traverse the garden.

The man straightens. The man turns. The fox doesn't hide this time. They share something, though the fox doesn't know what. A moment. An understanding.

You and I are one and the same. You and I exist on the edge of things.

The man heads for the forest. The fox can only assume it is his home. By nightfall, the fox will have found its way back into the house.

Wait for me! Wait for me! Wait for me!

Jack and the fox head for the village, Jack ahead, the fox behind. And even if Jack seems to be fleeing, he must know that, in some way, he needs the fox.

Since the common, their fates have been intertwined. The fox had been drawn back to Jack by its nose, led by its whiskers. The fox had nowhere else to go.

The fox would find a way to repay Jack. It just didn't know the way, quite yet.

I need your help, Jack says. I don't have any keys. And suddenly, the fox knows the way.

It's simple, with a little perseverance. Jump. Boing. Roll over. Jump. Boing. Roll over. Jump. Land. Jump again, climb a bit, crawl through a hole and tumble out into a dusty, desolate place.

The light is blocked by cardboard and white paint on the windows. A plum has gone mouldy in the middle of the floor. The fox doesn't know what it is looking for. The fox doesn't know what state it is in.

Outside, in the alleyway, Jack is nowhere to be seen. The fox must have taken too long. They must have been accidentally separated, again.

No matter. The fox exists on the edge of things. So it runs, sometimes on the road with the rats and the rabbits, sometimes through the woods with the weasels and the deer.

The hedgehog is waiting on the forest threshold when the fox returns. It seems out of its depth, but it still won't back down when the fox approaches.

A human on the patio, in a cloud of sweet smoke. Night is descending, and the darkness makes the figure hard to see. The fox creeps closer.

It's the girl from earlier, the one the fox had heard through Jack's bedroom door. The sister. She sniffs, wipes an eye, throws something glowing on the patio and stamps on it. Then, with reluctance, she goes inside.

The fox slips in with her. In a chaos of steam and running water, beeping timers and clattering pans, the fox crawls beneath the dining table. It can see Jack's legs, and it tries not to feel frustrated. It tries not to feel left behind.

The family take their seats. The girl is called Charlotte. The man is called Dad. Jack is chewing, and the fox is trying to get his attention. The food smells of lemon and cheese and earth-grown vegetables.

Dad is trying to speak, but his mouth is full. The fox creeps forward, looks up at him. His white hair hovers above his head, creating a halo effect in the harsh light above the dinner table.

'Did you know,' Dad says, stiltedly, 'that they've reintroduced wild boars to the Forest of Dean?'

Flecks of oil escape his lips and dribble down his chin. On the other side of the table, Jack sighs. Charlotte shifts in her chair, swallows a mouthful.

'They should reintroduce wildcats,' she says. 'Or wolves.'

The fox creeps back to the other side of the table. Jack's feet are firmly planted on the floor.

Behind the fox, above the fox, Dad is laughing. 'I don't think the farmers would be too happy about that,' he says.

'If you could bring back one animal, what would it be?' Charlotte asks.

The fox edges forwards, pokes its snout out from beneath the table. It is watching Jack now. He looks hot, bothered. Sitting at this table is a statement, from him. He hasn't done it since he's been home.

Dad has stopped chewing long enough to consider the question. 'I've always felt a kinship with mammoths.'

Charlotte laughs now. 'You are a bit of a mammoth.'

Jack looks down, into his bowl. Then down further, beneath his bowl and the table, into the eyes of the fox.

He does not jump. He does not look frightened, or surprised, or disappointed. Does he look relieved?

'In the Late Miocene era, there were hedgehogs as big as dogs,' Dad is saying. 'Hunted by barn owls as big as humans. Imagine that.'

Jack's hand, the one not holding a fork, is beneath the table. At first, the fox thinks Jack intends to push it away. But his hand extends, then rests on its ruff.

Jack doesn't quite scratch the fox's chin, or tousle behind its ear. He simply holds his hand steady in its fur.

Ask about foxes, the fox wants to whisper. Ask how big the foxes were.

'I got a job interview,' Jack says, almost to himself.

The conversation stops. Jack looks up, realises that Charlotte is looking at him. Dad is looking at him, too.

I'm here, the fox wants to whisper. But Jack has retracted his hand.

'It's this Friday,' Jack says, averting his eyes again. 'Just a phone thing. First round. But it sounds hopeful.'

Humans don't know how to express what they want. Jack wanted to say something else, but is talking about interviews instead. Dad is talking about mammoths, but mammoths aren't the meaning of what he's trying to say.

'Oh,' says Dad, absent-mindedly, at Jack.

'Eh?' says Charlotte, pasta sliding sleepily off her fork. 'Why are you looking for a job?'

The mood in the room shifts, suddenly. The fox senses it, like the bubbling over of water, or the dimming of lights.

Jack's eyes dart back and forth, as if making calculations. Behind the fox, Dad has tuned out. He stealthily spits out a mouthful of pasta.

'You had too much work on,' Charlotte says, also making calculations. 'Mum was missing. You didn't come home.'

'She's not missing.'

'You didn't know that,' Charlotte says. Her voice is breaking. 'You didn't come home for two whole days.'

Dad is sizing up the fridge. He pushes his chair back, folds up his napkin and leaves the table. Neither of his dinner companions seem to notice.

Jack is busy stuttering. He is scratching the coarse, wiry stubble on his cheek as if there are mites on his skin. I remember that feeling, thinks the fox.

Jack is drumming his leg on the floor as if he wants to chew it off. I remember that, too.

'Jack,' Charlotte says, coolly. 'Do you have a job?'

Jack can barely say no before Charlotte explodes.

She says he's selfish. She says he's unbelievable. She says she doesn't know why she asked him to come back, when they'd managed this long without him. She says that she deserves better, that Dad deserves better, that she's glad Mum isn't here to see the coward her son has become.

She says she used to look up to him, but now he's never looked so small.

Dad has taken some tomatoes out of the fridge. He finds a sharp-looking knife on the counter, resting on top of a leather carrying case.

He holds it up to the light, inspecting the patina. Then he carries it over to the chopping board.

It is Jack's turn to explode.

He says he didn't want to come back. He says he was perfectly happy where he was. He says that Mum's the selfish one, that Dad gave up his right to deserve anything from him long ago, that Charlotte doesn't have a clue how hard he was working in that job.

He tells her about how much was riding on his every calculation, and she makes a disparaging remark about reading some Heidegger. He tells her about his twelve-hour days, entire weekends on email, and she tells him that his priorities couldn't be clearer.

He brushes her off. This wasn't a part-time pub thing. He had a team, he says, people who listened to him. He was building something, not that she would care. He'd been fired, last Thursday. Not that she'd care about that, either.

'You're right,' she replies. 'I don't.'

Dad has started chopping, quick and carefree movements. The fox whimpers a little. No one else seems to care.

'You used to be smart,' he says. 'Don't blame me for your wasted potential.'

'Don't you dare,' she says, rising from her chair. 'I will not accept your pity.'

Dad has suddenly stopped chopping. He makes a guttural sound, but they can't hear him over their bickering.

The fox, trapped beneath the table, is panicking. It can see something that Jack and his sister cannot.

'You wouldn't know hard work if it bit you in the—' Jack is saying, when the fox bites him on the hand.

Jack swears. But the bite has the desired effect, in pulling him out of the argument, in turning his attention to the room.

When he sees Dad, he seizes up. Charlotte stops shouting, turns.

Dad is standing in the kitchen, facing them but not seeing them, holding his arm like it isn't attached to his body.

Behind thick glasses, his eyes enlarge. His legs begin to buckle. His body sways.

A dark red line splits one finger. His whole hand is covered in blood.

'Dad!' shrieks Charlotte, already moving.

'Oh my God,' says Jack, turning whiter than white.

Charlotte is now in the kitchen, holding on to her father's arm, steering him towards the sink. There are cries coming from both of them.

Jack remains rooted to his chair. He is unable to do anything but watch.

fourteen

Jack had always been an early riser. His days would begin before half of the city had woken up, before the other half had gone to bed. In this between time, before the daylight, Jack would rise from his orthopaedic mattress and stretch. He'd brew a coffee from a plastic pod, work up a sweat on his stationary spin bike. Then he'd take a cold shower, shave and dress as his smart speaker blared out a morning digest of the day's bad news. As the sun rose, as the city came to life, Jack would walk to the bus stop, catching up on his emails on his phone. A productivity podcast on the bus. Atomic Engagement. Execute Like an Executive. Jack would still be listening to a squeaky-voiced serial entrepreneur at 1.5× speed as he arrived at the office long before his colleagues, to prepare and get ahead before the meetings were scheduled to begin. Meetings with colleagues, meetings with clients, meetings about meetings, in wine bars and wellness boutiques and wherever else would swell the expenses and bloat the company card, meetings to organise more meetings, until either colleague or client retired or died.

Jack had set out with good intentions. Hadn't he? The finance route might have been a thinly veiled rejection of his father, the city a repudiation of Mole End, but that hadn't meant that he'd lived his whole working life out of spite. He'd enjoyed himself at his far-flung university, but he'd felt truly at home the moment he'd moved to the city where he'd make his living. He'd made friends on his graduate scheme. Not just Hugh, but other friends, nicer friends, friends he didn't work for. They'd go clubbing together on Friday nights, sometimes meet halfway between their flats for hungover Saturday brunches. He'd had a girlfriend, for a while. They used to sit shoulder to shoulder in bed on Sunday mornings, she doing a crossword and he a sudoku, both drinking a takeaway coffee from the roastery down the road. He loved getting lost, walking down side streets and craning at blue plaques on walls, never recognising the names of the artists or authors who'd lived in these buildings but still getting that starstruck feeling that something important had happened here. He loved to feel like he was at the centre of things, finding an overcrowded pub to sit out the two-hour queue for the restaurant everyone wanted to try, cold beer in one hand and plastic buzzer in the other. He loved the city in winter, when the Christmas lights were strung up, when every patch of open land seemed to turn into a German market of wooden huts laden with colourful trinkets, where everything smelled of mulled wine and toasted hazelnuts sold from carts. He loved the city in summer, where every inch of every park and every common was taken up by people with the same idea, a bit of sun, and you couldn't move for fear of getting hit with a frisbee or a popping Prosecco cork.

He loved the city, at first. He didn't know when he'd lost his way. The friends he'd liked the most switched careers or started families or settled down in villages like the one his parents had chosen. But while the grown-ups around him shifted their priorities, Jack kept his head down, working hard, rubbing at the boundary which separated work from life until there was no longer any difference between the two. Jack felt a sense of duty to the junior colleagues he managed, enjoyed the exhausting thrill of late-night brainstorming sessions, got a kick out of feeling as though the future of the company rested on his straining shoulders. And yet, as the years went on, true enjoyment dropped out of the equation. His vision was so tunnelled towards a computer screen, he stopped looking up, out of windows. He started to think of himself not as a person, but as a series of tasks to be ticked off.

Jack had never been a good sleeper. And by the time he'd taken the job at Hugh's new company, sleep felt like a luxury he couldn't afford. How had he ended up like this? He couldn't really afford his flat, couldn't find the fun in anything, couldn't recall exactly what it was that he'd wasted the last ten years chasing. Ten performance reviews where he'd been told that he worked harder than anybody else, but had never once been asked if he was happy. Was he happy? Even after all this time, he felt like he didn't belong. He worried that his shirts didn't fit him properly, that they made him look like a boy in men's clothing. He constantly googled 'imposter syndrome', cross-referencing the markers against his own long list of self-diagnosed flaws.

Jack had always found it difficult to step out of his comfort zone. He'd always been not so much buttoned-up as folded neatly and put away in the back of a drawer. So many times in his life he'd been desperate to join the conversation, but couldn't find a way in. At school, he'd loved maths, but had never once had the courage to raise his hand. At university, he'd sat in his room while his flatmates congregated in the kitchen, so afraid was he of thinking of what to say. Forever in fear that, if he opened his mouth, he'd come out with the wrong thing. When he'd first started working, it was like he'd found a purpose. He fitted neatly into a role, which made him feel as though he finally knew what to say. People began to look up to him. People listened. Then he started working longer hours, and he found himself with less time to talk.

He dated rarely, those short-lived situationships ending with messages which described him as 'emotionally unavailable'. His friends dropped off, and he stopped suggesting that his little sister, now a teenager, come visit him for weekends in the city. They messaged occasionally, instead. Charlotte would send him unintelligibly ironic memes. He'd reply: 'lol'. Jack would send her articles he found interesting, or useful, from broadsheet newspapers or economic think-tanks. She'd reply: 'lol'. Jack never went back to Mole End, and he assumed that his mum would find the city overwhelming these days. He placated her with a bi-monthly phone call in which he told her that everything was fine. And everything *was* fine, apart from the migraines, apart from the panic attacks, apart from the sleepless nights and the weekends which would stretch by without him talking to another human being. If Jack was lonely, if burnout was reducing him to cinders, if his eyes burned sometimes at night when he lay alone in bed and scrolled until his screen said, 'You're all caught up! You've seen every post from the last three days,' he'd learned to manage it on his own. And if Jack ever stopped to picture the company going bust, ever daydreamed about losing his job or his apartment and being forced to start all over again, somewhere else, he'd learned to suppress one simple fact: that the thought didn't make him feel scared, so much as relieved.

'Are you awake?' Jack whispered, to the fox. But the fox wasn't there, on his stomach, or anywhere else in sight.

Jack had always been an early riser, and today he rose even earlier than usual. Truth be told, true to form, he'd barely slept at all. It had taken him a long time to move from the dining table the previous evening, and when he did eventually climb the stairs, it was as if he was no longer in control of his own legs. He'd taken the new postcard with him, like a talisman. The caption simply wished them *Bonjour*, from the Alps. The message on the back, more of the same. He sat up for hours at his desk, poring over the postcard, obsessively trying to trace his mum's journey and make it make sense. Alderney was a stone's throw from France, so what? A three-hour ferry down to Guernsey, a transfer to the smaller island, a connection to Diélette and a rental car to the mountains? Jack pictured his mum yodelling on stage with an oompah band, or giggling her way up in a ski lift with a young and bearded snowboarding instructor. What was it all for?

Afterwards, in bed and staring at the ceiling, the woods shrieking that same shriek, Jack's brain had simmered over that same scene at dinner. There was something else he couldn't shake, too, something which had burrowed into his mind in the village and refused to climb back out. Blood. Matted fur, laboured breathing. A rabbit. A vague memory of one, of an early morning like this, of its wounded leg caught in barbed wire. Of Jack not wanting to look, not knowing how to help. Of his father having the answers, knowing exactly how to set it free. Something saved. Something shared. Jack must have imagined it. He tried to sleep, but spent most of the night listening out for the fox. He'd left his bedroom door open, to let the fox in. But the fox had spent most of the night elsewhere, and when it eventually entered his room, it did so only to crawl straight under his bed. Now Jack crouched on his bedroom floor before sunrise, rubbing his haggard face and trying to coax the fox out.

'I know you're under there,' he said.

Although, he didn't. He didn't know anything. And he was close to giving up, close to climbing back into bed for more sleep which wouldn't come, when two lighter-like eyes opened and illuminated in the darkness. The fox slithered across the carpet like a sea creature, crawling out from under the bed. Then it was sitting on his bedroom floor, not looking at him.

A whispered conversation in the half-light.

'Are you sulking?' Jack said.

The fox's ears flickered, registering the question.

'What have I done?'

The fox didn't look at him.

It's what you haven't.

'Come on,' Jack said, incredulous.

The fox bristled. Jack softened his tone.

'OK,' he said. 'I'm sorry I tricked you.'

The fox looked at him now. Its golden eyes were like torch beams.

I don't care that you tricked me.

'Then what is it?'

Who are those people? the fox said. *The man who can't say what he means? The girl who cries when she's alone?*

It took Jack a moment to understand that the fox wasn't talking in riddles. But Jack didn't say 'my family'. He didn't feel like the word captured the nuances of their situation.

Why won't you help them? said the fox, when Jack didn't answer. Its voice was only a vibration. *You helped me.*

'It's more complicated than that,' said Jack, crossing his legs, hugging his knees to his chest.

Nothing is complicated, said the fox.

'I wish that were true.'

They both stayed silent for a moment. The fox looked at the open bedroom door, then back at Jack.

I came here because I thought you were a good person, it said, with hesitation. *Not all people are good.*

'Thought?'

They seem good, the fox continued, gesturing at the door with its snout.

Jack looked at the door. 'What about me?'

The fox seemed disinclined to answer. It looked down at its forepaws, kneaded them into the carpet. Jack shook his head in disbelief.

'My dad is—' he began.

I don't think you know him, the fox interrupted. *I don't think I know you.*

Another silence. Jack clasped his hands together, exhaled. 'I can't believe you're guilt-tripping me.'

The fox didn't say anything. It simply left the room. And Jack didn't have the chance to say something that he wouldn't have said, anyway: that he did feel guilty. Jack had spent much of the night teetering on a knife's edge, thinking about his dad in the kitchen, blood pouring from his hand. Jack had always been squeamish. But the cut had been clean, not too deep, nowhere near as bad as it first seemed. Jack had sustained worse injuries in the kitchen, in the past. His dad had only needed a plaster. And yet, it felt as if the whole thing had opened up a gaping wound which was harder for Jack to ignore. It had been Jack's knife, left out on the counter. He should have been more careful. Maybe, all this time, Jack had been oblivious. Maybe he'd made a miscalculation. Maybe, so many miles away and on the other side of a mobile phone screen, he hadn't allowed himself to realise how bad things had become. And maybe he hadn't wanted to. Jack's dad had always been forgetful. He'd always been distant, unfocused, easily distracted. He was forever covered in cuts and bruises, forever saying that misadventure was the very heart of adventure. He was never easy to talk to. He was always, reliably, infuriating. But he was never like this.

Downstairs, in the kitchen, the fox was nowhere to be seen. There were signs of life, though. The kettle was warm, the back door slightly ajar. On the patio, in the rising light, the figure of his father. Standing, as ever, with his back to the window, staring off into the woods. Should Jack join him? What would he say? If Jack were truly the opposite of his dad, he'd have the words. He'd be someone open, someone easy to talk to. Never detached, never difficult, never far away. I'm falling apart at the seams, he could say, to his dad, to the one person with whom he'd never shared much common ground. I want to talk to you about it, because I know that you are, too. Last night's dinner was meant to be an attempt at that. Preparing a plate of food was one side of a conversation, something that speaks for itself. When you're eating it, you don't have to say a word.

'Good morning,' Jack said, tentatively.

He stood on the patio in his pyjama bottoms, a mug of instant black coffee in his hand. His dad, ahead, was little more than an outline in the lingering darkness, framed entirely by the sinister suggestion of the woods. Their vastness, the fact that the trees seemed like teeth and the darkness behind them like a roaring mouth, used to stop Jack from venturing outside before sunrise. But with his father stationed between himself and their expanse, they didn't seem so scary. His dad clearly either hadn't heard him, or had decided not to turn. He took a sip from his own mug of milky tea, continued to stare into the trees.

'I hear you,' his dad said.

Jack paused by the decrepit metal bench on the patio, its white paint flaking off patchily and discoloured by rust. 'Hear me?'

'Who?' said his dad, seemingly caught off guard. He turned now, and appraised Jack. 'Oh, you.'

147

Dark eyes behind gleaming spectacles passed over Jack's face, then returned to the woods. Jack stayed where he was, a step behind. He almost reached out, but found he was unable to move his arm. He put his hand into his pocket instead, dug his fingernails into his palm. This predawn was still and quiet, scored sporadically by lazy birdsong. Should Jack apologise? He wasn't sure exactly what for. He could say: I'm sorry for last night. He could say: I'm sorry for never coming home. But he'd have to addend it. The person I've become, the person I wanted to become, was never going to be close to the person you are, or wanted me to be. I didn't want to come home, because I didn't want to deal with the disappointment.

Jack, a man who had always taken things at face value, was rattled by the scene in the kitchen. He was starting to see things as they really were. Or, rather, he was no longer able to pretend things weren't how they'd been, all along.

'You're not wearing any shoes,' Jack said, after a long while.

Just below the precipice of the patio, his father's feet were trampling the grass. Beige socks with a hole in one toe, kneading themselves like paws into the dry mud. Jack imagined the earth opening up between them, the pair of them on either side of a canyon, too far apart to hear each other.

'Neither are you,' his dad said, without taking his eyes off the forest.

Jack looked down. He noticed now, that he was barefoot. The early morning was mercifully cool, the stone cold beneath his feet. He stretched out his toes, nearly said something else, then turned his eyes to the house, behind. In the living-room window, he could just about make out the dim triangles of the fox's ears. It was watching them. Caught in the act, it disappeared, soon emerging through the back door and creeping, tentatively, over the paving slabs towards them. It looked at Jack, briefly, then looked at his father. The fur on its tail seemed to be growing back with every hour that passed, pluming above its rump like a question mark made of smoke. Jack's hand stretched out in warning, but the fox didn't seem bothered. It simply wandered out on to the lawn, passing Jack, then passing his father. Under the pinkening sky, the fox stretched into a downward dog, its black paws out front, its chin tilted high, its mouth curled into an easy smile, any hint of reproach long gone. Jack watched his dad watching the fox. His dad could see it, too. Jack was sure he could see it.

What are you talking about? said the fox, it's voice carrying like a spark along a wire.

'Nothing,' said Jack.

'Shoes,' said his dad.

And Jack's mouth opened, his eyes unable to leave the back of his dad's head. 'You can—' he said, but his dad didn't turn. 'You see it?'

He's here, said the fox, to Jack's dad.

Jack's dad tilted his head ever so slightly. Was he nodding? The fox fixed Jack with the glowing embers of its eyes.

He's got something he wants to say to you, it said.

Jack stared, for a while, dumbfounded. 'Me?' he said, eventually.

The fox rolled its eyes. Jack's dad still didn't turn.

'What are you doing out here, Dad?' Jack said, to his dad. 'It's barely even morning.'

The fox padded over to Jack's dad, looked up at him. *I'm sorry*, it said. It looked at Jack, then back at his dad. *For not being here.*

'I couldn't sleep,' said Jack's dad.

The fox turned to Jack, its face suddenly soft. *It's alright*, the fox said. *I was never there.*

Jack swallowed. He found his voice catching. 'Same,' he said.

How are you? the fox said, to Jack's dad. *I'd really like to know.*

'So,' said Jack's dad, quietly. 'Here we are.'

The fox turned back to Jack, nodded in understanding. *Tired*, it said. *Tired of being confused.*

Jack looked down at the patio, closed his eyes. 'I've been thinking.'

The fox looked back up at Jack's dad. *Can I help?*

Jack's dad tilted his head, turned slightly. 'Thinking?'

The fox looked at Jack. *This helps*, it said. *Talking helps.*

'Yes,' said Jack. He opened his eyes again. 'About the rabbit.'

But there's so much to say, said the fox.

'The rabbit?'

I can't deny that.

'We rescued a rabbit,' said Jack, looking off into the woods. 'Remember? It was stuck in a fence.'

And not enough time to say it.

His dad was silent for a while. He might have been remembering the rabbit. His mind might already have moved on to something else.

'No, we didn't,' he eventually said. His voice wasn't exactly stern, but what he said seemed final.

There's never enough time.

Jack sighed, shook his head in frustration. He felt like saying: I'm trying. He felt like screaming: how would you know?

'Well,' said Jack, casting around for something to say. 'I guess we remember things differently.'

The fox looked at Jack, then his dad, then Jack again. It looked concerned. But before it could say anything more, a sound split the air. A shriek, which seemed to emanate from everywhere at once. Inside Jack's brain, yes, but also from the house behind him and the forest ahead, from deep in the dawn sky above and low in the dry earth below. The same shriek he'd been hearing, every night since he'd been back. He stared into the dark, greedy maw of the woods, straight-backed and stiff-legged. His father hadn't moved.

'I suppose that's a rabbit, too,' said Jack, shifting uncomfortably on his feet, casting furtive glances at the back door.

Jack's dad finally turned. He looked over his shoulder, straight at Jack, his stare holding nothing but Jack's eyes. Behind the thick lenses of his glasses, the icy pools of his dad's own eyes were totally clear.

'You know what that is,' he said, without anger, like a teacher might prompt a pupil.

And Jack, who didn't want to answer, who didn't know why he would answer, answered.

'It's a barn owl.'

fifteen

Gerry had always been an early riser. His days would begin before everyone else had woken up, in the hours before the world had scared its creatures away.

In this between time, before the daylight, Gerry would rise from his old mattress with caution, careful not to wake Hazel. He'd kiss her on the cheek, and she'd mumble sleepily.

He'd pad downstairs, brew some tea, decant it into a Thermos. Mole End would be warm and quiet, his burrow, his earth. Within its creaking walls, he'd pull on his boots.

Then he'd set off walking. Somewhere devoid of other people, somewhere he and only he could be up before the lark. Listening to the birds as they stirred in the trees, watching the sunrise behind them.

He'd take his binoculars, would write down what he saw in a little leather notebook. He'd doff his cap to the deer, who watched him with interest, never treating him like an outsider.

Never somewhere quiet.
The dawn chorus sees to that.

Gerry would be home, again, before the world had woken up. Although the world, the real world, never really slept. Humans did, while nature carried on in the darkness, under the stars, beneath the leaves.

He'd set to work in his garden, watering his crops, or pulling up that which might serve as breakfast or lunch. Radishes. Spring greens. Cucumbers and carrots, beetroot and broad beans.

Slugs are a pest,
but even those he can't kill.
He scatters eggshells instead,
coffee grounds, from coffee
he doesn't even drink.

Often, when he'd tended to his garden, he'd keep going. Step over the threshold, into the woods.

Forge onwards and forage to see what he could find.
Elderflowers. Oyster mushrooms. Chestnuts and chervil,
brambles and bilberries.

As the sun rose, as the human world came to life, Gerry
would trudge back home and fill the kitchen sink with his
soil-speckled findings.

More tea, a piece of toast. A crossword with Hazel. Then
Gerry would wash, put on a shirt and walk down to the
greengrocer's to start his day.

> He is always
> at home
> in the earth.

Being a grocer wasn't Gerry's calling. And he wouldn't call
it a vocation, didn't subscribe to his brother's belief that your
job should be the measure of your worth.

He'd never been apprenticed to a grocer, hadn't grown up
with grocers, hadn't had a father who would have shown him
the ropes, even if his father had been the sort of man to hang
a sign above a door saying 'PENWICK & SONS'.

His father wasn't a grocer. His brother wasn't around. And
Gerry, who felt he was worth more than any job, still enjoyed

the simple pleasure of working with things which had been pulled from the earth.

He liked packing fruit into crates, vegetables into brown paper bags. He didn't like exchanging money, or small talk, exchanges of any kind which had to be done with other people.

> I can't do it
> without you,
> I can't do it.

Gerry had never been a good sleeper. His mind might have been nocturnal, yet people still expected him to be present in the day.

He'd spent so many hours of his life awake when his family was asleep. Though his son, even as a child, was just as early a bird as him.

He'd creep downstairs as Gerry brewed his tea. His black hair mussed by sleep, made evening blacker by the dim light. Johnny's hair.

They'd say quiet hellos, Gerry and the boy, but not much more than that. They were never much for father–son conversations.

It had been easier when the boy was younger. But the boy

grew bored of nature guides, of the treehouse his dad was trying to build him.

As time went on, Gerry became the background parent. The boy's mother came to the fore, became the one who did the talking.

> Gerry in the garden.
> Gerry's son in the house.

When Gerry went out birdwatching, or foraging, he'd often wonder if his son would like to come with him. But he didn't want his son to say no.

When he'd asked his son if he'd like to learn how to fish, his son had said precisely that. No, in a voice which was already breaking.

He supposed there'd been no harm in asking. From then on, he went out alone, spotting things and sniffing them and picking them, imagining what he'd tell his son about each one, if his son was by his side.

That's garlic mustard, he'd say. Another name for it: Jack-by-the-hedge. But he never said it, because his son was never with him, because he never asked his son to come.

Did other people find it easy? To ask things, to say things out loud? To grab the stalks of the thoughts in your head and to pull up their roots, to bring them out of the soil and into the sunlight?

Gerry's son in the city.
Gerry in the wild.

Gerry had always been an early riser, and today he rose earlier than usual.

He was careful not to wake Hazel. He padded downstairs, brewed a tea. He couldn't find the Thermos. He wouldn't pull on his boots.

Hazel wasn't here. He couldn't remember what he'd done to make her leave him. But he did know that he'd been told not to go off on his own, so he stuck to the garden.

Dawn approached. Gerry stood staring at a bird bath, drinking in the glitter of the still-remaining stars on its undulating surface.

Behind him, a squirrel
abseiling down the drainpipe.
Ahead, the apple-pip eyes
of a hedgehog, hiding.

It didn't alarm Gerry when a gelatinous mass of lesions and pustules seemed to cohere, croaking, in the bird bath.

Or, rather, the warty lump itself didn't alarm Gerry. Gerry, who'd held frogs and toads and far uglier things, wriggling and rescued, between his fingers before returning them to whence they came. He was made of sterner stuff.

No, what alarmed Gerry was that he couldn't remember this: the difference. What makes a frog a frog, and a toad a toad?

> Frogs are smooth and slimy,
> Toads, dry and warty.
> Frogs have long legs.
> Toads, short.

He remembered that toads were poisonous to dogs. That a dog which licks a toad might froth, might vomit, might shudder and collapse.

A dog which licks a frog would be just fine. But Gerry was no dog, and licking this particular frog-toad would yield no useful answer.

Gerry had always spoken to animals. People wouldn't believe him if he told them that the animals had always spoken back. They'd think it was a symptom.

He didn't mind. He still supposed there was no harm in asking. I'll put the question to the toad-frog itself, he thought. Perhaps it would like a pumpkin seed.

159

> Sorry to ask, he says.
> Are you a frog or a toad?
> The amphibian puffed like a bellows.
> *He should decide*, it says.
> *It's his story.*

'I hear you,' said Gerry, taking a sip of his tea, because he knew that the canny creature was talking about the angry young man.

But the angry young man wasn't here, in this bird bath. And Gerry couldn't remember if his brain was supposed to be an ocean or a lake, a stream or a river.

He couldn't find a Thermos, let alone an entire ocean. He didn't know when he'd lost his way.

> Everything is a little
> too much to remember.
> Let's start with one thing.

Gerry had always been good with his nose. So, he smelled the black coffee long before he heard the sound of bare feet hitting the patio.

Gerry smiled slightly, felt Johnny's presence. He'd stood behind him, on this very patio, on a morning just like this. As far as rehab goes, he'd said, this'll do nicely.

How nice to have Johnny here with him. How strange to realise that that was all so long ago, and so far away.

'Hear me?' said a voice behind Gerry. It wasn't Johnny's, no matter how hard Gerry tried to make it so.

Who? Oh, you.
Too-whit, too-whoo,
what shall I do?

The presence of the angry young man became a prompt, as these things often did, and Gerry remembered the regrettable scene in the kitchen.

Gerry had never been a big eater. He wasn't one for feasts, for cheese or grease. He'd was even less hungry, nowadays. He was more easily overwhelmed.

He found himself looking at a plate of pasta and not knowing where the plate began or the pasta ended, plate being almost the same colour as pasta, pasta being almost the same colour as plate.

He'd wanted something fresh, something brighter. But he supposed he hadn't mastered the mechanics of that fancy sharp knife. There was now a plaster around his fingertip, which tapped against his mug of tea.

The other day, he'd picked up a fork, and hadn't a clue how

to use it. Something so simple, knocking the wind out of him.

> You're not wearing any shoes,
> says the young man.

The comment pulled Gerry away from the kitchen and back to the patio, his eyes on the woods.

What could he say to that? What could he ever? They'd always thought the opposite on everything, he and this young man.

Because, when he really thought about, he knew exactly who this young man was.

> Neither are you, says Gerry,
> because he'd heard the boy's footsteps,
> and had nothing better to say.

Who are you? he wanted to ask, though he thought he almost had the answer.

Where's Hazel? This one was more elusive. His short-term memory was better: he could picture the postcard, the pasta, but not the last time he'd seen his own wife.

> Speeding in a van
> at the foot of a French mountain.

What's the word for pharmacy?
Pharmacie. It's *pharmacie*!

Chunks of their marriage had extricated themselves from his memory.

Large swathes of their life together were peeling away into nothingness, like wallpaper detaching itself from the walls of a derelict old house.

He knew she wasn't actually in Alderney, or the Alps, but he didn't have a clue where she really was. He stared off into the woods.

Between an old man
and a young man,
a fox appears.

Gerry didn't know where the fox had come from, seeing as the forest was ahead of him. But the fox was here now, slinking from behind him and stretching out on the grass.

It looked up at Gerry with fiery eyes, familiar eyes, and it snickered cheekily in the way that foxes tended to do. It seemed to want to know what they were talking about.

'Shoes,' said Gerry, because he didn't like not telling the truth.

The young man
says nothing.

It was as if the fox was trying to say something. The young man was trying to say something, too.

Gerry's head was trying to say something else. You know him, it was trying to say. You know who he is.

Gerry closed his eyes, listened. Could he really be blamed for forgetting? He hadn't heard that voice in years.

What are you doing out here, Dad?
It's early.

Gerry's son had been gone for a long time. A lifetime, it felt like. But time wasn't so trustworthy any more.

Time had been a stream, once. Time had become a wider, deeper body of water, something to drown in. And his son was so far away, so far out on the banks, that there was no way he'd reach him before he went under.

Who was he? What had he become?

A fox.
Himself.
And his son.

The fox seemed to be apologising on his son's behalf. So Gerry apologised, on his own behalf, to the fox.

What else did the fox want to know? How he was? What would help? Talking helped. Being present, being made to feel as if he were present, helped.

Out here, on the patio, he was part of something. Out here, with his son, it seemed much harder to drown.

> A rabbit.
> We rescued a rabbit.

Gerry's mind might have been a cage, his brain a river. But he hadn't forgotten everything.

In the mornings, his memory was sharper. Which is perhaps why he remembered what happened. A whimper, a pair of pliers. A rare hug, between him and his son.

But no rabbit. They'd never rescued a rabbit.

They couldn't argue the point, wouldn't have been capable. The barn owl broke through the silence between them.

> *Oh–o–o–o–o,*
> *that I never had been bor-r-r-n!*

Gerry usually felt a kinship with the creature, but he didn't share its pessimistic outlook. If anything, Gerry was jubilant to have been born.

If anything, Gerry wished he could bathe in his life, wished he could remember every moment, wished he could dunk his head under the surface as if he was apple bobbing and let his entire existence fill his lungs.

He remembered running barefoot through the woods with Johnny. He remembered, often, a simpler time.

> Old Brown.
> Billy Wix.
> Ascalaphus.

The barn owl shrieked, and the boy said it was a rabbit. The boy still had so much to learn.

Gerry turned to him, looked at him, and felt, mainly, time. A grown man stared back at him, frown-lined, sunken-cheeked, with pale blue moons of eyes he'd have remembered even if everything else was gone.

There was so much Johnny in him. There was so much of himself.

> It's a barn owl,
> he says.

And for a moment, his son is just a boy, and they still have so much time.

sixteen

A man and a woman speed through a tunnel cut into the side of a mountain, neither of them speaking, both of them looking for the light at the end of it. The woman has dropped her bag at her feet, is gripping on to the door handle as if she's worried the entire van is going to fall apart beneath them, so rocked are her foundations.

'Shit!' Hazel had shouted, first of all. Gerry had only flinched.

It wasn't planned. They knew only this much: that they'd take the ferry from Newhaven to Dieppe, then drive the Ship of Theseus towards the Alps, via Der-Chantecoq and Lausanne. Things were foggier, from there. They'd drive to Milan, looking out for lynxes, wolves and brown bears as they progressed through Trentino. They might visit Venice, though the Ship of Theseus couldn't float, and Gerry didn't much like crowds. Beyond that, they'd earmarked a number of azure lakes near

Zagreb. Then they'd aim vaguely for Bulgaria, then Turkey, then on and on and on. Everything seemed possible. Hazel wanted to go north, to Kazakhstan. Gerry, who wasn't one to keep up with current events, wanted to head south, through Tehran and Kabul and over the Khyber Pass. It didn't matter what obstacles they might meet. They'd go as far as they could go, perhaps even further, until the money in the jar ran out, until they found a place where they couldn't make more, until they had to put down roots, someplace, somewhere. They'd never really talked about going back. It wasn't a when. It was barely even an if. They didn't know where they were going, where they'd end up. They were chasing a feeling, the concept of flight, the general gist of an adventure whose route could be defined as Hazel and Gerry seeing everything this beautiful world had to offer. It wasn't planned.

How boring for it to have started with a conversation about provisions. They'd have to stop and restock the van, at some point. Was there anything they urgently needed? Hazel had hoisted her hiking backpack on to her lap and riffled through it. She reached the toiletries bag and saw something which set her mind ticking. A box of tampons, unopened since she'd packed them – how long before? Hazel hadn't brought a calendar with her. She ran through the days and weeks in her head, instead. How long had they been on the road? And how long had it been since—

'Shit!'

When Hazel had been sick on the ferry across the Channel, she'd blamed the sea, that old childhood friend turning against her. When she was sick in Dijon, she blamed a dodgy batch of mussels. Now, after being sick out of the door of a van at the side of a mountain road, it seemed harder to blame a stomach bug than what was enormously, abundantly clear. They sped through the tunnel, neither of them speaking, Johnny Cash blaring out of the radio as if to try to make the silence less loud.

'Could it be?' was said, on one side of the mountain. 'It can't be.'

'What's the word for pharmacy?' on the other. '*Pharmacie*. It's *pharmacie!*'

A flashing green cross in a seemingly deserted village. Gerry had a story for every new encounter. She had somehow not known that, in his early twenties, he'd backpacked to Périgord and spent some time sniffing out truffles. Not because he liked the truffles, but because he liked the pigs.

Gerry still remembered a little French. And as he stood in the *pharmacie*, baffling the woman behind the counter, Hazel was suddenly laughing so much that she nearly wet herself, and was so filled with love that her cup felt as if it might overflow after all. What did it matter? If it's happening, she thought, if it's *really* happening . . . would it be so bad?

'*J'ai un bébé?*' Gerry said, pointing at her stomach. '*Peut-être?*'

In spring, the swallow returns to lay its eggs. But Hazel wasn't planning on going back. It was Gerry who surprised them both this time, Gerry who insisted on being the sensible one. The Ship of Theseus was no place to raise a child. So, after what felt like a hundred hours and a thousand arguments, they decided to turn the ship around. It was something exciting, they told themselves. They knew it was. But as they retraced their journey through that dark tunnel, driving a van full of blank postcards past Lausanne and Dijon and the Der-Chantecoq lake, it was hard to pretend that this thing, this exciting thing, this intangible thing which would soon be called Jack, didn't signify a kind of defeat.

seventeen

Jack had set out with good intentions. In the days since that conversation on the patio, he genuinely made an effort with his dad. One of Jack's tenets in the city had been radical practicality. He was thinking of it vaguely now, of things learned in strategy seminars in boardrooms many miles away, as he tried to apply a similar strategy at Mole End. If he couldn't exactly connect with his father, he could at least try to fix him. So, Jack began preparing all of their meals, cooking dinners with a broad spectrum of vegetables and a tick list of lean proteins and healthy fats, blending memory-boosting spinach and spirulina smoothies even though they invariably went undrunk. He packed his favourite knife away, confiscated any garden tools he deemed unsafe, removed rusty rakes and shears which could have been a tetanus risk. He tried to get his dad's steps up, invited him on brusque walks to the village and back. But his dad always had an excuse. And though Jack had set out with good intentions, his frustrations began to mount with every day that passed.

Perhaps it was the job interview that he was dreading, scheduled for ten o'clock that very morning. Perhaps it was the olive branch he'd extended to Charlotte, which she'd summarily snapped in two and thrown back at him.

'It's been hard, yeah?' Jack had said, placing a just-brewed mug of green tea in front of her.

'Obviously it's been fucking hard,' she'd replied, pushing the mug away.

Perhaps it was the postcards from his mum, two more of which had turned up in the meantime. One sent from Trentino had detailed a stop-off between Milan and Venice. The latest had arrived this morning, from Zagreb, his mother having entered Croatia after crossing Slovenia overnight. Jack couldn't keep up, couldn't work out how she was sending them so fast. He'd run out of headspace to wonder what she was up to, out there on her wild goose chase. The mood seemed to be catching. Charlotte had lost interest after the second one arrived, wouldn't even look up Trentino on a map. Jack's dad, when he'd seen the Zagreb postcard, hadn't been remotely surprised.

'Of course,' he'd said. He hadn't cared to elaborate.

In the three days since their strange conversation, Jack had been paying more attention to his dad. He observed the same old behaviours, the ones which hadn't changed. The way his dad started every conversation with 'Did you know?', followed by the most banal nature fact you'd ever heard; the way he wiped his glasses and blew his nose with the same cotton handkerchief; the way he kept loose pistachios and pumpkin seeds in his pockets, forever blowing the fluff off them before munching them down. But Jack began to recognise new behaviours, too. His dad moving listlessly around the house, turning lights on and off for no reason, opening random cupboards he'd then never remember to shut. His dad, unable to work out how to answer the phone, or button the cuffs of his shirt, or unlock the front door when it had been put on the snib. His dad, furiously writing more and more Post-it notes, each one making less and less sense.

STORM COMING

Jack stared at that one, this morning, then balled it up and threw it in the bin. He turned to the fox, which was sitting patiently by his ankles.

'What do foxes eat, again?' Jack said, standing with the fridge door open.

We're omnivores.

'That doesn't answer my question.'

We eat earthworms, crane flies, gooseberries. Cigarette butts, used tissues, dead baby birds. That sort of thing.

'Right.'

The skittering claws of a scarpering fox. Jack watched his dad enter the kitchen, open a cupboard, pull out a cumbersome jar of pickled onions, remove the lid and start eating. He gave no sign of having seen the fox, but he gave no sign of having seen Jack, either. Over the last few days, the fox had been similarly cagey about whether it had spoken to his dad since that time on the patio. Jack wanted to ask: does he talk about me? But he never did.

Charlotte entered now, in an old black hoodie and a pair of galaxy-print leggings. She'd been doing yoga on the patio. From her one dangling headphone, Jack could hear the tinny sound of aggressive heavy metal. She crossed the kitchen, gave their dad a kiss on the cheek, then counted out a few pills on the sideboard. After handing him the pills with a glass of water, she pulled a box of luridly coloured cereal from a high cupboard and started pouring it into a bowl. Were those pieces of marshmallow? She largely ignored Jack, apart from when she pushed him out of the way of the fridge to get the milk.

'Big day,' Jack said.

Charlotte, pouring milk, fetching a spoon, looked at him with suspicion.

'My job interview,' Jack said, in explanation.

Charlotte rolled her eyes, crunched down a mouthful of cereal.

'You can go out, if you like,' Jack said.

Charlotte started to say something, but her mouth was full.

'Go shopping,' Jack said. 'Get some me-time. I've got this.'

Charlotte visibly cringed. But Jack knew that she'd taken no shifts at the pub since their mum had been gone, that even she must be feeling cooped-up by now. Charlotte chewed it over. Their dad, on the other side of the kitchen island, was chomping on a pickled onion. He placed a hand on the countertop and crouched, slightly, his eyes fixed on something that Jack couldn't see.

'Hello,' he said.

Charlotte swallowed, turned to him. Jack froze, took a step back, spied the fox on the floor behind the island, looking up at his dad. From this angle, Charlotte wouldn't be able to see it. For now. Their dad, who realised that they were all watching him, widened his eyes. Then he gave Jack a look which seemed conspiratorial.

'Oh,' he said. 'Nothing.'

'Yep,' said Jack, quickly. 'Nothing.'

Charlotte looked between her brother and her father, put down her bowl, crossed her arms.

'You two are being weird.'

Jack looked at his dad. Jack's dad ushered the fox out of the kitchen, behind his closed legs.

'We—' Jack began.

'I don't care,' Charlotte said, moving the bowl to the sink. She left the kitchen without a goodbye, but dipped her head back in after a couple of minutes. 'Can I really go out?'

For Jack, the rest of the morning was spent upstairs hunched over his desk, while the fox chewed apple cores and a used printer ink cartridge from the upturned bin beneath. He grabbed a stack of Post-it notes from the kitchen, scribbled pointers and positive affirmations on them, plastered them around the room. I can do this! I am the future boss of my future boss! The fox is real, my dad can see it! The offer of the interview had turned up in his inbox on Monday. He'd applied en masse to a bucketload back in the city, lying on his

sofa, going for roles which seemed to be sensible and appro-
priately senior. His internet history was littered with searches
on potential interview questions and salary increases, or what
role he might be promoted to after his probationary period. He
trawled through trendy company names with dropped vowels,
pondering which collective noun would sum up how he felt
about them. A murder of firms. A misery of startups. Here,
at Mole End, he was already finding it difficult to remember
what he had done in his old job. He wasn't exactly sure what
the company he was interviewing for did, either.

Jack had a shower. He drank a very strong coffee. He sat
his dad down on the sofa in the living room, put the weather
forecast on the TV.

'Don't do anything,' he said. 'I've got a job interview. I'll be
done in an hour.'

Upstairs, drumming his fingers on the desk, Jack regarded
himself in the black screen of his blank monitor. Even though
the interview wasn't on video, he'd planned to smarten himself
up for a bit of self-confidence. He'd intended to dress for the
job he wanted, not the job he didn't have, but he'd left all his
suits in the city. He'd wanted to shave, but he hadn't had time,
not with all the prep he needed to do. So here he sat, in a too-
small varsity jumper from his university years, scratching the
stubble on his chin fast growing into a beard as he stared at the
ominously silent phone on the desk. The fox was sitting on the
bed behind him, assuming the role of cheerleader.

'You need to be quiet,' Jack had said, while the fox stared at
him with devoted eyes and upright ears. 'Not seen, not heard.
Got it?'

The fox played dead, rolling over with all four legs pointing stiffly into the air. Then it bounced back up, snickered, and ran in circles on the bed for a while. Now it sat back, looking quizzical.

Why are you doing this? it said.

'The interview?' Jack huffed, trying to make it clear he was too busy for questions. 'So we can get back to the city.'

In the blank monitor, Jack saw the fox heave a sigh. It rolled on to its back again, stared up at the ceiling, forepaws together on its chest as if in prayer.

I miss the city, it said. *I miss the glimmer of green algae on the surface of a canal. I miss the way the bats dance in pairs in front of streetlights. I miss the first frost on the common, the crunch of it under my paws.*

Jack stared at the fox's reflection, suddenly forgetting the interview entirely.

What about you? the fox said. *What do you miss?*

Jack was dumbstruck. He almost said: money. That's why I'm doing this. But he didn't miss money. It was just that money was what was missing, if Jack wanted to return to his old life, his real life, a life which ended easily at the boundary of his flat, his job and his yearly bonus. A hand-to-mouth childhood and a father awful with accounts had given Jack a complex, turned him into a teenager terrified of financial instability. He had hoarded money, fretted over it, vowed to manage it better than his dad ever did. But then he got used to it, so he stopped saving it. Money went quicker than he could put it aside, on overpriced moisturisers and expensive olive oil, weekend lunches at well-reviewed restaurants and post-work drinks at private members' clubs. And his flat, which he didn't picture as eerie and abandoned like his father's greengrocer's, but more like a museum after hours, dusty and echoing and high-ceilinged, filled with relics of a life lived by someone more successful than him. Jack had assumed things would always be the way they were. He'd believed that, with a little hard work, you could manifest anything. Even money.

'I miss . . . I miss . . .' *What do I miss?*

The phone on the desk began to vibrate. Jack might have called it manifestation, but he didn't feel relief when it started to ring. In the monitor, he affected a smile, minimised it, until he saw in his reflection the sort of calm, measured man a successful company might want to employ. He answered the call.

Deep breath. Big smile. 'Jack Penwick—'

I'm just going to patch you through.

A long wait. Jack's smile faltered. Then, a click, a pause.

'Jack—' he began.

Jack! The voice sounded entirely at ease.

'Hi,' Jack said. 'It's great—'

One sec, pal, said the voice.

More waiting. More breathy silence. Then, finally, another click, another voice.

Jack!

'Hi,' Jack said. 'It's great to be here.'

Great to chat, great to chat.

Jack knew what the company's co-founders looked like, having tracked them down on social media, but he found that he'd totally forgotten their names. All he remembered was their profile pictures, one of the founders shown making a best man's speech at a wedding, the other crossing the finish line of one of those charity marathons which involved muddy puddles and obstacle courses. Speaking to them on the phone now, Jack could only imagine them within these frames of reference. A pinstripe waistcoat and high-gloss tie, microphone in hand, or soaking wet, covered in mud.

So, Jack. Let's kick off with a bit about yourself. Tell us something interesting about you.

I was betrayed by people like you. Jack hadn't yet thought about it in those terms, but that's what it was. Betrayal. Hugh and Hugo had stabbed him in the back, and he'd thanked them. An icy trickle ran down his spine. It moved with the sound of a brown envelope being slid across a glass table.

'I have managerial qualities,' Jack said.

There was an uncomfortable pause.

Oh, yeah? said a voice.

'That is,' said Jack, with a slight stutter, 'I am a good leader.'

He'd got off on the wrong foot. The fox was standing proudly on the bed, the orange-and-white fur of its tail puffing out behind it like a mushroom cloud.

Yes you are! it said. *You're nailing it!*

On the end of the phone, someone asked another question.

'I'm sorry,' Jack said, closing his eyes. 'Could you repeat that?'

A pause.

I said, what in particular would you say it is that makes you a good leader?

'I am a good leader because—'

Sorry, let me stop you there for just one second.

A murmured conversation with an assistant. Two voices, then three. Jack made a fist with his left hand, kept a smile on his face. How many people were listening in? And did it already sound like they were bored?

Sorry, one of the interviewers said. *Why are you a good leader?*

Radical practicality. He picked the Post-it note on top of the stack in front of him, proceeded to read it aloud. 'I believe in being an active listener.'

Jack swallowed, drily. He was desperate for a glass of water, found himself looking around for one, tugging at the loose neckline of his jumper. Talking always made him nervous. Talking with stakes involved was his worst nightmare. Even when he was managing people, even during dutiful one-to-ones with junior staff, Jack would always have to psyche himself up. Hosting meetings or giving company-wide briefings was a personal nightmare, leaving him sweaty-palmed and filled with with a throttling anxiety. Jack's dad was quiet, too, but he never seemed nervous. Why couldn't he have imparted that sense of ease to Jack, rather than endless facts about foxes and owls? Here's one which had stuck in Jack's mind. In both species, the family connection is severed when the children are grown. From that point on, fathers and sons only see each other as competition for food.

'And I'm ruthless,' said Jack, puffing out his chest. He deflated it a bit, worried about coming on too strong. 'Fairly ruthless.'

The interviewer paused. *And you are aware this is a mid-level role?*

Jack's smart watch was buzzing on his wrist. The screen was telling him his heart rate was elevated, to take a breather.

'Mid-level is my middle name,' he said, with a forced smile.

He didn't know what he meant by that. The fox let out a snickering laugh, then rolled over and covered its muzzle with its forepaws. On the other end of the line, perhaps the longest silence so far. Jack pictured his interviewers drumming their fingers against their chins, one set of hands well manicured, the other caked in filth. He looked down for a Post-it note which might help him in his current predicament. The one on top of the pile had been written by his dad.

SPEAK TO HIM

The room behind Jack was spinning, his ears ringing. He'd missed another question.

'Sorry?' he said, voice faltering, breath coming short.

They didn't repeat it. *Jack*, one of them said, instead. *How do you think this interview is going?*

Nowhere, Jack thought. I'm going nowhere, and I have nothing to say, because I come from a long line of men who don't know how to talk to one another. He remembered rescuing a rabbit with his dad, but he drew a blank on shopping for suits with him. They'd never played football with jumpers as goalposts, never talked about life and life lessons over a pair of perspiring pints. They'd never talked about anything at all, in any context. Never then, and never since.

The interviewer's question had been like a stethoscope, and Jack suddenly became aware of the workings of his own body.

It was like they'd asked how he was feeling, physically. If they had asked that, he'd have said that he felt so trapped in this varsity jumper that he was ready to tear his way out of it, that the muscles in his shoulders and the back of his neck were so tense it was as if he'd been gripping an electric fence. If he tanked the interview, he couldn't go home. But what was left in the city, for him? Even before he'd been burnt, he'd been miserable. Hugh and Hugo loomed large in his mind. His thoughts got muddled. He imagined them in shiny ties, with mud-caked faces. Jack felt out of place here, at Mole End, but that wasn't the issue. The issue was that he didn't feel in place, anywhere.

'I think—' I'm going nowhere.

'I think—' I have nowhere to go.

'I think—' I've made a miscalculation.

Jack eyes alighted on the fox, which was off the bed, standing on spindly hind legs, pawing at the window. It was snarling at a cloud. No, not a cloud. A plume, billowing up from the lawn. Silently, as if pulled by a cord, Jack left his office chair and stood beside the fox at the window. Through the thin pane, through the lattice, was an overhead view of an overgrown garden and the wide expanse of forest beyond. Beneath a washed-out sky, beneath a canopy of green leaves which fluttered lightly, Jack's father cut a lonely figure. He was standing in his usual place at the edge of the garden, staring off into the trees. Jack was so used to seeing him in a shirt, buttoned up, with a belt and a pair of practical trousers, that the sight of him in pyjamas, outside and in the daytime, was unnerving. He briefly disappeared from view, along with the trees ahead of him, both obscured by a grey haze, then a monstrous black cloud. Smoke consumed the entire garden. In blaring snatches, through the black cloud, Jack could see the roaring fire in front of his father.

'Thank you for this opportunity,' Jack said, calmly, into the phone. Then he hung up.

eighteen

Having a routine will help,
the doctor had told Gerry.
The angry young man made that hard.

No, that's not right. The angry young man in Gerry's house was Johnny. No, focus. His son. The angry young man was his son.

It occurred to Gerry, as he sat at the breakfast table trying to do the crossword, that he should tell his son about his diagnosis. There was a lot the boy had missed.

It was Hazel, under instruction from the doctor, who'd procured the smoke-white card that Gerry now kept in his wallet.

Problems with my memory.
Please be patient.

Before Gerry could show it to his son, the post was causing chaos in the hallway. Another one had arrived. This time from Zagreb.

Of course it was. She was following their old route, the one they'd never stopped planning, the one without a fixed end.

If this was a memory game, Gerry didn't like playing it. He didn't know why Hazel was doing this to him. Or doing it without him.

It was Hazel who ensured people were careful with their words. Not a 'suffering from', but a living with.

Which was it, for her? Was she suffering from Gerry, or living with him?

The doctor had a name for it.
But Gerry wasn't paying attention.
In his defence, he was looking at a tree.

Gerry could imagine what was happening to his mind, like a tree growing in reverse. Branches spiralling backwards, leaves shrinking inwards.

Some days, he was in full bloom. On those days, he felt his mind was blossoming, was flourishing, was growing into something new.

Other days, the trajectory was downwards, not like an oak or an alder reaching up to the sky, but like a mighty trunk becoming a fragile sapling becoming a seed.

On those days, his mind took root like a leafless plant hunkering down for winter. On those days, he'd wonder: is something happening to my mind?

The oak and the alder.
The alder and the oak.

Gerry entered the kitchen, saw that his son was already there. Perhaps now was the time to tell him. Perhaps not.

His son hogged the fridge. Gerry crossed the kitchen and found breakfast elsewhere.

Charlotte entered, gave him a hand with his medication. Gave him a look which said: my brother is driving me mad.

Gerry would stay out of it. While his children argued, he stooped to watch the fox on the kitchen floor.

It tried to shush him, but he was never good at following social cues.

Hello,
says Gerry,
but the fox runs away.

Gerry was moved around Mole End like a piece of furniture. Sometimes, they put him in the garden, like a bird bath.

Right now, his son was plonking him on the sofa, like a cushion. He told him not to do anything for an hour.

What else had the doctor said? Write notes. So, back at the kitchen counter, Gerry wrote a note. He'd tell his son about his diagnosis. Right after his son's job interview.

SPEAK TO HIM

He heard his son making preparations. He made himself scarce, lest his son pick him up and put him back on the sofa.

Are you lost, little hedgehog?
I'm alright, the hedgehog says.
I hope you're alright, too.

Gerry stood in front of the raised beds where he carefully cultivated his vegetables, speaking quietly to a hedgehog in the undergrowth.

His daughter had told him she was going into the village,

that she wouldn't be out helping him on the veg patch this morning. The hedgehog would have to do.

Gerry offered it a pistachio. As it chewed, it asked, *Can I get you anything? Can I help?* Gerry told the hedgehog that his son had banished him to the garden.

The hedgehog's little black nose goes sniffle, sniffle, snuffle. Its little black eyes narrow as it asks the question. *Do you want me to sort him out for you?*

I'm OK, Gerry assured the hedgehog. He's stressed. He's got a job interview.

The hedgehog didn't seem to understand. It was putting on a brave face. A hedgehog, out in the open at this time of day, was most likely in distress.

Gerry knew what to do. In these situations, Gerry always knew what to do.

A full meal of meaty cat food
mixed in with porridge oats,
dried sultanas, mealworms
and poppy heads.

Gerry told the hedgehog to wait, then headed back inside.

He should have told it that hedgehogs have been around for

twenty million years. Longer than sabretooth tigers. Longer than woolly mammoths. You'll outlive me, he should have said.

Was this true? They said that hedgehogs were now vulnerable to extinction. Same here, Gerry thought, as he crossed the patio and entered the kitchen.

He followed the labels. He found porridge oats and sultanas, but the cat food was nowhere to be seen. He wrote a note, in lieu of a shopping list.

NO CAT FOOD

Perhaps he should tell Charlotte. Had she gone to the shops?

His son was busy, with the interview, with all his hard work. Johnny was hiding somewhere. Gerry would have to check the shed.

Hazel had flown the nest, had begun their great migration alone. Like a swallow. Like a swift.

The shadow
of the shadow
of the shadow.

Johnny wasn't hiding, Gerry remembered. Johnny had grown up.

And yet, Gerry had always trusted these glasses. He had worn the same sturdy frames for years, refurbished time and time again by the same optician in the nearest town.

So if Gerry's glasses showed him his little brother, ducking in the undergrowth at the edge of their lawn, what was he supposed to believe?

> Johnny isn't allowed on the lake.
> Not without a grown-up.
> Johnny is only three.

Gerry's memories were so vivid, it sometimes felt as if they had sprung back to life.

As if moments from years gone by were being projected on to what was really in front of him.

As if his past and his present existed, together, at exactly the same time.

> I'm seeing things.
> But that's all anyone is seeing,
> all the time. Things.

Time was a lake. So, yes, the view through the kitchen window was Gerry's back garden.

But it was also the garden that he and Johnny used to play in, outside their childhood home in Cumbria. At the end of the garden, through the trees, the lake where they used to paddle their boat.

There they were, right outside the window. He and Johnny, on the verge of capsizing. Brothers in arms, on the open seas.

Dad might hit you for that. Mum won't say a word.
So what? Was it worth it? Was it ever?
The ice-cold water says yes.

Those first ten years of Johnny's life were probably the best of Gerry's. It felt like nothing mattered. It felt like there was nothing but them.

Their father forced them into church every Sunday, made welts on the backs of their hands if they sniggered or yawned. They still tried their best to make each other laugh.

Outside, away from stern faces and stiff pews, they played characters from their favourite books. Gerry was the wise old owl. Johnny was the big strong badger. They made quite the team.

On the lake or in the woods, they were united in adventure. They stood together against misty mountains, against fearsome wolves, against grazed shins and bruised knuckles.

They were one and the same. They were two of a kind.

Careful, Johnny.
Don't let Dad see.

The shadow of the shadow of their childhood was their
father, who was always just within earshot, always looking
for an excuse.

He wielded his nastiness like a cane, balanced his superiority
on his upper lip. Like most cruel men, he thought he'd make
his mark by impressing his cruelty upon the world.

He'd take an almost-perverse pleasure in the wringing of a
rabbit's neck, the hunting of a quivering fox.

Tally-ho, he'd say.
Bloody good shot.

He'd tried to write his cruelty on to Gerald, his firstborn,
but the ink had never dried.

While men like Gerry's father were stuck in the past, his
elder son's dream was simpler. Less glass, more grass.

They both dreamed of Arcadia, but his Dad's green and
pleasant land would cast outsiders out. Gerry's Arcadia
would have room for everyone.

Gerry's father didn't care. He just wrote his cruelty on to Johnny instead.

> The other kids made fun of Gerry.
> So Gerry stopped talking to them.
> Stopped talking to people entirely.

Gerry looked away from the window, took off his spectacles and rubbed his eyes. He chalked it up to having a moment.

Where am I? Clarity, please. Silence, too. He looked around, saw the labels on the cupboards and the note on the counter. I'm in my kitchen.

Next to the note, a postcard. Gerry picked it up, saw the empty bench and the towering mountains. *Bonjour*, it said. From the Alps.

> More beneath it.
> *Buongiorno* from Trentino.
> *Zdravo* from Zagreb.

Gerry wasn't prone to anger, but something about the postcards peeved him.

Or maybe it was thinking of Johnny which made him mad. It didn't matter. He couldn't make sense of things, and frustration played havoc with a temper he didn't think he'd had.

His wife wouldn't abandon him for the Alps, not without
saying goodbye. Gerry turned the postcard over, trying
to decipher the puzzle, trying to work out what she really
wanted to say.

Something wasn't right. There had to be more to it than this.

It hurt his head.
J'ai mal à la tête.

Gerry had always been good with his nose. Which meant he
was surprisingly good at sniffing out deceptions.

Why play games? Why not tell him where she really was?
What bothered him more than the tricks was his wife's need
to play them.

Gerry listened out for any sign of his son, looked out of the
window for a Johnny who wasn't there. Was it Hazel playing
tricks on him, or his mind?

He picked up the rest of the postcards. He crossed the patio,
traversed the lawn towards the shed. He went through the
motions.

The kindling, the logs, the jerry can and the box of matches.

Checking the bonfire
for the hedgehog,

197

> for any hedgehog,
> as one must always do.

Gerry stood at the edge of the garden, on the threshold of the forest, and looked through the postcards again.

Something wasn't right, and Gerry realised what it was. These postcards weren't from his wife.

It wouldn't matter, then. If he started a fire. If he tossed the postcards into the flames.

A fox jumps from a porch and lands on a lawn, with an effect like diving into cold water. The air is filled with an immense pressure. The smoke makes it hard to see.

The human, on the other hand, moves with a single-minded grace. Jack is focused only on the present danger, racing towards his father.

The fire burns. Jack beats the smog away, eyes watering, shouting and coughing and calling out for his dad.

He reaches him. He grabs him, pulls him by the elbow, back from the flames. Jack's dad allows himself to be led.

Winds change. The smoke is carried the other way. The bonfire, it turns out, is not that big.

Only a misstep away from disaster. There's a jerry can by Jack's dad's ankles, closer to the flames than it should be. To a fox, it means nothing.

A fox will watch an entire garden burst into flames, today. A fox will watch everything burn.

'What are you doing?' Jack shouts, wiping his sweaty forehead, his voice cracking. 'We have to put this out.'

'What does it matter?' his dad replies, in a childish voice.

Jack seems off-kilter, and his father's tone seems to catch him off guard.

It occurs to the fox that Jack's dad is like a thrown stick, always in need of fetching. The fox can tell that Jack doesn't want to have to father his father.

'It's a pyre,' Jack's dad says, as if Jack were genuinely curious.

Jack closes his eyes, tries to breathe without coughing. 'A pyre?'

'Yes,' says his dad. 'For the badger.'

The fox creeps over the lawn, avoiding their gaze, trying to get a closer sniff of the fire. There's no badger upon it. Only burnt wood and brittle paper.

'Jesus Christ, Dad. A badger?' Jack says.

'I saw a dead badger.' His dad turns, points a crooked finger at the road, furrows his brow. 'He was—' He sounds confused. 'They must be bringing him later.'

The fox knows that Jack wishes he hadn't sent Charlotte away. What is Jack supposed to do with him, without her?

He settles on nothing. He does nothing.

The fox stares at the flames and wonders what a badger would look like on a pyre. It imagines the barn owl giving a eulogy. It imagines placing pebbles over the badger's eyes.

There are swallows on Jack's dad's pyjamas. Inky-black, fork-tailed outlines against an unbroken blue sky.

The hedgehog is hiding in the undergrowth, watching the fire from another angle. The fox slinks over to it, settles in the long grass.

The fox had grand ideas of saving Jack, just as Jack had saved the fox. But what would the fox save Jack from now? The city was never the enemy. And the fox doesn't know if anything can save Jack from himself.

Jack is wound up so tight, it's a wonder he hasn't already snapped. He stares daggers into the back of his dad's head.

His dad's glasses are filled with flames. The fox can't tell if he's watching the fire, or watching the fox. Despite the intense heat, the fox shivers.

'What's wrong?' says Jack's dad, not turning.

The fox thinks, for a moment, that it is being addressed. But Jack's dad is only talking to Jack.

'What's that?' Jack says, looking at the postcards which are curling into husks within the fire. 'Why are you burning those?'

Jack steps forward, crouches, tries to grab the postcards. They're too hot. They burn him. He swears, sucks his fingertips.

'It's a trick,' his dad says, in that same childish voice. 'They're not from her.'

Jack stands, turns, faces the house. He clenches his fists, then raises his arms and interlinks his fingers behind his head. From the other side of the fire, the other side of his father, the fox can almost hear Jack's silent scream.

'Let's go inside,' Jack says.

'I'm fine here,' his dad replies.

Jack grabs his dad by the elbow. 'I'm not asking.'

'I'm—' Jack's dad says, trying to shake Jack away. 'The pyre.'

'Dad,' Jack says, loudly, turning his father around by force. 'Can we live in the real world?' he says, looking his father in the face. 'For once?'

'You don't know the real world,' his dad says, firmly but quietly. 'You've never seen the wild.'

'Oh yeah?' spits Jack, seeming livid, looking fit to burst. 'And who am I, exactly?'

The fire sputters in the brief silence that follows. Deadly stillness, as if the forest itself is holding its breath.

'What?' Jack's dad says.

'Who am I?' Jack says, again, a vein pulsing in his forehead. 'What's my name?'

'I—' his dad begins, but cannot answer. He wriggles instead, tries to break free. Jack is gripping both of his dad's elbows.

'Tell me who I am,' Jack says, louder, not letting go of his dad's arms. 'And you can stay out here.'

'You're—' his dad is squirming, moving more erratically. 'I'm confused.'

The fox doesn't see vindication in Jack's face. His cheeks are red, and the fox doesn't think it's the heat of the fire. His eyes are watering, and the fox doesn't think it's the smoke.

'Who am I?' Jack shouts.

'I know it,' his dad says, still on the other thing, still sorting through his thoughts. 'You're J—'

Through the heat, through the fury, the slightest gleam of hope in Jack's eyes.

'Johnny?' his dad says.

And it all falls to pieces. Jack practically howls, letting go of his father's arms in the process.

The hedgehog rolls into a ball. And Jack's father, who was unsteady already, falls backwards now that he isn't being gripped.

Jack, says the fox. He's going to—

But it's too late. Jack doesn't notice the jerry can until it's been kicked. And while the fox had lunged to stop it, the can didn't need to fall far in order to ignite.

A moment of silence. Then, the garden explodes.

A fox's eyes are reflective, like a cat's. A fox's eyes have vertical pupils, which narrow into slits. Even in the darkest of times, a fox can see everything.

The fox sees this: a fire, becoming what Jack had foreseen from his bedroom window, something hellish and huge. Flames catching in tinder-dry grass and leaping into flowerbeds, over discarded garden tools, up the side of wooden planters.

A flash of its own near-death, before the fox crouches in the long grass. Through the grass, Jack, terror in his eyes, holding his father once again, disappearing into a rolling wall of black smoke.

Then, brief glimpses in the chaos. A hedgehog fleeing. Jack's father wriggling free. Jack tipping the bird bath, searching for a hose in the smog, desperately trying to curtail the blaze by stamping on errant patches of flame.

And Charlotte, standing at the front gate. Mouth agape, tote bag spilling open on the ground where she'd dropped it.

'Oh, my God.'

nineteen

'I can explain,' said Jack.

Holding a watering can in one hand, shielding his watering eyes with the other, he could barely make out who he was speaking to. At the gate, through the smoke, Charlotte's horrified face was shifting in and out of view.

'What the hell happened?' said Charlotte, already slamming the gate open, taking in the spitting patches of fire and the scorched lawn.

'It was him,' said Jack, gesturing at the house, his voice tight. 'He had a moment.'

'A moment?'

Jack was distracted. He couldn't get that name out of his head. Johnny. It figured that his father would be fixated on the past, oblivious to what was right in front of his eyes. Your brother's gone, he felt like saying. I'm here. But his dad was gone, too, so Jack surveyed the mess he'd left behind. Most of the grass on this side of the house was black or glowing orange, the raised beds which had previously held his dad's prized vegetables almost entirely burnt to a crisp. The shed looked like it had withstood a nuclear blast, a burnt-toast smell hanging heavy in the air around it. Jack had thought he could handle it. How had he let things come to this?

'I don't know.' He shook his head, gesticulated, tried to seem convincing. 'You know what he's like.'

Charlotte was busy running towards the house. 'Is he alright?' she said. 'Where is he?'

'He's fine,' Jack said, dazed and blinking. 'He's . . . in the house?' Though he was trying to sound sure, he couldn't keep the question from his voice.

Charlotte crossed the patio in a few strides, turning to Jack at the back door with the fire in her eyes. 'I was gone for just an hour,' she said. 'That's all the time you had to give to him.'

'It was closer to two,' Jack said, pulling at the sleeve of his jumper.

Charlotte's voice rose. 'You said you'd watch him.'

'I said I had a job interview,' Jack squealed. 'He was supposed to stay in the house!'

A piece of blackened trellis toppled off its frame, sending out a flurry of embers.

'It went badly, by the way,' said Jack.

'I don't care,' said Charlotte, stamping her way inside.

In the house, the bonfire smell was just as strong. An apocalyptic haze hung over the back porch, the dining table, the kitchen beyond. Charlotte rushed through the living room, calling their dad's name. Then she was in the kitchen, doing the same. Jack followed behind her like a scolded puppy. He wanted to explain that the fire wasn't his fault. But Charlotte had already gone upstairs, so he ran after her, taking the stairs two at a time, ignoring the conspicuously missing picture frame which he must have passed a hundred times since he'd been back.

At first, Jack wasn't sure why he stopped in the door of Charlotte's bedroom. Maybe it was because she usually kept the door closed, unless she was sitting at her desk, gesturing impatiently for him to move along. Without her in it, Jack had a brief opportunity to enter and inspect his sister's habitat. Framed on a shelf, a picture of her in a school play, made up to look like the Phantom of the Opera. A bookcase in which old-school romance novels rubbed shoulders with volumes of Chomsky and Derrida and Barthes. A vintage horror movie poster behind the bed, partly obscured by a threadbare hedgehog teddy which she'd had since she was a child. On the desk there were a number of university prospectuses, the pages downturned on a seemingly random selection of courses. Anthropology. Plant Science. International Animal Law. Next to these, Jack settled on the thing which had really caught his eye from the landing. It seemed anachronistic, sitting next to Charlotte's sleek laptop and streaming headset. A physical diary, written in pen.

Jack glanced at the door, heard Charlotte entering their parents' bedroom, still calling their dad's name. Jack traced his fingers on top of the open pages, contemplated the potential fallout of reading his sister's diary. He was better than that, he tried to convince himself: he was observing it as a curiosity.

As he leafed through the pages, making a slow calculation, synapses firing in his head, his stomach started to rotate like meat on a spit. Jack picked up the diary, held it close to his face in one trembling hand.

'You're kidding me.'

It wasn't his sister's innermost secrets which had elicited this reaction. It was the handwriting. And when, on a hunch, Jack opened the top drawer of her desk, he found exactly what his subconscious had been expecting to find. Beneath a ring light and a gaming console was a stack of postcards. Turkey. Tehran. The Khyber Pass and the Galapagos Islands. All the places their parents used to talk about. All unwritten, all as pristine as if they'd been printed yesterday. Some of them still in their packaging, from where they'd clearly been bought online. It was in this moment, shaking with silent rage in Charlotte's bedroom, staring so intently at a stack of postcards he almost burst a blood vessel, that Jack's sense of déjà vu suddenly revealed itself for what it actually was: recognition. The first postcards, from Alderney and the Alps. They used to hang, in a picture frame, above the stairs.

'Charlotte!' Jack yelled.

His sister appeared in the doorway, first looking frustrated. When she saw the diary in his hand, anger washed over her face. As her eyes moved to the postcards, her colour began to drain.

'I can explain,' she said.

'You'd better.'

twenty

A man and a woman step through the heavy front door of a ramshackle old house, followed closely by a besuited man holding a brochure. The estate agent toggles a light switch which doesn't turn on or off. The daylight through the mottled window above the stairs is dusty, unfiltered. The couple look up at the staircase, at the peeling wallpaper and the partially rotting wood. Her hand rests on top of her stomach. His, on the small of her back. The estate agent coughs, looks longingly over his shoulder, towards the front door.

'As you can see, it needs a bit of work.'

The couple aren't listening to him. They creak their way upstairs and stand on bare floorboards in the doorway of what could be a bedroom, then another, and another. This could be a studio. A sewing machine would go here, a mannequin right there. The bathroom is a museum of black mould and dripping pipes. The kitchen downstairs looks like it hasn't been used in ten years, and hasn't been cleaned in twenty. In a spot where their scuffed, gouged and ludicrously heavy dining table will one day stand, Hazel and Gerry stand arm in arm and stare out of the long windows at the overgrown garden, the woods beyond. There is no obvious point where the lawn ends, meaning there is no obvious point where the woods begin. The scale of the forest itself is overwhelming, and there's something dangerous about the darkness between those thick, knotty trunks. Hazel, the born romantic, feels its pull. Dangerous, but inviting. It looks like a place to get lost in, they say. A whole world outside their back door. They'd be settling, yes. But they'd be settling somewhere wild.

'The price is competitive,' the estate agent says, now eyeing the back door. 'You're our only viewing.'

Hazel is looking at Gerry, at the forest reflected in the lenses of his glasses. She already knows that this house will be the next step in their adventure. So what if the pipes leak, and the windows rattle, and nocturnal things scurry about behind the walls? Nothing has changed. Hazel is still a sucker for imperfection.

What do we seek in the country? Stability. A village, and in that village a wonky old house on a hill. Hazel's eccentric aunt, the one she'd lived with in the city, had died childless. What a surprise, when a phone call from a lawyer informed Hazel that she'd been left everything. Far from a fortune. But enough to help them buy this, a shell of a home acquired for a song at an auction where everyone else had wanted to flatten it and build something more modern.

Hazel and Gerry moved in almost immediately, surprising themselves at just how quickly they made a nest of their new life. It felt like the future was beginning around them, their Roberts radio crackling out dispatches on computers and compact discs, but Hazel and Gerry were never especially futuristic. His hair was already turning white at the temples, and he'd developed a penchant for moth-eaten jumpers. Hazel looked a lot younger, and her Doc Martens and safety-pin piercings seemed woefully out of place in a place like this. She stopped wearing so much eyeshadow, but even when she started cutting her hair short to be practical, she'd dye it an even brighter shade of red in defiance.

They tried their best to ingratiate themselves with the other thirty-something villagers, though they couldn't have felt more out of place among all these rugby-loving men and their horse-obsessed wives. They weren't exactly a hit at the local pubs and village fêtes, with Gerry's uncomfortable mumblings and Hazel's foul-mouthed anti-capitalist tirades. So they spent their time at home instead, sanding, stripping and scouring every long-neglected nook and cranny. Gerry created his utopia in their garden. Hazel made a house that might just be able to cope with a newborn, swinging around power tools that probably weren't meant to be used by people as pregnant as she was. Mornings and evenings were spent planting, walking, watching the birds. Like primitive people, Gerry would fish and forage, then Hazel would cook up the spoils. Not the fish, mind. He threw them back into the river, still alive. He'd been a vegetarian as long as they'd known each other, could grow every kind of carrot but couldn't cook to save his life. It was as if, once something was dead, it ceased to interest him. He'd leave it all in the ground if he could.

In that ground, they put down their roots, and when things got lonely, or difficult, and Hazel wished they were still out on the road, Gerry showed himself for what he was: her anchor; her breakwater; her port in a storm. Or, no, he was her mighty oak, like the one they took to taking picnics beneath, down the way, by the river a short walk from the house. When Hazel felt sick, he brewed her fresh ginger tea. When Hazel felt sad, he held her in his strong arms until she'd forgotten what was getting her down. He always managed to be buoyant, because the beauty of his world was always around him, wherever they were. He wrapped his branches around her, made himself a hollow in which she could shelter. Eventually, his rose-tinted view of the world started to rub off on her, like moss from bark. If Gerry was always there, things could never be so bad. Being sensible started to suit them. When Gerry christened the house 'Mole End', Hazel even insisted on hanging a street number on the front door, 'in case the fire brigade couldn't find us'.

Hazel got bigger. Dreams, generally, get smaller. And the time for questions was brought to an end when their newborn son suddenly arrived one winter afternoon, raven-haired and blue-eyed and strangely averse to crying. Jack. Their son was called Jack.

They say time flies, like a bird. Hazel had never quite agreed. Time sinks, like a stone, like a baited hook dropped from the side of her father's boat. She didn't miss her childhood after it had happened, her formative years spent around stinking troughs of guts, pinching eyeballs out of fish heads with

214

fingernails that would reek afterwards no matter how much soap you scrubbed them with. But like that baited hook, the deeper Hazel sank into her life, the faster everything seemed to disappear above her. Now, years after she and Gerry had stood silently in the kitchen of the house that would one day be Mole End, she often found herself longing to be back beneath that tarp, leaning against the side of the boat between the cages and the nets, the ocean patting her on the back. Or once again on that clifftop, the sea spray filling up her cup. She never did see a sea eagle.

Charlotte arrived some years later, time sinking further between. And though she loved her children, Hazel sometimes felt like motherhood had erased her. Like the Ship of Theseus, the old Hazel had gradually been replaced, that adventurous young woman dismantled bit by bit until she'd become someone she didn't recognise, someone who barely existed but as an extension of others. This couldn't be the end of her adventure. That's why she knew she needed to go.

A whispered conversation in the half-light, a few weeks ago. Hazel had stood in that same spot in the kitchen, staring out of the window. Pressed against the dining table where she now spent most of her days, watching her husband, wondering what she was going to do. Are you OK? Charlotte had enquired, though she must have already known the answer, because since things had changed, they generally avoided asking each other the question. Perhaps her daughter thought that her mother, so distant and diminished of late, had fallen under the same spell as her father. Like Gerry, she'd taken to staring at nothing. Like Gerry, she'd started loitering at the edge of the garden, looking for something beyond the trees. That early morning, the morning that Charlotte found Hazel at the back window, she'd decided to come out with it.

'Are you OK?'

No, I'm not. None of us are.

'There's something—' Hazel had started, but stopped herself, tripping over her own words. She didn't know how to say it, didn't want her daughter to think her selfish. Out with it. 'There's something I have to do.'

A pilgrimage, Hazel told Charlotte. One last adventure, before it became impossible, before everything that might be about to happen came to pass. One last leap into the unknown. When a swallow's last brood leaves the nest, it has no purpose left in the place in which it settled for summer. Its journey begins again. But Charlotte was still here at Mole End, and Hazel knew why. Hazel said she was sorry, said that Charlotte should be the one going on adventures. She would, she promised. But, to Hazel's surprise, her daughter urged her to go, first.

'Get lost,' Charlotte had said, with a small smile. 'In the nicest possible way.' She'd held on to Hazel's wrists. 'While you still can.'

Relief had flooded Hazel, meeting an opposing tide of guilt.

'I think you need this,' Charlotte had said. 'And I think that he does, too.'

Hazel hadn't understood. How could this help Gerry? But Charlotte hadn't been talking about Gerry. And while Jack hadn't even been factored into Hazel's thoughts, so absent was he from the family's day-to-day existence, now it hit her, with all the force of a wave breaking against a rocky outcrop. Hazel's desperate need for freedom, the old impulse to steal away on her father's boat, the yearning which made her take flight when life on the ground got hard, could be an opportunity. For though her son was as stubborn as his dad and as single-minded as she was, he had a sense of duty, and a soft spot for his sister. Charlotte claimed that Jack wasn't happy in the city. Charlotte claimed that, on the rare occasions when they spoke, Jack seemed despondent at best, crushingly lonely at worst. Jack was blind to anything but his job, his rulebook and his safety net, but he'd come to regret it if he wasn't persuaded to see things as they were. Charlotte claimed that she knew better than Jack about what Jack needed. And Charlotte had decided that Jack needed to come home. Jack and Gerry, under the same roof, without Hazel as a referee. Imagine that.

The postcards had been Charlotte's idea. She decided she'd post them herself, after insisting that Hazel didn't tell her how far away she was going, and in what direction. She'd said: you've told me enough about your adventures for me to get a little creative. She'd said: leave it to your daughter to throw your son off the scent. Hazel got the impression that Charlotte would relish the mischief. The pleading phone call she'd place to Jack, shortly after Hazel's departure, was also her idea. Hazel had a recollection of her daughter as a precocious four-year-old, spooking her teenage brother by pretending that she could hear the voices of imps in the woods. Charlotte had inherited her mother's dramatic flair.

Hazel had a practical head, and no wish to abdicate her responsibilities, so she handled the call to the doctor, the stockpiling of Gerry's medication, the Gerry-proofing of the house. Rugs and wires rolled away to limit trip hazards, the house furnished with her old family photos to jog his memory and keep him comforted. Many times, she wondered if she was being cruel to Gerry, or fair on Charlotte, by leaving. But she never wavered. Because even if she didn't yet know exactly where she was going, she knew that going was something she had to do.

'I won't be gone too long,' she told Charlotte. 'And you'll always be able to reach me.'

And she'd left. She'd finally done it, putting all those miles between herself and Mole End, miles and miles and miles. Now she lay, curled up in this faraway place, wracked with guilt and soaked with rainwater, remembering a life unlived. Of all the places to end up, she'd found herself here.

twenty-one

'She tricked me,' Jack said, through clenched teeth, his hands clamped to Charlotte's desk.

His sister's revelation had made him incandescent with rage. Now she stood there in front of him, still looking like she was holding back.

'She shouldn't have had to,' Charlotte said, tentatively.

'*You* tricked me.'

'It's not my fault that you don't know your own mother's handwriting.'

Jack closed his eyes, massaged his temples. For someone with an analytical brain, he felt pretty stupid for not having questioned the first-class British stamps affixed to the post-cards. He pictured Charlotte, hunched over her desk, forging messages from their mother. He pictured his dad, losing his grip on reality in the garden, Jack gripping on to his father's

219

elbows and shouting in his face. He tried to picture his mum, somewhere else, but he couldn't even conjure up an image of where she might be. Things were spiralling out of control. As Jack was shaking his head and muttering under his breath, Charlotte was backing out of the doorway and looking off down the landing.

'Where's Dad?' she said, mostly to herself.

'Where's Mum!?' Jack shouted, entirely at Charlotte.

Charlotte sighed, looked at the ceiling. 'She's—'

'In Alderney?'

'Further.'

'The Alps?'

'I think—' Charlotte said. 'Further.'

'Where, then?' Jack said. 'Trentino? Zagreb?'

'Further,' Charlotte said, then hesitated. 'I think. She didn't tell me.'

'Great,' Jack said, incredulously, flinging his arms wide. 'And when is she coming back?'

'She didn't tell me that, either,' Charlotte replied, panic creeping into her voice. 'But it's been nine days, and, and—' She checked her phone. 'Look, she said she'd message. And she hasn't.'

'I don't understand,' Jack said, starting to pace and rub his brow. 'She said you'd always be able to contact her. But her phone's been off all week.' He pointed at his own phone. 'I've messaged her, a lot. I've called her, a lot. It rang through. Every. Single. Time.'

A pause. Charlotte played with the hem of her hoodie, spoke almost under her breath. 'I bought her a burner.'

'A burner?' Jack grabbed two handfuls of his unwashed hair. 'This isn't a spy film, Charlotte. This is real life!'

'I know,' she said, but she was distracted, looking down the landing again. 'We need to find Dad. I'm worried.'

Jack shook his head, stared off out of Charlotte's bedroom window. 'That's rich,' he said. Then he shrugged. 'He'll be in the garden. He's not exactly hard to find.'

Charlotte left the doorway, headed towards the stairs. Jack chased after her.

'This conversation isn't over,' he said, in the voice of a school prefect.

Charlotte turned at the top of the stairs. She looked on the verge of tears, an expression entirely unfamiliar to Jack. It made him stop in his tracks.

'I've been trying,' she said, her voice choked. 'To hold it all together.'

Jack felt a stab of something. 'Look,' he said, stiffly. 'I get it.' He paused. 'You're not old enough to deal with all this.' I should have been here, he thought. 'Mum should be here,' he said.

This didn't seem to go down well. 'I'm not a teenager any more!' She was the one shouting now. 'Not that you've noticed.'

'Well, you're still here,' he said. 'You could have left a long time ago. I could have got you work experience. I could have got you out of here.'

'You're so oblivious, Jack,' she said.

'That's not fair.'

'I'll tell you what isn't fair,' said Charlotte, gripping the banister. 'Me staying here, helping Mum and Dad and keeping

house like Mrs fucking Tiggy-Winkle, while you're off pretending to have the perfect life in the city.'

She descended the stairs.

'I thought you liked—' Jack began.

But Charlotte had already moved on, climbing back up the
stairs with her already-wide eyes bulging.

'Don't you dare tell me I like it here.' Her voice was brittle,
her finger jabbing at his chest. Then she pointed to the stairs,
as if Jack's old life was at the bottom of them. 'Especially when
you *hate* it *there*.'

'That is not true.'

'I'm your sister,' she cried. 'I can tell when you're unhappy.
I can tell when something is destroying you.'

'I'm busy!' Jack shouted. 'And, yes, I'm stressed.' He steadied
his voice. 'It doesn't mean I'm unhappy.'

'Well, guess what?' Charlotte said. 'I'm stressed. And I'm
unhappy. We all are. And I know that you are, too.'

She didn't wait around for an answer. Jack followed her
down the stairs.

'I thought—'

'I know what you think,' she said, re-entering the kitchen,
disturbing the pots and pans hanging from the low ceiling,
peering out of the windows, behind the door. 'That I'm lazy.
That not moving out was the easy choice.'

Jack stopped in the kitchen doorway, made a face behind her
back that said: yeah, basically. Charlotte kept talking.

'Do you think Mum can handle all of this on her own?' she
said. 'And who would she call, when she can't?'

'Well—' Jack said. 'She could—'

'Where's Dad?' Charlotte cried, actually cried, stamping her foot, tears spilling down her cheeks.

'He's just so difficult,' Jack said, still on the previous point. Thinking of the scene in the garden made his heart race.

'You think I don't know that?'

'He actually likes you!'

'You never give him a chance.'

Charlotte looked at the back door, then set off towards it. Before stepping outside, she turned once again.

'Do you know how old I was when you went to uni?' she said, quietly.

'What's that got to—'

'I was seven,' she said. 'I wasn't even a teenager when you moved out for good.' She shook her head, turned her eyes to the ceiling. 'And it was fine, even if you visiting once every six months didn't exactly equate to a brother–sister relationship.'

'It's not only—'

'Then you stopped visiting, and that was fine, too.' Her voice was breaking. 'You were off living your big life.' The tears were flowing now. 'But you forgot about us.' She could barely get these next words out. 'You forgot about me.'

Jack wanted to protest, but it was hard to do so when his memories of Charlotte were so sparse. He'd hardly seen her in the years after he moved to the city, save for the rare occasions when his mum brought her along on her already-rare visits. For a brief patch, when Charlotte was in her mid-teens and he in his late twenties, she used to come up and stay with him, get drunk on cheap tequila with her responsible older brother. She actually ran away, once, turned up on his doorstep in the city, in the rain. Jack had been concerned, had asked if she'd had enough of their dad. She'd brushed him off, had been in strangely high spirits. She'd just been bored, she said. She'd fancied an adventure. She'd always had a flair for the dramatic. It was a long time since Jack had invited her to visit. If she ran away now, he supposed she'd run to someone else.

'Charlotte, I—'

'Do you understand how much it takes out of you, watching him, watching what's happening to him, day after day, week after week?' Charlotte seemed furious that Jack had made her cry. It seemed like she couldn't stop talking. 'Things are not fine. Things are far from fine, even if you stay far enough away to pretend it's not happening.'

'That's not—'

'I would love to have the opportunities you've had,' Charlotte said, finally, the tears drying up. 'But one of us has to be the grown-up. And it isn't you.'

Jack didn't know what to say. And he didn't have to, because Charlotte had already left the house, was tearing through the garden, shouting for their dad. Left all alone again, Jack swayed a little in the middle of the kitchen. The pots and pans swayed with him. Where had the fox gone? Just as he remembered it, it appeared, in through the back door his sister had left wide open.

Jack, said the fox, apprehensively. *He's*—

'I didn't forget about them,' Jack said, vacantly, to himself, to the fox. 'I just didn't—' he said, choking on the words. 'I didn't know.'

Through the open door, beneath the sound of his sister's panicked refrain of Dad, Dad, Dad, came the rhythmic rasping of crickets, like an orchestra tuning up. Jack could feel their vibrations in his jaw.

Jack, said the fox, again, nervously darting to and fro on the kitchen tiles. *Your dad is—*

Jack began to feel as if he was re-entering his body, re-entering the room. Now he saw the swaying pots, the agitated eyes of the fox, the freshly minted message on a Post-it note on the kitchen island in front of him.

'Dad?' Charlotte was still shouting, her voice getting closer. 'Dad?'

When had his dad written this? Jack took a step forward with a lump in his throat, held on to the top of a stool to steady himself. As he read the note, as he realised what had happened while he hadn't been paying attention, Jack found himself caught between a lone fox and a stricken sister.

Jack, said the fox, looking up at him from the kitchen tiles below.

'Jack,' said his sister, from the back door.

He's gone, said the fox.

And Jack turned to Charlotte, who stood by the dining table, wiping her eyes and biting her lip. 'He's gone.'

twenty-two

Did you know?
Shrews often die of shock.
The thunder of a car going past.
The roar of the human world.

The fire roared in front of Gerry, and the Alps burned in its flames.

Gerry thought of an old song, of falling into a burning ring of fire. He heard coughing, felt a hand on his elbow, and was pulled back violently. Hazel?

No, his son. The angry young man. It wasn't like him to overreact. It wasn't like him to take a fire and turn it into an inferno.

> What am I doing?
> Why does it matter?

A few days before, Gerry had walked into the village with Charlotte.

She'd had a coffee. He'd had a milkshake, with whipped cream on top. They'd laughed about the rotten-looking green juices his son had been making, the ones Charlotte had taken to pouring down the sink.

On the walk back, they'd stumbled upon a dead badger by the side of the road. It had made Gerry sad.

Judging by his son's voice, the thought had made him sad, too.

> Did you know the badger?
> Gerry wants to say.
> But a fox in the grass
> runs off with his attention.

His son was talking about the postcards, the flaming falsehoods in the fire. But Gerry was distracted by the blazing eyes of the fox.

Gerry knew about foxes. He knew that foxes weren't pests,

that some farmers actively encourage them. Foxes won't eat your crops, but the rats and rabbits they eat will.

He knew that any fox rehomed near a pheasant shoot will be killed to protect the pheasants, which will then, in turn, be killed.

He knew that certain chemicals will throw hounds off a fox's scent. Hazel had taught him that one.

> I know where I am.
> I'm fine where I am.

The fox yipped quietly, but Gerry didn't know what it was trying to say. His son yipped louder. Saying: let's go inside. Saying: I'm not asking.

His son had always been like this. He could never relax, could never stand still, could never appreciate the crackle of a fire or the low hum of nature. Perhaps he'd like a pumpkin seed? Perhaps he hadn't noticed the fox?

His son never looked. He lived in the city, and city folk liked to talk instead. Gerry wanted to say that the city was a kind of indoors, but he was scared of appearing unkind.

He wanted to say that the city had a convertible roof, and that most people in the city kept the roof closed. But he was scared of not making any sense, of being made fun of.

He wanted to say, more than anything, that all he'd wanted was for their home to be a kind of anti-city. After Johnny, all he'd wanted for his son was a kind of safety net. A kind of cocoon.

He kept quiet, and his son kept talking. He was asking more and more questions, and Gerry was getting more and more confused.

'Cold line' is a hunting phrase.
The faint, barely perceptible scent of a fox.
Gerry understands. He's following his own cold line,
searching the undergrowth for hints of himself.
Chasing after traces of his mind.

His son was asking who he was, and such a simple question could have made Gerry laugh.

But to be confused, to be distracted, to be put on the spot, suddenly seemed more likely to make him cry.

I know the answer, but it's escaped me.
Can I get back to you?
Can I tell you that I love you another time?

Things aren't set in stone. The smallest creatures undergo the greatest transformations. We are all of us, always, in flux.

Gerry stared at his son and watched him transform, again.
From his son to an angry young man. And from an angry
young man to Johnny.

> Johnny got a brand-new cricket bat,
> so he didn't come to the woods any more.
> Preferred hitting things with wood instead.
> Preferred his willow dead.

Was it toys that came between Gerry and Johnny? Was it
things?

Gerry couldn't remember a single one of his childhood toys,
but he did remember the books that they used to read, and
the precise series of moves it took to climb the alder in his
parents' garden.

It wasn't long before Johnny stopped climbing trees and
started climbing ladders. Even then, he wanted to get ahead.
If Gerry had been reared on roots and salad, Johnny was
nursed on nickel and copper.

Johnny was a badger, but he had the eyes of a magpie. Gerry
was never anything but a barn owl.

> The order, Strigiformes.
> Two hundred birds called 'Owl'.
> Split, by science, into two families.
> True owls, and barn owls.

Gerry often thought that the other kids were the true owls. They hooted together, and watched from on high.

He took Johnny under his wing. Johnny allowed him into his sett. When they were still young enough to still read those talking-animal books, they painted their faces accordingly, played in the woods.

Gerry, with his circular glasses, the barn owl. Johnny, brash and tough, a little stubborn. Doomed to end up as roadkill.

What was Gerry's son, then? Gerry had always said that he was like a magpie, because he'd always been attracted to shiny things.

But he was also so much like his uncle and so little like his father that he could have been a cuckoo in the nest.

> Barn owls might seem scary, tawny owls endearing.
> But it's the barn owls who get beaten up in the wild.
> Lo and behold, the tawny owls fight back.
> Gerry was never a tawny owl.

Who were the boys that used to beat him up? The Snargets? The something-elses?

He supposed it didn't matter now. If Gerry's memory was a lake, in moments like this, he'd catch a glimpse of the shore.

And he'd know that all that was very long ago, and that he'd been lost for a very long time.

There's nothing worse than remembering that you can't remember things. Than staring through eyes which suddenly deceive you. Than having an argument with the brain inside your head.

> Gerry the barn owl.
> Mobbed, teased and picked on.
> Relying on his younger brother for help.
> How embarrassing to watch Johnny fighting his battles.
> How embarrassing when Johnny started picking on him, too.

Johnny? Is it you? It can't be you. Where am I? Where's Hazel?

Like a shrew keeling over at the side of the road, Gerry felt overwhelmed, then overcome.

> The thunder of a car going past.
> The roar of the human world.

The fox was barking. He imagined it was Johnny, shouting for help in the undergrowth.

Had there been a hedgehog in the fire? Was a flock of darting swallows pummelling him from above like a

hailstorm, like an airstrike, like a driving rain of spears
in battle?

Gerry had nothing with which to shield himself. He tried to
run, but he was being held in place.

> Shrews can simply drop dead
> upon finding themselves out in the open.
> They'd rather die than feel exposed.

Who are you? It wasn't his wife. It wasn't Johnny, even if it
looked like him. It was his son, and his son wasn't angry, he
was afraid.

And he had a right to be afraid, and he even had a right to
be angry, because Gerry had never been much of a father.
Hadn't he tried with the boy?

He remembered the alder, the oak. He remembered
attempting to build that treehouse. He remembered pushing
the boy on a swing, saying: I'll catch you if you fall.

> Down, down, down,
> and the flames went higher.

A tumble. An explosion. A wall of flame and a
ceiling of smoke.

Gerry had always been good with his nose. But his
nostril hairs were singed, and the inside of said nose felt
roasted.

Unable to see a thing, unable to hear a thing, Gerry bolted
from a garden which was now on fire and found himself back
inside the house.

Had the angry young man set the fire? Gerry didn't
recognise the stranger floundering in the smoke. But
he recognised his daughter, and he knew that she'd
banish the intruder.

He left her to it. In the kitchen, he set about looking for his
wife.

The Alps and Alderney.
Alderney and the Alps.

At the counter, a deep breath. Sense replaced nonsense.

His son had made a mess of the garden. His daughter was
sorting him out. His wife was nowhere to be seen, and she
wasn't where she said she was, because she'd been bored by
Alderney, and because the Alps had never been an end point
for them.

Where else could she be? He thought of the Isle of Mull
and the Galapagos Islands. He thought of Dieppe and the

Der-Chantecoq lake. He thought of Turkey and Tehran, Kazakhstan and the Khyber Pass.

And he thought of the French woods, and the French pigs, and the clarity of his memory of those months surprised him.

> It's a simple toss-up.
> Pigs are better at finding truffles,
> but dogs are less inclined to eat them.

Think, think. Hazel had never been to those woods. She'd never met those pigs, though she had enjoyed their story. Pigs in Périgord, she'd said. It sounded like a band she would have been in as a teenager.

But she wasn't in Périgord, with the pigs, and she wasn't on the Isle of May, with the puffins. So where was she?

Gerry stood by a dining table which had withstood three decades, staring out of the long windows as he and Hazel had, that first time, all those years ago.

Gerry stared at the burning garden, at the woods beyond. The point where lawn ended and forest began. The overwhelming scale of a forest, the imposing yet inviting darkness between the thick, knotty trunks.

What had they always called it? A whole world outside their back door. A place to get lost in.

To get lost in. To get lost in. To get lost.

> Barn owls mate for life.
> Barn owls hunt in pairs.

So it was with Hazel, who understood Gerry better than anyone else. She'd loved him without complaint, so he'd loved her without question.

Female barn owls are a third bigger than the males. And so was Hazel, in spirit. Larger than him. Larger than life. Yet growing smaller these last few years, because of him.

Now she was lost, and Gerry thought that might be his fault, too. Was she out there? He hoped she wouldn't have just left him, so she must have got lost.

If she was lost, and the woods were a place to get lost in, then the answer was obvious: Hazel must be lost in the woods.

> Nothing for him here,
> if she's out there.

It didn't take much decision-making. Gerry was a man of action. All he needed to do was pack a bag and pull on his boots.

While an argument unfolded on the burnt lawn, Gerry gathered his things and wrote a note, which he left on the counter.

> How long had she been gone?
> Time is a lake, not a river.
> Days could have been weeks.

While the fight raged on outside, Gerry sneaked out of the back door with a backpack on. He crept across what remained of the garden, behind the shed, towards the long grass at the edge of the lawn.

He turned. He saw his son. He saw his daughter. And he saw a fox, seeing him. He thought about saying goodbye. But what would it achieve? What was one more thing left unsaid?

Gerry faced the forest, the yawning emptiness beyond. He saw a place to get lost in. He saw a great darkness, ready to swallow him up.

He took a deep breath, and stepped over the threshold.

> The fox watches Gerry leave the garden.
> The owl watches Gerry enter the woods.

twenty-three

As Jack stood with his sister in the kitchen and stared at a sky-blue Post-it note, he found it hard to imagine anything worse happening than this.

GONE TO FIND HER

Charlotte put her hand to her forehead, breathed deeply. Jack scratched the wiry hair on his cheek.

'I know what you're thinking,' he said.

'You definitely don't,' said Charlotte, her voice wavering.

Jack swallowed. 'OK,' he said, rubbing the bridge of his nose with his free hand. 'We need to find him. Obviously, we need to find him.'

'Well, where would he have gone?' said Charlotte, dipping in and out of the hallway, looking for signs.

The woods, whispered the fox, from the back porch. *He went into the woods.*

'The woods,' said Jack.

Charlotte's head reappeared around the kitchen door. She looked horrified. 'How do you know that?'

'Where else?' Jack says. 'For him, that place has always held all the answers. Of course he thinks he'd find her out there.'

They both looked in the same direction. The back windows, the burnt garden beyond them and, beyond that, the wilderness. The jaws of that forest which had always terrified Jack, and the even more terrifying prospect that their father was out there, swallowed up by them. Charlotte didn't seem to doubt that that's where their dad would be. Just scared. Acres of woodland extended beyond Mole End. But while the forest might have been their father's natural habitat, he wasn't as capable as he used to be. Their dad wouldn't think of it like that. He hadn't wandered out there aimlessly. No matter how misguided, he would always follow his nose.

'What are we going to do?' Charlotte said, quietly.

What were they going to do? Jack's better judgement said that they should call the police, make a statement, wait around. But they were already losing time. What would his dad do? He already knew that. Jack thought of himself on a common in the city, what felt like months ago, placing a call about an injured fox. And he saw that same fox standing on the back doorstep, its eyes like searchlights beaming back at him. He wouldn't have approached the fox on the common if it weren't

240

for everything his dad had taught him. If it weren't for his dad, he'd have stayed on the bench.

'I'm going after him,' Jack said.

This wasn't radical practicality. This was something else. His need to go after his father was stronger than caution, more important than rules. The need was so heavy that it broke straight through the bottom of his safety net and kept on falling.

'I'm coming with you,' Charlotte said.

'No,' Jack said. 'You stay.' He spoke calmly. 'He might come back. Stay, please. You'll find out where Mum is. You're smarter than me.'

Charlotte looked reluctant, but she nodded, called the number she'd dialled. Jack listened to her talking to their dad's doctor in worried tones. He left her, went upstairs and changed as quickly as he could. He stuffed his running ruck-sack with a head torch and a first-aid kit and any other useful items he could find, returning to the kitchen to hunt for dried fruit and slow-release carbohydrates, anything to give him energy. He filled a bottle of water. He checked his phone was in his pocket. Charlotte handed Jack a number of pill boxes and a sheet of scribbled instructions. Jack nodded gravely, tried to give her a hug which turned into a shoulder-bump, then zipped up the rucksack and headed for the back door. The fox was already waiting for him on the lawn, nodding its head in encouragement.

'I didn't know,' Jack said, to Charlotte, from the doorway. 'About any of it.' He turned, but only barely. 'I mean, I should have known. I should have asked.'

What was it she'd said? Run away. It's what you do.

'We'll talk,' he said.

He didn't wait around to see his sister's reaction. The fox was darting about on the grass, its tail swishing about in anticipation.

Are we going? it said, in a sparking voice. It hopped on all four legs, looked back at the house. *Where's your sister?*

'She's not coming,' Jack said.

The fox's brows knitted together, its eyes searching the back porch. *Did you say goodbye?*

'Goodbyes always come too early,' Jack said, drily. He was already striding down the lawn and towards the tangle of bushes.

Right, said the fox, after him, sounding pleased. *Better to never say goodbye at all.*

Jack was already at the edge of the garden, already having second thoughts. The forest looked endless, remorseless. Jack looked back at Mole End, felt as if he were straddling a widening chasm, over a ravine which he might just fall into. Behind him, a failed interview, a wasted decade, a city in which he'd long ago lost his way. Ahead of him? The unpredictable. The unknown. The wild.

Jack stepped forwards, but only to avoid falling. The fox rocketed to his side, rocked backwards and forwards like a greyhound awaiting the boom of a starting gun.

Are you sure about this? it said, with creeping agitation. *Lone foxes die alone.*

'I'm not alone,' Jack said.

And he took another step. From the slope and into a hedge,

through the hedge and into the bracken. He stepped over the threshold, into the forest, and he started walking. The man who was going somewhere. The man whose life had very nearly begun.

The swallow barrel-rolls through the sky above an orchard in which two humans strike up a conversation, but the swallow doesn't register the humans; it is looking for food, though it is not finding any, for it feeds on horseflies and bluebottles and they're nowhere to be seen at this time of year – tiring to be so hungry – it settles on a telephone wire instead and there finds another swallow, and those swallows, together with yet more swallows, fall from the wires and rise from the orchard in a cloud and begin to fly south, six thousand miles of togetherness, through France and much further, feeding over fields and rivers, sleeping in reed beds, no longer starving but replete by the time they arrive at the southern tip of Africa, then – pause for winter – back again, a journey of six weeks, of two hundred miles a day, the same process repeated for ten years, or twelve years, as many as sixteen, which is how one lone swallow happened to perch on a telephone wire above the orchard where those two humans first met, and how, over a decade later, that very same swallow happens to hunt flies over a shallow river by which those very same humans are swinging from an oak tree with their young son (their son!), and the swallow, which has nurtured many broods of its own, which has watched its own pink and squealing progeny spring forth from its own tiny speckled eggs, might just think that (perhaps, something like) every life is a long journey, and you don't have to travel six thousand miles over six months to feel like you've made it somewhere, and wouldn't it have been nice to have stopped moving, to have spent a year not on the wing, to have roosted in a wonky old house on top of a lumpy hill and to roost there, still, to have had a rest – the swallow perches with tiny feet on a thin branch and watches the family for a while – but soon its regret has fluttered away and it can think only of the scarcity of horseflies, of bluebottles, and of the many miles it took to get here, to this river, to these flies and these people, and yet still it nods its vermilion head and falls from a branch and rises from a forest in which a fox skulks and does it all again, because who wouldn't do so if the choice was all of this, or none of it?

part three

WILD

twenty-four

Winter. A man sits at a dining table with a baby in his lap. The boy had woken with a nightmarish shriek, so the man had carried him downstairs, sat patiently with him at the table while the early morning darkness yawned behind them. He's telling the boy a story, even if the boy is too young to understand it. It's dark outside the window behind them, but they're wrapped up in the warmth of the house, the steam from the man's mug breathing condensation on to the windows. The man informs the boy that he was born frozen solid. The man tells the boy that they had to defrost him, like a fish from a freezer. But his eyes never thawed. That's why they're so blue. The boy gurgles, eyebrows raised, looking like he's hanging on every single word. And his mother, who arrives downstairs with the morning sun, laughs from the doorway. Not at the story itself, but at the fact that a man who'd never wanted children found it easier to talk to a baby than he ever had to anyone else.

Hazel knew that baby magpies are born with blue eyes. Gerry said the same was true for fox cubs. Would Jack's eyes change over time? In the years since moving to Mole End, Hazel had started wearing glasses. In the years since that first night at the pub, then on the crest of an open field, half sub-merged in a weedy hedgerow, she had mastered the mechanics of Gerry's beaten-up binoculars. She'd long since had a pair of her own. She'd long since felt that, as the years unspooled like a rope slipping away from her, so fast that trying to keep hold would burn her hands, she'd been watching her life from a distance, through a pair of fogged-up lenses. Here, now, she held them to her eyes and adjusted the sights, peering through two perfect circles, thirty years into the past.

The first six months of Jack's life were spent in a bubble, another perfect circle, in the guise of an imperfect old house which seemed like it would probably collapse if a wolf tried to blow it down. Then, to pay the household bills, to pay for the countless repairs, Gerry got a job at the local greengrocer's. He was taken under the wing of its owner, Monty, whom he'd met on the crest of another hill on another early morning, who was just as keen as birdwatcher as him. Gerry had a friend. But Gerry, quite suddenly, was no longer at home. Gerry would spend his days opening up early and closing down late, and Hazel would spend hers on her own except for Jack, doing her best to curtail her swearing, fixing her eyes on the endless forest on the other side of the window whenever she began to feel trapped or short of breath. Hazel was quieter than she used to be, because she had fewer opportunities to speak. Jack was quiet, too, ever ready with a gummy smile but as strangely reluctant to laugh as he was to cry. Old ladies in the village said he was the best-behaved baby they'd ever met. One such old lady, Monty's wife, Bea, became Hazel's only friend in the village, then her go-to for help with Jack when Hazel felt the urge to go back to work.

Designing dresses felt like folly now. And for all his good intentions, Gerry was never very good at keeping house. Her husband could catch sticklebacks and salmons, but he couldn't screw in a lightbulb. He could build a shelter out of twigs and turf, but he'd be stumped if you asked him to put up the ironing board. Was Hazel defined by being a mother? She'd broken down in front of Jack, once, early on. At the dining table, him watching curiously from his high chair. Gerry was at the green-grocer's and she'd been trying to sew but had pricked her finger, not a deep wound but enough to draw blood. A mug of tea had been brewing on the tabletop, and Hazel remembered thinking that the infusion looked like blood in water, like something to lure a shark. Time seemed to sink faster at such moments. On good days, the house felt like a life raft on a choppy sea. But sometimes it was like an anchor, dragging her down. Or, no. Perhaps the house was a bucket, and she was a crab. Trapped, yes. But with only herself to blame.

Hazel could fix anything. It was a point of pride. She learned to rescue a leaking pipe, repair a broken fence and, of course, bring any tattered item of clothing back from the brink. She used to be a maker. Now she was a mender. Her skills became domesticated over the years, her sewing used on children's socks and sock puppets rather than stockings and silk slips. She got a part-time job at the haberdasher's in the village. The haberdasher's! She could feel her younger self rolling her eyes as she adjusted the scarlet waistcoats of ruddy-faced landowners with expanding waistlines and helped aghast old women get red wine stains out of damask tablecloths. It wasn't like the village had a dry-cleaner. She spent days boxed in between endless spools of thread and growing mountains of clothes. Sometimes, all those garments pressed in on her. Sometimes, she felt tangled up in those spools. She'd speak to Gerry about it, but they were both too tired to talk, one exhausted from work and the other exhausted from everything else.

Little comedies became important in a life which was smaller than the one they'd imagined. The blank postcards they'd collected on their travels were framed, hung above the stairs. They still had no one they'd send them to, Hazel being a self-appointed orphan who'd lost her favourite aunt, Gerry avoiding the subject of his father and being long out of touch with his only brother. Yet though they were fairly friendless and more than fairly broke, they were never unhappy. How could they be, when they had those little comedies? Sometimes they played at being farmers on their modest patch of land, sowing seeds in second-hand dungarees. Baby Jack was 'Boggis', she 'Bunce' and he 'Bean'. Even now, she and Gerry drank from those same mugs they'd been given as a wedding present, she from 'Mr' and he from 'Mrs'. They slept in each other's bedsocks because they were comfier, would compete to fill in the Sunday cross-word and trade answers like contraband. Jack would watch all the while through those curious, icy eyes, as if he were Little

Father Time, older than the pair of them, longing for the words with which he could take part. In the years to come, those little comedies would turn into tall tales. The adventures she and Gerry had planned would morph into stories to be told to Jack and Charlotte, even if those stories never truly felt like fiction. One day, we'll see the Galapagos Islands. One day, we'll cross the Khyber Pass.

There was still time. And by the time Jack could speak, his curiosity had turned into a quiet inquisitiveness, questions he'd whisper into his nearest parent's ear. It was usually his father who'd take the teacher role: telling him which bird was which; how to climb alders and oaks; why, when they caught those fish, they should always throw them back. That's not to say that Jack wouldn't ask Hazel questions. It was just that, as his father's answers were limited to the practical, he'd go to her for more philosophical enquiries.

Where does a fox go when it dies?

To a big forest, with lots of other little foxes.

How do I make friends with the other boys at nursery?

Just be yourself, Jack. They'll find it hard not to love you.

What are you making, and why's it taking up the whole table?

A wedding dress, remember? Your dad and I are getting married.

twenty-five

I've always wanted to go on an adventure!

The fox's enthusiasm irritated Jack, because he'd rather
be anywhere but here, in any situation but this. He'd
mainly been prevaricating around the edge of the woods, so
far, scared to get to the heart of the matter. Sticky red things
were clinging to his trainers, clingy brown things sticking
to his arms. Keeping his eyes mainly on the ground, he saw
dry dirt, twisted branches, animal droppings. Burst tyres and
trampled iron fences, broken guttering and forgotten, water-
logged gloves. But even in the places where the human world
had found its way in, this forest remained an old kind of wild.
It seemed to be endless, ageless, to go on for ever in every
sense. Roundabout Wood. The forest's actual name, not some
lazy attempt at whimsy, as Jack used to assume when his dad
referred to it. Google Earth had proven otherwise. Within this

wood, the village was a glorified clearing, surrounded by trees. His childhood home was nothing more than a needle mark in a patchwork quilt of rusty brown and thirsty green thrown loosely over the surrounding hills. Jack had no idea which direction to walk in. He simply walked forwards.

'It's not an adventure,' he said, gritting his teeth.

Jack had never liked taking risks. Even in daylight, even on a warm and clear day like this, the forest seemed filled with threats, able to arouse a primal fear in him. Predators seemed to lurk behind every tree trunk, each rustle among the leaves suggesting a swooping raptor or a falling tree about to flatten him. He feared, mostly, how much he'd fucked everything up. Top dog had become runt of the litter – he already knew that. But his mind was racing over a painstakingly put-together career which he'd thought he wanted but now felt like a long path taken after a wrong turn. Over a fox which he'd thought was imagined but turned out to be real. Over a family which had needed him, which had had to resort to subterfuge simply to get him to come home. Jack wanted to believe that the feeling burning in his cheeks was anger, at being lied to by his sister and his mum. Really, it was shame, because they had to lie in the first place.

Jack stopped suddenly, stubbing his toe on something soft but firm. The fox, which had been parkouring off stumps and proclaiming this the best day yet of his short life, stopped, too. They'd reached the road, were standing obstructed by something on the pavement.

What's that? said the fox.

At first, Jack had thought it was a sandbag, the sort they

leaned against pub doors and garden gates down in the dip of the village when the river burst its banks. But it hadn't rained for a long time, and it could just as well be a dead badger. Badgers don't look like badgers when they're dead. The black bleeds into the white, making the whole thing grey. Up close, Jack could see the stripes that ran like road markings from the dead badger's ears down over its eyes and stopped at the end of its snout, above a curled mouth crusted with dried blood. Roadkill was a fact of life around these parts. Jack was well used to the sight of pulped squirrels and mashed foxes, or dead deer looking strangely intact, straight-legged and stunned, in ditches and lay-bys. Had he ever seen a badger alive? This one looked like a stuffed toy, the dull eyes like buttons, the body tightly bloated as if packed to the brim with cotton wool. He thought of what his dad had said, in the garden, about a pyre. Over a stile, in an arid field, a pheasant barked as if it was choking or clearing its throat. Feeling suddenly nauseous, Jack stared along the road as it sloped down into the village.

'Where are you, Dad?'

Back into the woods, retracing their steps. The fox was quieter from then on, giving Jack time to think. Where in the woods might his dad have ended up? The old oak was the obvious suspect, the swing by the river. He'd aim for there.

Poor badger, said the fox, finding its voice again after a while. *Out here should be safe.*

'Out here is the same as back there,' Jack said, trying to load a map on his phone. 'With a worse signal.'

Out here is the great outdoors, said the fox, relaxing its hackles. *Nothing can get us, out here.*

Jack snagged his sleeve on a thorned branch, swore to himself. 'The great outdoors are not that great.'

No mange, no motor vehicles, the fox continued, either not hearing him or wilfully ignoring him. *No pollution or pest controllers.*

'Those things don't bother me.'

No people.

Jack ignored the fox. 'Where is my dad?' he asked no one.

You don't know the real world, said the fox, not quite in response.

Jack stopped walking, looked down. 'What?'

The fox averted his eyes. *That's what he said,* the fox stuttered. *Your dad.*

'I know what he said,' said Jack, looking off into the trees.

You should act on instinct, said the fox. *You should follow your nose.*

'I don't need your input.'

I think he was right, said the fox. *I don't think you know where he is. Or how to find him.*

'I don't care what you think,' said Jack, clenching his jaw. 'And don't pretend you know the real world, either. You've spent your whole life stealing half-eaten kebabs out of bins.'

They bickered like this, on and off, walking in circles, tracing and retracing their steps as Jack tried to find his way back to an oak tree he only half remembered from a childhood he'd devoted every effort to forgetting. He walking some distance behind the fox, swearing intermittently as he tripped over protruding roots and got caught up in low-hanging branches. His previously pristine trainers were soon streaked with dirt, his

T-shirt damp with sweat. The straps of his rucksack cut into his shoulders, his bare legs and arms scraped and stung. They reached a small clearing, a tall tree over a trickling stream, where the fox decided they should rest. Jack picked at the knotted bark of the tree, trying to figure it out. Beech? Birch? No, birch was white. But then, so was the eucalyptus tree in the back garden of his city flat, after it had shed its red bark.

Maybe the fox had a point about the real world. About whether he knew it, or not. Or, no, his father had made the point, and Jack had always made a point of doing precisely the opposite. If his dad could track a muntjac deer or string a hammock together out of reeds, Jack had thought he'd find his skills in a stable career, indoors, in last-minute presentations or hours-long meetings. If his father could commune with nature, Jack would commune with banking apps and smart speakers. If Jack were to draw on his adult experience of the wild, 'experiences' were all he'd have to go on. Butchery for someone's stag. Axe-throwing for a work Christmas do. A few hours of foraging bought by his ex-girlfriend, during which he'd pretended to enjoy bitter nettle tea and eye-watering wild garlic pesto. His dad had once wanted to teach him to fish, but he'd never taken up the offer. Jack of no trades. Master of absolutely nothing. This was not his domain. This was the real world.

'OK,' said Jack, eventually, sliding his back down the tree until he was sitting, stiffly, on the ground. 'We can rest.' He sighed. 'Then we can do things your way.'

The fox sat expectantly, blinking at Jack. It cocked its head. *My way?*

'The real world,' Jack said, gesturing vaguely. 'We'll follow our noses.'

The fox nodded vigorously. Then it sniffed the air once, twice, three times. *He was here*, it said.

'What?' Jack said. 'You're making that up.'

Thick black lashes blinked over shining eyes. The fox's tail looked near-full, bushy and white-tipped. *I'd never lie to you.*

'Right, of course.' Jack looked around, suddenly keen to save face. 'He's been here.'

Avoiding the fox's watchful gaze, Jack sniffed the air, rubbed some dirt between his fingers as if trying to commune with the earth itself. He looked for prints, tried to think like his dad. What would his dad think? What would he do? There were fresh-dug holes at the base of the tree which might have harboured a badger, or a rabbit, or a mole. Setts and warrens. Earths and forms. Jack couldn't remember how to tell the difference. He couldn't remember the last time he'd seen a rabbit, in real life. The animals in the city were limited to pigeons, squirrels, foxes and rats. Once, bafflingly, a horse tied to an old-fashioned caravan behind the IKEA at the end of the bus route. There were city farms, parks with temperate gardens, but in recent years he'd kept nature at arm's length. He'd never cut sprigs of rosemary from the communal herb garden outside his flat, in case foxes had urinated on it. He'd never gone to the local deer park, wary of the risk of catching Lyme disease from ticks. You could rewild a common, or a golf course, or the grounds of a country estate. Could you rewild a human being?

We should eat, said the fox. *For energy.*

Finally, something they agreed on. Jack pulled a small bag

of dried apricots from his rucksack. He chewed on one, held another out for the fox. He checked his phone, messaged Charlotte to say he was still looking, asked if she'd heard anything. He looked up, put his phone down. The fox was a little way off, trying to get its mouth around something cow parsley-like on the water's edge.

'Don't eat that,' Jack said, quickly, loudly.

The fox stopped, turned. *What?*

'Don't eat that,' Jack repeated, as if it was the most obvious thing in the world.

Why?

'Do you know what it is?'

The fox looked back at the plant. *It's—* The fox paused, studied it from a different angle. *Meadowsweet.*

'No, it's not,' said Jack, patiently. 'It's water hemlock.' Jack held out the dried apricot again. 'And it's very poisonous.'

The fox retreated, took the proffered food. Jack swallowed, chewed another, not meeting the fox's eyes.

'What?' he said, eventually, impatiently.

How did you know that? the fox said.

Jack was suddenly bashful. 'I don't know,' he said, looking away, swallowing his mouthful.

Now you're following your nose.

'Maybe,' Jack said. 'But we're no closer to finding him.'

The fox had started distractedly chewing a thorn from its forepaw. *You could climb this tree*, it said, looking upwards, paw in mouth.

Jack could see its paw pads, a smiling curve crowned by four soft little discs. 'What?' he said.

Climb the tree, said the fox, taking its paw out of its mouth. *Get a better outlook.*

'A lookout?' said Jack. He turned, tested the strength of the leaning trunk. 'Yes. Right.'

Aware of the fox's eyes on him, Jack cleared his throat, then stood up and dusted off his hands. He grabbed the trunk tightly. He hadn't climbed a tree since he was a child. Grunting, he pulled himself off the ground as he would if doing a muscle-up on the monkey bars at the gym. Then, with a wheeze, he swung ape-like on to the first branch. Struggling, he pulled himself away from the ground and over the branch, his stomach muscles aching and his forearms burning. He was barely more than head height off the ground, but already he could see more clearly. The stream beneath them ran downhill. Down the slope, from above, Jack could see a good swathe of the woods around them. He looked, through the trees, for his dad. He already felt closer to him, up here in the air. He'd enjoyed all of this, once. The side of nature which gave you dirty hands and bruised shins. The rough bark beneath him, and the gurgle of the source of the stream beneath that. The quiet of it all. That was what he had missed, he now realised. Not talking to anyone, not performing anything. Even cooking, alone in a kitchen, he'd never found a quiet quite like this.

'Did you know?' his dad had said, knee-deep in river water.

Jack had got a Subbuteo set for Christmas. He'd asked his dad to play with him, cross-legged on the living-room floor, but his dad had said he couldn't, he wouldn't be any good, and, besides, he was about to go foraging. Then he'd wavered, squatted down on the floor next to him. He didn't suppose, he

262

imagined Jack wouldn't, want to join him? This one time, Jack
had said yes. In this memory, which had come out of nowhere,
they were both wearing waders, both wading out into the ice-
cold current.

'Your game is named after the Eurasian hobby,' his dad had
said, eyes skimming downriver for horseradish and water mint,
for hints of skittering fish.

'The Eurasian what?' said Jack, splashing for the sake of
splashing.

'*Falco subbuteo*,' his dad said distantly, trailed a hand across
the surface of the water. 'The inventor wanted to call it "Hobby",
but he couldn't get the trademark.'

In this memory, in which they were both wearing waders,
in which they were both wading, Jack had found a plant at the
edge of the river and had fondled its white frills and said: Dad,
what's this? And his dad's face had gone grave, and he'd waded
over and washed his son's hand for him.

'Water hemlock,' he'd said, a twinkle in his eye. 'It'll kill you
in fifteen minutes. Even touching it can be deadly.'

Jack was horrified. His dad seemed excited.

'You know what else they call it?' he's said. Then he'd affected
a pirate's voice. 'Dead man's fingers.'

A crack. The branch supporting Jack shifted, snapped beneath
him, and he fell forwards, leaving the memory behind and
landing, with a yell, face first in the beginnings of that stream.
The drop winded him – not too far to fall but far enough to
hurt. He landed on his knees and his palms, scrabbled around,
his hands plunging into the wet mud, his face hovering inches
away from the sodden leaves and a spout of trickling water. He

breathed in the wet cardboard smell of mulch, spat out some sandy grit. He rolled over on to his back, allowed the wet earth to hold him. It was confusing, to fall. More so, to feel like he'd enjoyed it. The soil between his fingers was soothing, not like a mud spa but like something more fundamental, more ancient. A men's magazine had once told him of bacteria in soil which, in contact with skin, caused the brain to release serotonin. His dad had once told him something else, that pigs aren't physically capable of looking up. That if a pig wants to see the stars, it has to look for them reflected in the mud. Jack held his hands up in front of his face, blocking out the dappled sunlight. His fingernails were dirty, but he didn't feel an instant urge to scrub them as he usually would. He smeared the extra mud, which caked his fingers, across his cheeks like a jungle commando, like a bona fide wild man.

Tendrils of white sky split the canopy above, like forked lightning. Then the view was obscured by the fox, whose curious face filled the space where the trees had been. The fox didn't seem bothered by the mud on Jack's face, just as it was unbothered by the fall and the broken branch before. It simply blinked down at him and dropped on to its back, stretching out the length of its warm body against Jack's arm.

What do you see? it said.

Jack opened his mouth slightly, but he couldn't verbalise what he felt. A sense of something fresh, springing forth.

'It's—' said Jack. 'It's hard to explain.'

twenty-six

A woman stands in her upstairs bathroom, being fixed into a handmade tartan wedding dress via a system of extravagantly oversized safety pins.

'Don't hurt yourself,' she says, to her young dresser.

'I know what I'm doing, Mum,' he replies.

Hazel hadn't lost her sense of drama, the lurid colours and loud mouth which had defined her adolescence and persisted through her twenties. Now it had been channelled into other outlets, a dress like that which had no place in a village like this. And though making her six-year-old son chief warden of the safety pins might have been infringing on a few child labour laws, there was no one else she'd want by her side but him.

The wedding was cheap, because it had to be, and small, because they wanted it to be. Both bride and groom had rejected their parents' piousness long before, so they kept it well away from the village church. Hazel and Gerry weren't getting married for the occasion, nor even to share it with their families, or all except their closest friends. They weren't getting married because of Jack, either, though years later Charlotte would try to get a rise out of him by saying that it was no surprise they hadn't been married when he was born, seeing as he was a total bastard. No, as Jack walked Hazel down the aisle towards Gerry, father and son both squirming beneath their suits because they didn't like being the centre of attention, it felt like their final step in becoming a family. And that felt like something worth celebrating.

Little comedies. Jack interrupted the ceremony to tell everyone he needed a wee. Hazel tripped on her way down an aisle which was really just a slope of uneven grass, had the smattering of guests in stitches. As she'd traversed the garden of Mole End, towards the floral arch that Gerry had made himself, she could pick out every single face in the audience. One or two cousins, a couple of her former bandmates, a few of Gerry's old comrades. Bea and Monty, both beaming at her. And Johnny, standing right beside her future husband, fulfilling best-man duties when neither of them had thought he'd even get the invitation. When was the last time the brothers had seen each other? Years, probably. There were purple bags under Johnny's eyes, and his hands shook when he searched his pockets for the rings. But he was here, and Hazel could see in Gerry's face how much that small detail meant.

'I do,' said Gerry.

'I really bloody do,' said Hazel.

It was a formality, really. They'd done the legal bit in a registry office a few days before. Bea and Monty were the only witnesses, Jack sitting patiently between them. But while neither Hazel nor Gerry were great ones for parties, they embraced that formality with enthusiasm, then held a reception in the garden, because celebrate is what they'd decided they'd do. Gerry's speech was comically dull, meandering through a number of nature facts which weren't especially relevant to the occasion, stopping entirely halfway through when he got distracted by an inquisitive bullfinch. Hazel was the only one who cried. Johnny's speech, on the other hand, was loud and overfamiliar, unrehearsed and filled with empty words. He looked skinny beneath his shirt, sweat beading the boundary between his tanned forehead and greasy hair. Hazel did her speech last, feeling she'd saved the day, even if she did need to make Jack plug his ears for the especially sweary bits. As evening descended, Hazel's old guitarist and drummer put on a rough-and-ready show, and even Gerry had a go at dancing.

Bea got plastered on cheap red wine, had to be taken home early. Jack fell asleep under the flower arch, was swaddled in blankets out there in the garden so he didn't miss the party. Gerry took Johnny aside, thanked him, asked him if he was doing OK. They spoke in hushed tones at the edge of the garden, Gerry touching Johnny's arm, Johnny baring his teeth a little too wide. Then Johnny brushed Gerry's hand away, slurred something Hazel couldn't hear, swaggered off to try to chat up one of Hazel's cousins. Hazel never did find out exactly what words were exchanged between the brothers. No time to dwell on things. Morning came. The guests left. And the grass in the garden, which had seemed trampled beyond repair, began to creep out of hiding from the flattened earth.

Married life, it turned out, wasn't so different from what had come before. And though they'd settled here, Hazel and Gerry's minds still roved far beyond Mole End. Where next? Jack was more than big enough for a little adventure, which meant living in a van for a couple of months would be a piece of cake. They talked to Jack about it, unfolded great maps on the dining table. If they hiked through western Spain in search of vultures, they'd simply slather him in sun cream and take him with them. We'll make sure one doesn't carry you off, Gerry had joked, confounded when his careless comment gave Jack nightmares. For every plan they made, obstacles overcame them. Jack's schooling was an issue. Money was more in the way than ever. With bills to pay and a kid to parent, they couldn't afford petrol, let alone plane tickets or ferry fees. They thought they might at least head back to the Scottish islands, finally see those sea eagles. That never happened, either. When things did change, as they were about to, those dreams which had been getting progressively smaller would dwindle away to nothing.

Adventures became hypotheticals, stories to be told to their wide-eyed son. The expeditions they did manage would only take them as far as the woods outside their house, at the oak over the river which could be reached through the bracken and down the slope at the end of their garden. Gerry crafted a swing out of a reclaimed piece of timber, Hazel threading it with sturdy rope so they could hang it from the tree. It was an intrepid thing, that swing, set on the steepest part of the bank.

Jack always needed to be lifted on to it, a good hard push before he sailed off into the open air. If you didn't get it right, you'd end up face first in the river. As he did, many times. Yet he'd always shout: again, again!

At that oak, over that river, Hazel and Gerry could make-believe, close their eyes and pretend they were anywhere else in the world. But they could also do the opposite. Open their eyes and look around, see their little slice of the wild and be content. They could say, as they sometimes did: if I could be anywhere else in the world, I'd be here. Years later, when things had changed again, Hazel would wonder how Jack remembered his childhood. Did he look back fondly, despite the distance he'd since put between himself and it? Perhaps he wasn't old enough yet. It was only once those crabs in those buckets were long gone that Hazel had realised how much she missed them. But she didn't need to be back on the open ocean. When Hazel was out of sorts, when she felt she'd been beached or poached or caught in a net, it was never the water she was actually yearning for. It was a moment in time, which now felt like a lifetime ago. Her family. A rope swing over a river. An oak tree in a forest, a short distance from their house.

The knock at the door came one morning, many months after their wedding, too early on a Sunday for it to signify anything good. Gerry and Hazel shared a puzzled look over the dining table, the crossword they'd been trying to complete resting between them. Their son was fast asleep upstairs. They were never expecting guests. Gerry frowned, swallowed his spoonful of muesli. Then he stood, wiped his hands on his practical trousers, and headed for the front door. Moments went by without a sound. When he returned to the kitchen, looking startled, he had a visitor in tow.

'Sorry,' said Johnny, hair uncombed, shirt unwashed, hugging his arms to his chest despite the fact it was high summer. 'I had nowhere else to go.'

twenty-seven

Can you hear that?
Hear, here. Here.
Hear here.
Here.

Here came Gerry, to the rescue.

And while Gerry might not have been totally with it – he
knew in himself that he wasn't, because he knew that he
wasn't himself – he knew how to track, and he knew that
Hazel was in need of being tracked

Gerry used to say that he couldn't communicate with
anyone, except for Hazel. That wasn't strictly true. He could

communicate with these woods, commune with the real
world right in front of him.

Gerry knew who he was, once, but he didn't know exactly
who he was now. So he assumed this new, old role, the
role of the tracker, and he tracked his quarry like any good
tracker would. Well. Well, well.

He used his nose, and his eyes, and what was left of his mind.

His mind.
A wilting thing.
A dying flower.
A drooping.

Here's what Gerry saw, as he made his way into the woods,
out again, back in, through thickets and under fences and
over stiles, following scents and sounds.

He saw gorse as sharp as rapiers. He saw tall and yellow
Oxford ragwort standing to attention. He saw goldcrests and
whinchats and dunnocks darting between hedgerows like
arrows fired across enemy lines.

He took a little leather notebook from his jacket pocket,
noted the sightings down. He heard a voice, and saw the
frog-toad, or the toad-frog, which he'd met in a bird bath.

Perhaps yesterday, perhaps longer ago. It waved him on his way.

There was a frog,
a whole lifetime ago.
A captured frog. Or was it?
A captive toad, perhaps.
Johnny's cruelty.

When Gerry was younger – that is, not so young that Johnny
and he still played owls and badgers, but young enough
to still mess about in the woods – he'd stumbled upon his
brother and his brother's friends at the dump.

And the dump wasn't a dump but more of a pit out in the
middle of nowhere where people left rusted barbecue buckets
and bits of old furniture, where people dumped things, hence
why they called it 'the dump'.

He'd stumbled upon Johnny at the dump and he'd stumbled
upon Johnny's friends at the dump and they'd been poking
a squealing frog or a screaming toad with pointy sticks
and when Gerry had said: no, no, no, don't do that, they'd
pushed him down a short bank and it had hurt for a long
time.

But what hurt more than the scrapes was the realisation that
his little brother wasn't his little brother any more, because
his little brother had never been one to hurt anyone or
anything.

Am I looking for Johnny?
Is Johnny living at the dump?
If not there, perhaps a wigwam
in the woods, like a charcoal burner.

Get a grip, Gerry, thought Gerry, as he took a breather in a small clearing, against a tall tree over a trickling stream.

There are no charcoal burners in these woods. There's no Johnny in these woods, either. The dump was long ago, and far away.

No order. Gerry grasped at things. The best orienteer these woods had ever seen, unable to find his way. Was it normal, to always feel this lost?

Lizard's leg
and owlet's wing.
Love is a burning thing.

Hazel always loved listening to music. Gerry preferred to read.

It was harder, nowadays. He mostly stuck to his old nature guides. They didn't have a plot, so there was no danger of getting to the second half of the book, as in a novel, and finding the first already melting away.

A squirrel raced past, asked what he'd been reading. It was gone before he could answer.

Gerry was envious of animals with faster brains than his. He wished for bigger eyes, a keener nose. A mind which wouldn't run away from him.

He could still read a forest, though. Especially one as familiar as this. When he was out there, he felt as he always had.

His mind.
A rising thing.
A blooming flower.
A blossoming.

Here's what Gerry knew. He wasn't looking for Johnny. He was looking for Hazel. He'd follow her anywhere.

He knew that these were footprints, and that this scrap of wool was likely to be from a fleece caught and pulled on a thorn. He knew that these were old traces, and that they'd only remained because the days were so dry, so still.

He knew that he would not give up looking until he'd found her.

Is she here?
Is she somewhere
like this?

As Gerry spent the afternoon picking his way through the woods, he chewed on some wood sorrel he'd found growing in the elbow of a hawthorn.

He was never much of a cook, always a forager. Preferring things raw and gritty, chowing down on celery and carrots he'd grown himself, not bought from a supermarket. His wife said he ate more like a pet rabbit than a human.

But his son liked to cook with his mother, so Gerry picked things for their culinary exploits. He watched from the dining table as his son and his wife turned veg from the garden into feats of gastronomy.

On the inside,
Gerry only feels happy
outside.

As Gerry picked his way through the woods, he felt content, freed of the constraints of the home where he'd been kept, for weeks, like a house pet.

He felt every shift in the breeze, felt every crunch of every twig beneath his boots. And he felt the slow arc of the sun across the sky, saw the point behind the trees where it was planning to bury itself.

Time was water, so it moved in a fluid way, running forwards like a stream, yes, but expanding and contracting to fit the vessel that confined it.

A splash,
then a squeeze.
Day becomes night.

Evening was descending, and Gerry was descending a short slope into a clearing sheltered from the wind.

He settled under the overhanging roots of an old tree, treated himself to a foraged dinner. He was well used to wild camping, and the night was a warm one.

The bivouac bag he'd brought enveloped him like a hug.

Snug
as a bug
rolled up in a rug.
Snug as a hug.

Gerry came from a different generation. His own father had never hugged him, so he came to believe that his own son wouldn't have a need for hugs.

When another child came along, she had an instinct for sniffing out affection, for knowing what couldn't be said. Charlotte would say: I love you, Dad. And she'd hug him,

and he'd stand awkward and still until she'd removed her
arms.

That didn't mean he didn't like it. From time to time, he'd
even hug her back. But his son? It was too late to start now.

Gerry puts his arms around himself
and thinks of what he'd have done differently.
Under the moonlight, he drifts off to sleep.

twenty-eight

Two men stand on a patio. One is drinking black coffee. The other, milky tea. They stare out into the fathomless depths of the forest ahead of them, listening to the birds converse. The man with the coffee takes a sip, turns to his brother.

'As far as rehab goes,' he says, that old snake-charm slowly coming back after days lying alone, in the dark, in the small bedroom upstairs, 'this'll do nicely.'

Hazel, watching from the doorway, had to quell a gnawing sense of apprehension. For the first week of Johnny's visit, Jack had politely given up his room. Now that the boy's uncle was showing no sign of leaving, Hazel and Gerry had moved him to the fold-out sofa in the living room. He was making himself at home, there and throughout the house, as he tried to sort out whatever sticky situation he'd got himself into in the city.

Gerry had once been a father figure to Johnny. They'd been so close as young boys, but had gone their separate ways as teenagers, were broadly out of touch as adults. Now, they were back together, and an uneasy equilibrium reigned. Gerry had taken Johnny back under his wing, while Jack, ever on the edge of things, watched from a distance. Jack treated the uncle he'd never really had with trepidation, hiding from Johnny when he tried to say hello. Yet whenever Johnny was holding court at the dining table, Jack would hover in the kitchen doorway, fascinated by his uncle's easy manner and eloquent way of speaking. When it was just the two of them, Jack would ask Hazel breathless questions about this relative stranger. What does he do? Where does he live? And why is he so different from Dad?

Johnny had been in a sorry state when he turned up. Talking nineteen to the dozen. Eyes like cigarette lighters, smouldering in a sunken face. He'd tossed and turned in bed for the best part of two days, then devoured the entire contents of their fridge when he'd just about come back to life. When asked to explain his presence, Johnny kept things vague. Something to do with money, with work, with bad investments. He just needed somewhere to lay low for a while. He'd be gone before they knew it.

How many times had Hazel met Johnny? She remembered an excruciating Easter at Gerry's parents', and a lunch he'd taken them to at an uncomfortably posh city restaurant. Both occasions were years ago. Each time, she'd left feeling nonplussed. He had so much charisma, so much going for him. So why did seeing him make her husband so sad? Even now, knowing the reason why, she couldn't help but enjoy her brother-in-law's presence. Gerry might have been the gentle one, the sensible one, perhaps the cleverer of the two, but he'd have been the first to admit that it was Johnny who'd been gifted all of the charm. Gerry was usually only funny when he didn't mean to be, but Johnny had a wicked sense of humour which could never fail to make you laugh. He perked up. He got his colour back. And his presence galvanised them, like jump leads, for Jack as much as anyone.

They hadn't expected this: Jack and Johnny, playing video games on the little grey box the boy had begged his parents for the previous Christmas. They hadn't had the money. Now Johnny had bought him one, brand new, and they sat cross-legged together on Johnny's pull-out mattress, crashing fast cars and shooting bad guys. Mornings playing Subbuteo, afternoons of Scalextric, while Gerry wandered in the woods and mooched around the garden, casting the occasional fretful glance back at the laughter which drifted from the living-room window. They hadn't expected this, either: Johnny reading to Jack at bedtime, showing an affinity with a nephew who also wasn't very good at plucking the words off the page. All the self-confidence and that overabundance of charisma leaving him, as he sat on the edge of Jack's bed and stuttered out stories of a fox in a fantastic plum-red coat. Johnny, watching Jack fall asleep with something like regret. Gerry, watching Johnny, with something much the same. And Hazel, watching Gerry in the doorway of their son's room, wondering how it felt to see his brother so easily build the kind of relationship he'd tried so hard to have with his own son.

That uneasy equilibrium felt, for a while, like it could be sustained. But as time went on, it became harder and harder to turn a blind eye to what had changed in the months since Johnny had arrived. The bottles going missing from the booze cupboard, and the little plastic packets from the bathroom cabinet. The erratic way in which he acted, leaving Mole End in the early hours and returning late at night. Jack's new console which went missing, a loss Johnny blamed on his nephew just as he suddenly seemed flush with cash. The moods that came over Johnny, the way he started belittling his brother, then outright snapping at him. The way he tried to do the same to his brother's wife, then tried to play her off against her husband when he realised such bully tactics wouldn't work on her. Johnny had always seemed lost. Now, all of a sudden, he didn't seem to know why he'd ever come to Mole End, and his own presence there seemed to infuriate him. He was gathering a storm over the house he'd deigned to call home, and even Jack ceased to provide enough entertainment. Mole End, which was meant to be a safe haven, started to creak like a shack on the fringes of a hurricane. Then, one overcast autumn morning, the storm broke.

'Where's Jack?' Hazel had asked, when their son couldn't be found in the living room, or his bedroom, or anywhere in between.

'Where's Johnny?' Gerry had asked, more sternly, when it turned out his brother was missing, too.

The next hour was a blur. Gerry, at the edge of the garden, in the outskirts of the woods, shouting their names. Hazel, consulting her phone book, wondering who on earth to call.

Johnny had a mobile phone, but neither Hazel nor Gerry had its number, or much of a clue how it worked. She settled on the greengrocer's, the haberdasher's, the tearoom and the pub. Then the other pub. Soon, they were speeding down the hill towards the village, bursting through those pub doors only to be told that they'd arrived just too late.

'He had a boy with him, yeah,' the barman said, sounding disinterested. 'He was talking about an oak tree.' He raised an eyebrow. 'Well, slurring.'

By the time they'd reached the oak, the wind had picked up. The river roared like a braying crowd, its surface goose-bumped by the whipped-up air. Gerry marched forward like an advancing army. Even Hazel couldn't keep up with him. The rope swing thrashed about, creaking as it went. Above it, Jack crouched on a high branch, cowering in a tree he'd only climbed to impress his uncle.

'Go on, then,' Johnny was saying, from beneath him, swaying in time with the wind, barely managing to remain upright. 'Jump. Don't be boring.'

Hazel only now noticed that the grey overcoat which had become Johnny's de facto uniform during his time at Mole End was fraying in several places, covered in a patchwork of stains.

'You're being a wimp,' Johnny said, practically hiccupping. 'Guess the apple doesn't fall far from the tree.'

Several things then happened at once.

'Johnny!' shouted Gerry, in the most commanding voice he'd ever mustered.

'Gerry,' said Johnny, staggering backwards, turning his bloodshot eyes on his brother.

'I'm not a wimp,' said Jack, before dropping from the branch and landing, with a heavy thud, on the hard riverbank.

After that, several more things happened. And they seemed, to Hazel, to happen in quick succession, even if the events really unfolded over the course of the rest of the day. Gerry, grim-faced and stern-mouthed, scooped up a wailing Jack and carried him away. Hazel flew at Johnny, called him every name under the sun, while he teetered, wide-eyed, somewhere between apology and oblivion. They drove to the hospital, saw an X-ray of a broken ankle, saw it set in plaster, as Johnny sat outside in the waiting room, a cloud collecting behind his eyes. Hazel sat up on the hospital bed with Jack, who was already asking after his uncle. He didn't ask about his father, who at that very moment was standing over Johnny, speaking in a voice that was low but clear. Johnny had always been selfish, and Gerry had always taken the consequences of that selfishness upon himself. But this time was different. This was his son. And if asked to choose between Jack and Johnny, Gerry would say that he'd given his brother enough second chances.

'We're done, Johnny,' he said, with a detachment that pained him, with a voice he'd strive never to raise again. 'Clean yourself up tonight. I want you gone by the morning.'

twenty-nine

'Did you know?' said Jack, to the fox. 'You can track an animal by the angle of a broken plant.'

They were hacking their way through the woods, scrambling over roots and ducking branches, heading deep into the heart of a place which Jack used to fear.

'Look, here,' said Jack, crouching and pointing to a chewed-off stalk. 'Forty-five degrees. Clean cut. This was a rodent.'

The fox stared up at him like a well-behaved pupil, its attention held rapt. *Is your dad a rodent?* the fox asked.

'No,' said Jack, distractedly, staring off into the brush. 'But these plants are trampled.' He took a few careful sidesteps, to get a better view. 'Something big has been through here.'

Something human?

In the human world, Jack had never felt like an expert in anything. He was an imposter, spending every investor meeting saying things that sounded smart, pretending he hadn't spent the twenty minutes beforehand doing deep-breathing exercises over the bathroom sink. A weed, waiting to be rooted out. But out here, looking for his father, moving like a fox, it was like a valve had been opened. He was mystified by his ability to read the forest, as if his own brain were the imposter here. Jack had never been an expert in anything. And yet, here, years of seed money and growth-hacking were giving way to a budding expertise which felt organic, a knowledge which, having been exposed to sunlight and the water of a trickling stream, now sprang fresh and green from some dark recess of his mind. Things were coming back to him, a spring gurgling at the forefront of his mind which sounded a lot like his father. His father. A man still proving very hard to find.

As Jack spent the afternoon stampeding through the woods, his newfound confidence started to show itself as overconfidence. The serrated edges on the long grass at the edge of the field should have been sign enough that they weren't following a man, deer having a habit of chomping grass against their upper palette and sickling it away with a jerk of their neck. As they crept alongside the deer themselves, over a carpet of electric-blue cornflowers and past the secluded lake from which the creatures were drinking, Jack tried to convince himself that this was all worthwhile. They were having fun, he thought, as he breathed in a purple meadow, watched butterflies float up and out of the undergrowth and into the air like embers from a fire. They weren't wasting time, he thought, as he and the fox clambered about on a pile of stacked logs next to a faded sign saying 'DON'T CLIMB ON THE LOG STACKS'. How could they be wasting time? Jack was out in nature, fighting his fears. If he couldn't find his father, he could at least find himself. But even as he tried to convince himself of this fact, such aphorisms already felt like something which belonged to the old Jack, the Jack who sat at his desk in the city with a rictus grin and a can-do attitude. The forest wasn't something whimsical, no matter how hard Jack tried to make it so. This was the real world. And in it, they'd achieved nothing, wasted a day that was already running away from them.

'Did you know?' Jack said, as he chewed on a crab apple and winced. 'Earthworms have taste buds covering every inch of their bodies.'

The fox wasn't listening. It rolled about in the background, frolicking around in so many daisies and buttercups that the creature itself looked like part of a pattern on a kitsch table-cloth, its white ruff stained an ebullient yellow. Jack watched it, his stomach rumbling, thinking that he should have brought more food. He'd eaten nothing before the interview, and had been surviving on snacks since then. He craved the least forageable meal imaginable, a luridly coloured, MSG-infused takeaway in a plastic container, tossed with fruit pastilles and gummy bears, washed down with a taurine-and-aspartame energy drink. He downgraded his daydreams. He imagined a sandwich bag. Inside that sandwich bag, he imagined a sandwich. Cheese and pickle. He remembered himself as a strange little kid, remembered how he'd ask to make the sandwiches for his and his parents' hikes, remembered the pleasure he'd get out of carefully spreading butter on to soft white bread, of cutting off his own crusts with mathematical precision. His happiest memories might have been in the kitchen of Mole End, his mother ruffling his hair and telling him he was doing a good job. What would she say now? How disappointed would she be, when she finally returned?

What's this? said the fox.

Jack didn't know how long he'd zoned out for. But the fox was staring at him, and it seemed just as hungry as he was. It licked its lips and nodded at a bulbous mushroom which looked a little like an Italian meringue.

'A puffball,' said Jack, barely even thinking. 'And those ones over there are devil's bolete.'

Jack of some trades. Master of one: the mushroom.

Delicious, said the fox, tucking in.

'Did you know?' Jack began, resting against the tree. 'If the flesh inside a puffball has started to turn yellow, it'll make you sick.'

The fox spat out a mouthful of yellow flesh, then shook its head. It observed the encroaching gloom above them.

Do you think we should— it began.

'We're not giving up that easily.'

Not long after that, Jack had given up. Not easily. And not entirely. He just needed a rest, overcome by a mental and physical fatigue which felt all too familiar to someone who'd spent years burning himself out in a job totally inimical to his own wellbeing. Evening was descending, and the pair of them had ascended a steep hill, sitting shakily at the base of a tree on the breezy, exposed summit. Jack tried to breathe slowly, tried not to picture his dad out here, alone. He'd thought that finding his father should have been easy once he and the fox had hit their stride. It felt more like they were going in circles. They could have walked right past his dad, mere feet away. More likely, they hadn't even come close. It felt stupid, to suddenly register the vast size of these woods, the web of sprawling footpaths and intersecting bridleways so intricately interwoven that you'd feel lost just looking at a map of them. Jack had lost faith in their likelihood of success. He had also, at some point, lost his phone. He'd hoped for good news from Charlotte, but the fact that he couldn't contact her was something of a relief. He didn't want to let her down again. Besides, they had more pressing issues. Without a phone, without the help of GPS, they were lost, too.

'Let's just—' Jack said, trying not to let the acid fear rising in his throat get the better of him. 'Let's just stay here for a bit.'

Jack knew they should keep searching, but he found himself physically unable to get up. Muscles which he didn't even know existed were aching, burning coils where his neck met his shoulders, where his elbows met his forearms, where his hips met his thighs. His ankle was throbbing, as it always tended to when he'd overdone it. He'd broken it as a child, messing about at the tree with his uncle. The weakness was still there, but Jack's memory of the whole thing was hazy. All he remembered was that his dad had turned it into a big deal.

What are we going to do? The fox sounded just as rattled as him.

'I'm thinking.'

Jack's T-shirt was soaked, his gym shorts muddied, the mud he'd smeared on his cheeks now dried out and flaky. Unshaven since that last morning in the office, his stubble was morphing into a short, unruly beard which was at once itchily dry and oily with perspiration. He tried to move, but his body was too heavy. How does one track a tracker? Jack would have to go full wild man. He'd drink from the same lake as the deer, if it helped him find his father. He'd run barefoot through the forest, like he'd always wanted to. He'd tuck his trainers in his backpack and pad barefoot over soil and leaves and sticks, splashing through streams and skipping across fallen logs as the excited fox darted in and out of the trees around him. His legs were already stung, scratched and bitten to bits. And while Jack would be an even worse tracker on bleeding feet, he also couldn't go home until he'd found his dad, wouldn't return to Mole End with his tail between his legs.

Jack? said the fox.

It sat in front of him, ever-present and ever-glowing, now such a natural part of his personal landscape that it seemed an extension of Jack himself. Even with his eyes closed, Jack would have seen the quivering whiskers which sprouted not just from its cheeks but from above its eyebrows and behind its elbows, the fur which spilled out from beneath its ears and joined up around its throat like a ruff. The furry knees which looked like they belonged to Mr Tumnus, and the tufts which sprouted from between its claws, like the fingers of the Grinch. Its black-lipped grin, and its glowing eyes. Jack, who had closed his own eyes, now opened them. The fox remained, incandescent, almost frighteningly real. Jack reached out and stroked it, found comfort in its soft fur. It flinched, but never flickered.

What are you thinking? it said.

He was thinking that the fox's coat was the perfect

stress-reliever, so warm and pleasant-smelling. He was thinking that, in another life, it would have smelled of something sour, of something dying or something dead. But here, with him, the fox smelled like a lit match or a toasted marshmallow, with a fluffy tail which seemed to float like candy floss. At least that was one good thing. Jack wanted to thank the fox. He wanted to say that, whatever the outcome, he wouldn't have had the courage to go after his dad without the fox. That the fox had been like a spark to kindling, that, since they'd met on the common, his life had blazed in a way that it hadn't for years. But this wasn't the kind of thing that Jack said out loud.

'I'm thinking,' said Jack, eventually, 'that I don't have a clue where my dad is.'

I didn't want to say anything, said the fox, cheerily. *But I'm thinking you're right.*

The wind was warm and heavy, surprisingly relentless. Jack didn't have the strength to build a shelter, nor the knowledge to build a fire. He didn't know what flint looked like, let alone if you could still find it. Can rocks go extinct? Jack knew that there'd be whole subcultures on the internet devoted to surviving in the wild. With the help of his phone he could have hunted for information, gathered knowledge. But it was just him and the fox, in the darkness. So he sat against the tree, eyes closed, stroking the fox's fur, facing the thoughts he'd been running away from all day.

'I'm thinking,' Jack said, sleepily, 'that we found the real world.'

I think so, too. The fox was curling into a ball beside Jack. *Do you like it?*

'I'm scared,' Jack said, biting back his emotions, screwing his eyes even further shut.

The fox exhaled gently from its snout, shifted closer to Jack to get comfortable. *It's all part of the adventure.*

Jack couldn't help but snort. He shook his head. Then he opened his eyes, felt the length of the tree against his back, rested the back of his head against it. Above him, he saw the creeping moon, imagined the point above the trees where it would soon take its place. He yawned and stroked the sleeping fox's fur for a while, allowing himself to forget where he was. Then, despite his best intentions, he drifted off, too.

thirty

An arrowhead of scoffing geese flew overhead, just visible through the treetops. They were pointing Gerry towards a new day.

The sun was being throttled by humid clouds when Gerry's eyes snapped open. He felt like a boil-in-the-bag chicken as he fought his way out of his bivouac, as he rolled and stood and sniffed an armpit and turned his nose towards the morning.

Gerry only had to stand still to smell the honeyed aroma of lime flowers in one direction, to see a silver-washed fritillary flutter its leopard-like wings in the other, to know exactly where he needed to go.

He was not lost. Hazel would soon be found.

Enchanter's nightshade
puts him under
its spell.

Gerry had slept comfortably, though had woken quite stiff.
He'd spent the night dreaming of Hazel, the pair of them
taming an ibex and riding it over the Khyber Pass.

Moving was the best medicine. Gerry drove his way forwards
through a dream-like morning, nothing but him and the
forest, the melody of flowers and the sweet scent of birdsong
soothing every one of his aches and pains.

He walked, and he walked, and he walked. Above his
head, in the twinkle and the dapple of the sun, he heard
chaffinches and the chiffchaffs cheerily chiff and chaff.

The stench of petrol
pulls him back
to reality.

By the time he'd reached the road, Gerry knew that any trail
he'd been following had gone cold.

A badger had been here, and a shrew. But any trace of Hazel
had been carried away on the wind. Had he really been
following Hazel? Or had he only been following a feeling?

Gerry focused not on what he knew, but on what he could see. A squat bridge over a skinny river. Two pubs, one on either side of the bridge. An old church. A new deli.

A dusty haberdasher's, a dried-up village green, and a greengrocer's which had long been empty.

> 'It will be a home for owls,'
> said Isaiah, before Babylon fell.
> 'Never again will people live there.'

Memories sometimes charged at Gerry like stampeding cattle, thundering towards his mind without warning and leaving him trampled.

Here was one. His son, sitting on the counter behind those very windows, giggling as his dad shelled peas and popped them into his mouth.

Here was another. His nine-year-old daughter slipping her hand into his at the funeral of his old friend Monty, not being embarrassed to see him cry.

Two days later, a lawyer had handed him the keys to a shop that Monty was always better than him at running.

Gerry had only been good at running the greengrocer's into the ground.

> Squirrels who
> bury their nuts
> lose more than half.
> They can't remember the place.

Such thoughts put a dampener on Gerry's morning. He closed his eyes, stood on the verge and let his face soak in the sun.

Only happy inside when he was outside. He'd never be under a roof, if he could get away with it. He'd always be in the sun.

Gerry and Charlotte had been planting vegetables in the garden, recently. He found it calmed his mind.

> Charlotte?
> Where's Charlotte?

Gerry crossed the road now, looking for Charlotte, in search of Hazel. Seeking something, though his mind wouldn't settle on what that something was.

As he approached the greengrocer's, he had a sudden urge to cradle a marrow, or to bury his green fingers in a bucket of bright red strawberries, to pull out hands which smelled of nature's perfume.

Nothing more grounding
than that which grows.

But the greengrocer's was empty. Nothing here but windows covered in carboard and white paint, dusty floors and out-of-date post.

Gerry pulled some pistachios from his pocket. Shelled a couple, ate a couple, all the while staring at the unused shopfront, the impromptu noticeboard it had become.

All the while staring at
a bright green slip of paper
stuck to the glass.

Another memory approached, more gently, snorting and pawing its hooves in the mud.

His young son giggling on a rope swing. Over a river, under a branch. The swing affixed to a branch, the branch affixed to a mighty oak.

Oaks and alders.
Alders and oaks.

Gerry nodded sagely, as if someone had told him a secret.

Then he turned, and returned to the forest.

thirty-one

Spring. An oak tree next to a shallow river. A ten-minute walk from a wonky old house on top of a lumpy hill. A swallow dips from the treeline and catches a fly over the flowing water, then perches for a little while on a thin branch overhead. Beneath the bird, a boy in wellies kicks about in the shallows, trying to disturb the fish. His father doesn't stop him. He's standing, absent and absent-minded, up on the verge. Looking back every so often in the vague direction of the house, steadying himself just as often against the trunk of the sturdy tree. At the centre of the river, the water moves not like a billion droplets, but more smoothly and less agitated, like a single, billowing sheet. Over the surface buzzes a fat hoverfly and a thin dragonfly, like characters, the mother thinks, from Dickens or Dahl. Hazel glances from her son, laughing by her side, to her husband, paralysed in the distance, like a deer in headlights.

'Come and join us,' she says, to Gerry. With hesitation, he first wipes his eyes and then joins them.

They would never be the same as they were now. At the very least, within months, there'd be four of them. Hazel wasn't showing much yet, but here, standing in the river with the legs of her dungarees rolled up, the cool water was working wonders for her ever-present nausea. Wetting one hand in the water, she held the back of it against her forehead. Down here, deep in the woods, it didn't feel like a new millennium. Looking at the river, at the oak, you could have imagined yourself in any century before. But the faces of her small family were all change, and Hazel had a sure sense of something slipping away, like a handful of mud dropped into the water beneath her and carried off by the current, diluted into a shapeless cloud which would soon disappear out of sight. The new member of their brood was just about starting to kick, beating out a drumbeat against the walls of her belly as if signalling the arrival of something ominous, something marching through the woods towards Mole End.

Of course, the ominous thing had already come. A call, the kind that changes everything, in the middle of the night a couple of weeks before. Gerry had left for the city the very next morning, even though there was nothing else to do. No one left to save.

Gerry had never given up on his brother. Not even at the end, not even after what happened at this very oak, a couple of years before. And though he'd said in the waiting room that he wanted nothing more to do with him, Gerry had seen Johnny, once more. He'd taken a children's book with him.

He'd told Hazel that he'd wanted Johnny to look backwards, to remember a time when they both talked to animals. Gerry begged Johnny to make a change, to go somewhere else, to go anywhere. It must have been conspicuous, that he didn't offer Mole End. He'd thought he was protecting Jack. And though Hazel would never know exactly what Johnny said in reply, Gerry returned home diminished somehow, with a little less of himself. When that late-night call came, a year or so later, it had jolted Hazel awake. But Gerry had already been sitting there, wide-eyed in the darkness, as if he were expecting it. When he returned from the city that second time, after the funeral, even Hazel didn't realise quite how much of himself he'd left behind.

It almost seemed like how things used to be. The three of them, down at the river, beneath a swing beneath an oak. Gerry hadn't been keen to leave the house that day. Come down to the river with us, Hazel had begged him. It was Jack who'd said: some fresh air will do you good, Dad – ever a little old man in a ten-year-old's body. Gerry had often talked about an alder in his childhood back garden, a tree that he and Johnny would spend every day attempting to climb. The house had been sold long ago, Gerry's mum long dead, Gerry's dad having downsized in every sense. But Hazel wondered now, if that alder still stood, if she'd be able to find her husband's childhood home on a map, to see the tree still standing there. Perhaps Gerry was thinking of the alder in that moment, when he placed his palm on the side of the oak, when he snapped out of himself for just long enough to listen to his hopeful son.

'Can we go on the swing, Dad?'

Jack's ankle had long since healed. He'd seemingly forgotten the whole episode. Gerry, on the other hand, couldn't even answer the question. He simply nodded. But he moved, too, knowing the boy still needed a leg-up on to it, crouching and lifting the boy and helping him up the bank. Only when Jack was in his dad's arms did he reveal his true purpose, two silt-caked hands on the end of arms which reared up like pythons and smeared mud across his father's cheeks. Jack laughed a villainous laugh. Hazel winced, prepared to scold him, because she knew her husband wouldn't. But while Gerry didn't laugh, didn't join in with the mud fight, he didn't retreat, either, not into himself nor back to the house. He simply smiled a sad smile and held his fast-growing son aloft, wriggling wildly. A muddy Gerry placed a muddy Jack on the already-rickety swing, held by filthy ropes which showed no signs of fraying, even though they'd hung from that same branch for almost a decade. That oak, that swing. In this one memory was contained everything that the oak meant to this family, the tree that stood firm by the river which flowed through the middle of their life.

Though this oak would change throughout the seasons, it would always stay put. So would they, whatever obstacles they might encounter, whether it be a death in the family, another baby on the way, or a house which needed more repairs with every week that passed. Hazel felt an affinity with the oak tree for this reason, its steadfastness, even if she knew that she was more like the river, spread out beneath the children to soften their landing, carrying them along safely on her current. Gerry was the oak. Stubborn, hard to budge, but so solid and un-wavering and unchangeable over the years that it was as if his roots anchored their whole family into the earth. She supposed he'd been the same for Johnny. The strong roots. The support system, even when those who needed him didn't know that they did. When Gerry lost Johnny, those roots were disturbed. Something like rot set in. And though he stayed sturdy and stubborn, Gerry's exterior hardened. He became something calcified, something closed-off.

It wasn't how things used to be. The change which overcame Gerry in those weeks and months would set Jack off on an entirely new trajectory, one without oak trees, without swings, without helping hands from loving fathers. Family might eventually nurse Gerry some of the way back to life, but by then, too much time would have passed. Too much water under the bridge. Jack would be long gone, both in body and in spirit. And years later, when Gerry was uprooted again, his only son wouldn't be around to stand firm for him.

'Dad,' said Jack, laughter giving way to panic, his voice filled with a creeping trepidation, perhaps triggered by a sudden memory of that time before. He was worried that the rope would snap, that he'd fall into the river over which the swing swung, that if he did, when he did, the pain wouldn't be worth the leap of faith. 'I'm scared.'

'Don't worry,' said Gerry, his damp cheeks streaked with mud. 'I'll catch you if you fall.'

thirty-two

The birds are talking.
They say, *Keep it up, Gerry!*
They say, *You'll find her soon enough!*

Gerry wandered on through the forest, the smell of
approaching rain in the air, the traces of his lost Hazel
stretching ahead of him.

He passed a secluded lake and found, to his surprise, a snipe.
It bleated as snipes do, watching him with its beady doll's
eyes and bizarrely long beak, an avian Pinocchio.

In the morning sunlight, a linnet looked as if it were daubed
in blood, a starling seeming soaked in iridescent oil.

Their black eyes watched him as he forged on, his hips and thighs aching, his ankles throbbing, weighed down by a frame that seemed heavier than it used to be.

> The birds are talking.
> They say, *Get out of our house!*
> They say, *You humans are all the same!*

Perhaps it was the sight of the linnet, the thought of blood, that brought Johnny back to mind.

Johnny, like everyone, had grown up, although not grown old, not as Gerry had. His body would never feel heavy like this, would never sit on top of old bones like these.

Even at the end, Johnny had moved against the world like a man younger than he was, like a man younger than Gerry ever was.

> Gerry was never invited to parties.
> Johnny measured out his life in them.

When Johnny moved to the city, he became someone flash. Someone whose teeth gleamed, someone who wore a pin in his tie, someone who never came home.

Gerry left home later. When their mother died, he began to roam. He found himself in Périgord, then an orchard, elsewhere. He and his brother would rarely see each other.

When they did, it was only to share the misery of visiting their father.

There was a time when Johnny would arrive in a shiny car. Another time, a later time, when he came sallow-cheeked and sunken-eyed, in a taxi for which Gerry had to pay.

When he surprised them at Mole End, not long after their wedding, there was no pin in his tie. There was no tie at all.

> Pin feathers.
> Pity parties,
> perhaps.

Gerry and Johnny's father was wilfully distant. Their mother had been accidentally so. It fell upon the elder son to raise his younger brother.

Imagine seeing your little brother chewed up and spat out by a world which told him he could have anything. Imagine seeing the person who mattered to you most eaten alive by ambition.

I'm tired, Gerry, Johnny had said, after decades of ignoring his elder brother. I'm so tired.

> Johnny.
> Come back.
> Johnny! Stop it.

You'll get us into trouble.

It had been a fair day, the last time he'd seen Johnny. The week before Christmas, but the sky seemed to think it was summer.

And Johnny had coughed through his laughter and cried through his jokes, had been in over his head, had been back to work and buried under commitments and barely able to come up for air.

Run away, Gerry had said. Leave it all behind. But while Gerry was his big brother, Johnny always knew best. I'm not you, he'd said, with venom. I tried things your way.

Perhaps Gerry was just as stubborn as Johnny. He'd never given the city a chance. He'd never listened when Johnny said that he loved it, that he couldn't get enough. He'd never tried to help Johnny, in his brother's own domain, on his own terms.

Where would I go, this time? Johnny said. My options have run out.

He'd shouted at Gerry.
Live in the real world!
I do, Gerry had thought.
I wish you could, too.

They hadn't parted on good terms. Maybe it was naïve of Gerry to think he'd see his brother again.

He'd sat on the train back home and tried not to cry, glasses fogging up in an overheated carriage, other passengers averting their eyes.

He'd sat up in bed, that night, the following spring, and felt like he was waking from a nightmare he hadn't yet had. Then the phone started to ring.

> They would never
> be the same
> as this.

He could have helped Johnny. He could have said: come back to Mole End, try again. He could have done anything but leave him behind.

But he didn't. Johnny died, alone, in an apartment he couldn't afford. And how could Gerry ever recover, after losing something the world had trusted him to keep safe?

Life, after Johnny, lost a lot of its colour. His office didn't even send flowers to the funeral.

Life, more recently, had become something of a kaleidoscope. Gerry's surroundings would refract, rub against each other, refract again.

As if
a child is
turning a dial,
twisting a kaleidoscope:
he sees all of this,
all at once.

He sees himself, crying quietly on a train.

He sees the sides of the carriage slide down, his seat
becoming propped-up pillows, the speeding countryside
outside the window replaced by the walls of his bedroom,
late at night. The phone is ringing.

The ringing becomes a voice, and the voice becomes Johnny's,
and the bed becomes a sofa and the night becomes a day and
the room becomes a flat, back in the city.

The sofa turns itself inside out, becomes a coffin. The walls
of the apartment are flipped, become the confines of a
crematorium. A big picture of Johnny unfolds itself on an
easel at the front of the room.

Johnny folds himself back up. The walls fall down, and Gerry
is in a garden, and Gerry is a child, and so is Johnny. They're
running towards the alder at the bottom of the lawn.

But the alder becomes crowded, by another tree, then

another, then another. Trees are bursting out of the earth now, flinging themselves towards the overcast sky above.

> Gerry is in a forest,
> looking for his wife.
> Searching for his son.

Don't dwell on things. You're a man of action, not confusion. Better to see for yourself. Better to save your son, if you couldn't save your brother.

Gerry couldn't be the lighthouse Johnny had needed him to be. And though time is but a stream, Gerry's memory more a murky lake, he knew that history was at risk of repeating itself.

But how could Gerry save his son, if he couldn't save himself? And how could he save himself, if he couldn't find Hazel?

> Too-whit, too-whoo,
> here's what I'll do.

Gerry allowed himself to remember happier times. He and Johnny poring over those books they both loved so much.

He and Johnny, the owl and the badger, tearing their way through the woods, shrieking and roaring all the while.

He and Johnny, back in Cumbria, splashing about in the lake, racing each other to the tops of the hills.

Fells. They call them fells, up there, all the way up there. Back there. All the way back there.

Johnny! Stop it.
You'll get us into trouble.

Johnny was always faster than him. Gerry remembered racing him to the top of the fell, only to roll back down after him.

An entire kingdom laid out beneath them. A landscape which was no one's for the taking.

What do we seek in the country?
Magic.

Ah! Here it is, thought Gerry, stopping at the oak tree for which he'd been looking. He remembered it well.

He put his hands on his hips, considered its knotted trunk. He couldn't see the rope swing. He couldn't locate the river, either. He frowned.

This wasn't the oak. It must be the alder, then. He scratched his chin. He didn't remember his garden looking like this.

No matter. He was simply happy to be home.

> The oak and the alder.
> The alder and the oak.

Both things are true at once. Gerry is standing beneath the
alder. He is also standing beneath the oak.

He'd climbed both trees enough times to remember the
best first foothold. He steadied himself, and put his foot
in it.

If he could only gain a bird's-eye view, climb from branch to
branch and get a few feet off the ground, he might be able to
see where Hazel had gone.

He might be able to see where he was going. Or he might be
following a hunch, that Hazel was waiting for him, up in the
canopy.

Was she up there? Was the barn owl in its hollow, hiding his
son beneath the shelter of its wings?

Only one way to find out. Gerry began to climb.

> Gerry falling, as a child.
> You never learn, do you?

Gerry never got the chance to learn why they called it a fell, just as he never found the time to tell his son that he loved him.

He never learned what happened to that little boy, nor the name of the angry young man who'd replaced him.

> Johnny falling, never landing.
> I'll catch you if you fall.

He cleared his mind of memories. He focused on one thing, climbing, and he climbed.

Higher and higher. Quite high up, by the time he allowed himself to stop, to picture his brother, to remember what it felt like to play in that garden.

To remember the alder, still waiting for him, after all this time.

> Your foot
> goes here.
> Then, there.

Wait. If the alder was waiting for him. What was this?

> The oak or the alder?
> The alder or the oak?

Not the alder. Not the oak. The branches were all wrong.

The bark beneath his fingers was that of the beech tree he'd been at, the day before.

And yet, Gerry had reached out his leg for a foothold in the alder. Or the oak.

> A slip.
> Of the mind, yes.
> Of the foot, too.

No surprise, then, that Gerry's foot met nothing.

> Thin air.

Empty space.

> Deep trouble.

And floating in the lake of his memory suddenly felt like floating in time itself.

Gerry was suspended, knowing he'd messed up, powerless to turn back the clock.

> Then, through the air,
> towards the forest floor,
> he is falling.

Falling.

Falling.

Fallen.

Fell.

thirty-three

A woman stands in a kitchen, arguing with a young man. It's not a volatile argument. No screaming, no smashed crockery. That's not in the young man's nature. But in his sparse words, in his smarting eyes, in the way that his mouth curls into a near-snarl when he spits those words out, the woman can tell that he's reached his limit. He's coming from a place of genuine hurt.

'Why can't he just be happy for me?' the young man is saying.

'He *is* happy for you,' the woman responds, wondering why this is her battle to fight.

'You don't have to speak for him,' the young man seethes, pushing locks of raven-black hair out of his eyes. 'He can tell me himself.'

With this, the angry young man looks towards the other man in the room, his father, who is standing at the long windows on the other side of the dining table, pretending to focus on the garden. It's early evening, and the sky outside is dark. The woman looks from her son to her husband, thinks of saying something else in his defence. She doesn't know how to begin.

'Gerry,' she says.

'It's a Larsen trap,' her husband replies, turning, appraising his son, shaking his head. 'This offer. The kind of life you want to live. It's a Larsen trap.'

Hazel sighs, massages her brow with one hand. Jack looks as if he might spontaneously combust. Charlotte is playing with his old Action Man toys in the living room. Hazel can hear the plastic figures clacking against each other.

'What?' is all Jack can manage in return.

Hazel knows what Gerry is getting at, in his own round-about way. Gerry had always called Jack a magpie, on account of his penchant for shiny things. A Larsen trap is a cage with a captive magpie inside, used to trigger the territorial instinct of other magpies, to lure them in to see off the intruder. She knows that Jack's university offer, the springboard to making as much money as he can possibly make, is a Larsen trap to Gerry. His son is being baited, being drawn in by the other magpies and their shiny things, being tricked into the same gilded cage that his brother had been in, all those years before. But she also knows what her husband has never seemed to understand – that their son doesn't care about Larsen traps, about metaphors. That he's more than just a magpie, standing here in the kitchen, baring his teeth like a fox that won't stay captured for long. Jack is everything his father is not: logical, practical, factual to a fault. He has big dreams, but what he wants above all is his father's approval. Hazel wishes she could translate for Gerry. She wishes she could say to Jack: he doesn't want to lose you, he doesn't want to see you go down the wrong path. But it shouldn't be her job. So she wills Gerry to apologise, to at least say congratulations, even if he doesn't mean it. But Gerry says nothing.

'Why can't you talk like a normal person about it?' Jack says, to his dad, voice cracking. 'Why can't you be proud of me?'

Gerry has already turned back to the window. Within weeks, Jack will have moved out of Mole End. In the fifteen years that follow, Hazel will be able to count his visits home on two hands.

Turn the binoculars back, Hazel thinks. Adjust the sights. How many times had they had variations of this argument, throughout Jack's teenage years? Things had been simpler when her son was still a child. When her husband was still the sturdy oak, awkwardly accompanying Jack on voyages around the garden, spending the hours outside work rubbing Hazel's shoulders and running her baths. Whoever was crying, it was Gerry to whom they'd go for comfort and calm. Hazel remembered punching and punching Gerry's chest when she finally lost her fisherman father, confused by the intensity of hurt she felt at knowing that they'd now never put their differences aside. Gerry had done what he did best: spoken softly, scooped her up in his branch-like arms. She remembered him taking her into the woods for an anniversary dinner on a picnic blanket, the part of waiter played by their waif-like son, the illumination provided by fairy lights hanging from the oak tree above. The strong roots beneath them. After those two fateful days at the

319

oak, the one with Johnny and the one without, everything had changed.

Wondering who started it would be a fruitless endeavour. For one of them to have started it, there'd have had to be a tangible trigger. The widening gap between father and son was the opposite of that, a lack, a crack which began to show in the months after Johnny's banishment. It became a rift, after Johnny's death, when Gerry began to pull away from everything and everyone, including his son. In the years that followed, what else could it become but a chasm? In that respect, Gerry must have started it, though he didn't know he was starting anything at the time. He wasn't capable. He was simply retreating, turning away from the world which had taken his brother from him, going to ground like a wintering plant or a hibernating mouse. Jack was still too young to understand the new-spreading absence in Gerry. He couldn't grasp what had happened to his uncle, why his dad blamed Johnny, the city, himself. Jack's dad never asked him to come foraging any more, never even gave him the chance to say no. Gerry never asked anyone anything. He spent solitary mornings out in the woods, started speaking almost too quietly to be heard. His son, cursed with his uncle's sleek black hair and scrutinising eyes, bore the brunt of Gerry's cold-shouldering. It wasn't Jack's fault that he'd started to look like Johnny. That when Gerry looked at his son, all he could see was someone he'd never be able to save.

Gerry wasn't lost for ever. He'd come back to them, in his own roundabout way. His daughter, so full of affection, so devoid of shyness and awkwardness, would see to that. In summer, a swallow will build a nest of mud and straw and raise its young. When those chicks up and leave, the swallow will do it all again, perhaps even a third time, all of this in the space of a few short months. The journey continues. What was one more child, compared to all that? They hadn't planned this one, either. They'd assumed it couldn't happen again. Their daughter would be someone with 'old parents', Hazel already past forty, Gerry nearer fifty. If Hazel saw her life through a pair of binoculars, Gerry read his between the lines of a nature guide. So, when Charlotte was born, he likened her to a hedgehog. Her hair all spiked up, her face serious and downturned. Hedgehogs are born blind, their spikes sealed in a fluid-filled sac so that they don't hurt their mother on the way out. Gerry had told Hazel that. Jack had come into this world blind, without yet having any sharp edges. And while Charlotte would be wonderfully spiky from the get-go, the barbs Jack would grow were the ones that could really sting.

Charlotte and Jack's childhoods barely overlapped. When Jack was a moody teenager, Charlotte was a feisty toddler. She was born into a world without Johnny, a world in which things had already changed between her brother and her dad. And yet, she could cross that growing abyss with ease. She was the apple of her brother's eye, the only one who could coax him outdoors to push her on that swing or wade into that river. One of Hazel's most treasured photographs was of just that, taken on her film camera, a black-and-white shot of Charlotte on Jack's shoulders. The old oak is behind them, the distant hint of a planning permission notice pinned to a board right next to it. It hadn't meant anything to them, at the time. Their wild was becoming less wild, but their minds were on other things. Jack, turning vain, becoming self-conscious about the gap between his two front teeth, had recently stopped smiling in photos. But this picture was different. No matter what, Charlotte could always make him smile.

The same went for Charlotte's difficult old dad, who somehow always found it easy to be around her. She'd spend hours with Gerry in the garden, not talking, the pair of them plunging their hands into churned-up soil. Charlotte had never known a world where Jack and Gerry were friends, so she'd never bothered to question it. Jack would sometimes watch her, gardening with their dad, unaware that Hazel was watching him. The quiet jealousy on his face was plain to see. When Hazel encouraged Jack to speak to Gerry, he'd sneer and laugh. When Hazel encouraged Gerry to do the same, he'd redden, say he didn't think Jack was all that bothered about his old man. Gerry's head was in the clouds, or somewhere deep in the earth. Did you know, he told her once, that the muscles a hedgehog uses to roll into a ball are the same ones we use to frown? Hazel, unable to sit at the dining table with her husband and her son without the air being sucked out of the room, thought she could imagine that feeling. Frowning and frowning and frowning until your body had folded in on itself.

Gerry wasn't lost for ever. But by the time he'd poked his head back above the earth, the damage was done. This thing between him and Jack was a self-fulfilling prophecy, like a serpent eating its own tail. Jack drifted from Gerry, because Gerry had drifted from Jack. And when Gerry, eventually, tried asking his son to come foraging again, offering finally to teach

Jack to fish, Jack spurned him – just as Jack himself had been spurned, all those times before. There was a cruel irony in the fact that Gerry had sought to create Mole End as a safe haven for Jack, closing him off from the world and smothering him with stories, instead, until he became a sort of anti-Gerry, desperate to leave the woods behind. Straight-laced and risk averse, disinclined to scraped knees and muddy elbows, only happy indoors. A crueller irony, that the start of this rift coincided with Jack entering secondary school – that he was set up to fall in with the kids who gave him what he thought he needed. Jack started confusing popularity for approval, money for fulfilment. Like his dad, he began to value self-sufficiency – but Jack's self-sufficiency was all about making something of himself despite, or perhaps in spite of, the father who'd completely withdrawn the affection he'd never been particularly good at giving.

Maybe settling around here was part of the problem. Hazel had said it to Bea once, after dinner, between hiccups. This place breeds horrible boys. Horrible boys who come from horrible bankers, who'll grow up to be horrible bankers with horrible boys of their own. A backwards cycle, repeated indefinitely, and she'd dropped her son right in the middle of it. What did she expect?

Bea had poured her another glass of her homemade brandy. 'Don't be such an inverse snob,' she'd said. 'All teenagers are horrible.'

Hazel had laughed, had tried not to dwell on a particular raffle at Jack's secondary school, a fête where all the parents had been asked to contribute a prize. The mother before her had contributed a spa day. The one after proffered tickets for

a box at a Premier League football match. And Hazel? She'd
turned up laden with a basket of her and Gerry's homemade
preserves. She'd been proud of those jams and jellies. Gerry
had grown all the fruit, and she had spent weeks tweaking the
recipes. And yet she could still remember the way Jack's friends
had sniggered at the gifts, and no doubt at the weird-looking
mum who'd brought them. Her bright red crop of wiry hair,
her homemade clothes, those same old beaten-up Doc Martens.
She'd never forget the way that Jack had blushed and pretended
not to know her. Who are you? she'd wanted to shout, shaking
him by the shoulders. And what have you done with my son?

Mole End needed a new boiler. The land near the old oak
was fenced off, permissions approved for a new road, a fresh
development of new-build houses with a nice view of the river.
The village was always extending its boundaries, eating into the
woods. The Penwicks missed the chance to protest, barely even
noticed when the building began. It had been a long time since
any of them had taken a picnic down to that oak, had pushed
each other on that creaky old swing. Jack's voice dropped. His
mood dropped with it. And even when he started staying out
late, squirrelling away bottles of booze and frequenting pubs
with a fake ID, he was always too sensible to let his grades
slip. He was smart, well behaved at school, well liked by his
teachers. His university offer was a good one, and Hazel had
cried on her own when it had come through. She knew that,
for her son, it was a one-way ticket away from there.

'Why can't he just be happy for me?' the nearly-adult Jack
had asked her, in that argument to end all arguments.

She could have tried explaining to Jack, about Johnny. But

what good would it do now? They'd kept the details of his death vague, didn't exactly talk about him at the dinner table. Jack barely remembered his uncle, and was already propelling himself forwards into a life where there'd be no time for looking back. Time had run out. No one was more aware of that than Gerry, who'd sat at the very same dining table months before and asked her something along the same lines.

'Ask him yourself,' Hazel had said, to both of them, knowing neither ever would.

By that point, Jack and Gerry were hardly speaking to each other. When they did, it was in a passing mumble. They never argued, unless Hazel was there in a negotiating capacity. Both preferred to walk on eggshells, to simmer in silence. Hazel used to be able to fix anything. But she found herself increasingly unable to fix this strange feud between her husband and her son. Even if she'd locked them in a room together to iron out their differences, she knew they'd choose to stand in their own corners, totally silent, facing the wall.

'The kind of life you want to live,' Gerry had said, when things finally boiled over. 'It's a Larsen trap.'

Both Jack and Gerry would tell you that they had nothing in common. This wasn't strictly untrue. Gerry could survive in the wild without needing anything from another human. And Jack could survive in the great, wide human world, without needing anything from his father. The magpie flew the nest, and the chasm only grew. Jack's great failure, never impressing his father. His father, marking fatherhood down as yet another defeat in a litany of them which would characterise much of his later life. The greengrocer's was the next one, a poisoned chalice which passed to him when Monty, unexpectedly, dropped a crate of oranges and died of a heart attack. He'd had no children. So, a bewildered Gerry lost the closest thing he had to a friend and gained a shop which he didn't know what to do with. He was so busy, so stressed, that he didn't think twice about missing his son's graduation.

Hazel had always been close to Jack. She was always able to see through him, to penetrate his well-groomed facade. As a teenager, he'd still help her dye her hair every few weeks when the roots started to show, washing the lather out with the hand-held shower attachment over the bath. It had been Hazel whom he'd dragged around campus on his university open day, charged with an electric sense of purpose. Their places were reversed, she running to keep up with him, just as he'd had to do with her as a toddler. Even when he'd graduated, started working in enormous edifices of concrete and glass, became far too busy to come home, she'd visit him in the city. He would take her out for lunch at places in which she felt uncomfortably underdressed. But they'd talk, so she'd always leave with a smile on her face.

Time was a rope, slipping away. To try to catch it would be to blister your hands. Jack became the kind of man who was driven by promotions and profit and pats on the back from colleagues with double-barrelled surnames. The lunches dried up, the phone conversations got fewer and further between. His little sister – with whom he'd still been close even when he'd pretended, in his late teenage years, to be embarrassed when she asked him to take part in her two-person plays about goblins and ghouls – stopped getting messages, or invitations to stay at his shiny new apartment for the weekend. Visits home for Christmas were torpedoed by the need to work through the holidays, presents replaced by lavish IOUs. Hazel was losing Jack, only finding him momentarily again when she was lucky, in the rare occasions when she caught him on the phone, just home from the pub, in that sweet spot after two pints. He'd suddenly find himself able to speak. Love you, Mum, he always said, when he signed off those phone calls. He rarely asked about his dad.

What of his dad? Not that Jack would see it, but Gerry had long been back to his old self, making Charlotte giggle with his outlandish animal facts, taking Hazel and their daughter on woodland adventures to pick mushrooms which he promised wouldn't poison them. It was as if, after alienating his son, he'd redoubled his efforts not to ruin things with his daughter. He never complained, always welcomed her affection, was there with a sympathetic ear whenever she needed it. With Jack long gone and having lost interest long before that, it was Charlotte he now regaled with tales of his wild years — she laughed, when he called them that, but was enthralled when he told her of being tear-gassed at protests, of almost being flattened by hunters' horses. It was Charlotte, too, whom he and Hazel started to tell about their plans for a great adventure, showing her the old maps which would take them down the Oka- vango Delta, letting her trace the old route which would have taken them across the Khyber Pass. And Charlotte responded quite differently from Jack, back when they'd had those same conversations with him. Jack had humoured them. But Char- lotte, staring up at her parents with those chocolate-button eyes, believed unreservedly that their dreams would come true. Maybe that's why Hazel started believing in them again, too.

Gerry was never a realist. But he'd slowly come down to earth in the years since the pair of them had planned to roam the planet without a care in the world. He'd spent nineteen years and counting working at the greengrocer's, claiming that he was going to do something else with his days. When Monty died, that opportunity was finally, officially, taken away from him, and he spent the next decade working harder than ever. His back started to give him trouble. His eyes gave him more trouble than they had before. He came home drained, perpetually exhausted because he refused to give up his early mornings, his solitary walks in the woods. Business wasn't exactly booming. Gerry couldn't deal with people, was much better at shovelling soil and stacking shelves than he was selling himself or his wares. He was swimming upstream, losing loyal customers to the newly opened Whole Foods in the next village along. Still, his head grazed the clouds, floated right above them. He never complained, always seemed to be coping, which is perhaps why Hazel stopped paying attention to him. She was busy watching her own life pass her by, worrying that her son was in the process of forgetting his family. She missed all the signs that her husband was doing the same.

'It wasn't like I was on my own,' Gerry had said, when the police brought him home in the early hours of the morning.

Hazel should have noticed in the months before, every time he'd lost his train of thought or forgot where they kept the teabags, couldn't find his walking boots or work out which one was their bedroom. She should have taken it seriously, done something sooner. Perhaps if she had, it wouldn't have happened like that: him going missing, in the middle of the woods, in the middle of the night. Him returning a different man to who he'd been. How had she let this happen? When she and Charlotte called the emergency services, as they waited for the police and then, fear in the pit of their stomachs, for Gerry, it became clear that there were bigger problems than finding a buyer for the greengrocer's, or whether, this Christmas, Jack would decide to come home.

'It wasn't like I was on my own.'

Shocked to the core, Hazel stood statue-still in the kitchen. A stoic Charlotte was speaking to the two police officers on the porch, calmly taking in their practical next-steps advice. And Gerry, who'd pottered in through the back door, whose hands were filthy and whose hair was matted, didn't seem to understand what all the fuss was about.

'What do you mean?' Hazel had said, though she wished she hadn't asked. 'Where were you?'

'I was at the oak,' said Gerry, with a simple smile. 'I was with the owl.'

thirty-four

An owl, shrieking in despair as it takes flight from a falling oak tree. A dead badger, burning on a pyre made from nature guides and rotten apples. Empty eye sockets spewing fire, turning to ice. Jack saw all of this as he slept fitfully in the clearing, back pressed against the base of a black poplar, fox hugged tightly to his chest. Images which were hard to focus on flickered, flooding his brain, freezing and solidifying into something clearer. A forest. A cityscape of trees, a rolling metropolis of green and brown, through which Jack slowly walked. He saw them as his dad would see them – that is, the trees as they were, with tiny doors hidden in their roots, with tiny windows halfway up their trunks, with tiny chimneys poking out of the crooks of their branches, spewing out tiny plumes of smoke. Jack watched the bark of each one swing open like a doll's house to reveal families of rodents feasting in front of fireplaces, latticed blackcurrant tarts billowing with steam and towering fruit jellies that the kits and cubs couldn't help but prod with sticky paws.

A great togetherness. And Jack, watching from the outside, too cynical to join in. Hadn't he seen his whole life like this? Removed, emotionally disengaged, always a step back? Inside one of those trees, a tiny breakfast table. And at that tiny breakfast table, in his dad's lap, a tiny Jack.

'Dad,' said this younger Jack. 'Did barn owls exist before barns?'

A nature guide was open in front of them, resting on a page about owls. His dad laughed, taking off his glasses to wipe them on his jumper.

'Of course they did.'

'But where did they live?'

'Rock crevices,' his dad answered, placing the circular frames back on his nose. 'Hollow trees.'

Jack woke with a start, scrabbled to a seated position, sent the fox flying. It landed deftly, baring its fangs, then looked around, confused. Jack looked around, too, no idea where he was, no idea what he was doing there. It was bright, and a breeze was kicking up dust into his eyes. Trees were shaking their leaves, filtering the daylight through their branches. He was in the forest. He'd been looking for his father. It was daytime again, which meant it had been night. He'd fallen asleep.

'Oh,' Jack said. 'Oh no.'

It didn't convey the graveness of the situation, the fact that his dad may or may not have been missing for an entire night. Without a phone, Jack had no way to tell. His watch was dead, so he couldn't even tell the time. Jack swallowed guiltily, had to remind himself to breathe. Church bells were ringing in the distance, and Jack's panic almost gave way to a sort of peace. The morning was warm. Jack had slept in the woods. He considered, briefly, what it might be like to burrow into the ground, how nice it would be to stay out here, to hibernate until all of this had resolved itself. He imagined sleeping curled up in a pile of furry, quivering bodies, the grass above him frozen and the trees above that devoid of leaves. Everything stripped bare, ready for an awakening. As long as he stayed still, Jack kept telling himself that he didn't have to deal with any of it. And yet, the clang of church bells was rapidly bringing the real world into sharper focus. Jack shifted, cocked his head. Church bells. They'd be coming from the village.

The fox yawned, slowly stretched in front of him. *We should probably try and find your dad.*

Orienting himself clumsily, Jack slipped down the slope he'd climbed the previous evening and started walking once again through the woods, the fox following closely behind. Though his mind was bleary, the edges of his vision blurry, he felt strangely well rested, weirdly cleansed, and he stretched out muscles which didn't feel as tight as they should have been. He'd like to take a leaf out of the fox's book and be led by his nose, but he didn't have the time. He followed his ears, instead. Towards church bells. Towards traffic. He felt like the backs of his teeth were covered in moss. He hadn't packed a toothbrush. He hadn't planned on still being in the woods.

'We're here,' Jack said, the sound of cars sweeping past

indicating a busy road. Those wedding bells again. Jack counted in his head, deduced it must be Saturday.

The real world, said the fox.

Jack couldn't tell if it was being sarcastic. He climbed up the bank, peered through a bush. He knew he should go into the village and beg a stranger for change to use a phone box, check in with the police, call his sister and see what was needed before he climbed the hill home. Were phone boxes still a thing? Probably, here. Jack didn't want to have to tell the powers that be that he'd mislaid his phone and both of his parents, one after the other, in the space of two weeks. The thought of his mother intensified the fear roiling in his gut. He was so full of guilt and worry, he felt as if his insides had been hollowed out. But that wasn't all, if he was being honest with himself. His stomach rumbled. He didn't want to admit that what was driving him to the village, above all, was hunger. He and the fox were really drawn by the prospect of a crisp pain au chocolat and the fresh-poured foam on a flat white. He wasn't thinking straight. He'd just spent the night in the forest.

'Stay out of sight,' Jack said, as they fought their way through the bush towards civilisation. 'We don't want to draw attention to ourselves.'

Jack meant the fox, but he might just as well have been referring to himself. Filth had collected beneath his blunted nails, mud was still smeared across his cheeks. His beard was so itchy it seemed to be crawling away from him, his eyes so dry they were burrowing into his skull. Jack lurked beside the trees on the grass verge, staring across at the village church with its wedding guests congregating outside. The pubs probably wouldn't quite be open yet, but the deli or the village shop must have a phone. Would they call the police for him, if he asked? He still knew Mole End's number off by heart, but he already knew he wouldn't ring it. He couldn't allow himself to be seen like this. Everyone knew everyone around here. And everybody talked. His mum had told him that everyone in the village thought of the Penwicks as the lunatic hermits on the hill.

Jack used to feel ashamed of his parents. Now he'd managed to lose both of them, the thought made him intensely sad. At university, his friends were all sons and daughters of bankers and brokers and QCs and VPs. From time to time, they'd ask, what does your father do? At school, Jack had once proudly declared that his dad was a naturist, and the whole class had laughed at him. Your dad strips naked? Your dad's a flasher? Naturalist, he'd meant. Say very little, and you won't say the wrong thing. An older, wiser Jack evaded the question, stayed silent, let the Hughs and the Hugos speak about themselves, which is what they really wanted to do, anyway. He might say that his dad was a local business owner. He'd admit that he'd gone to a state school, but felt the need to follow up with 'a good one'. When they referred to Jack's 'country pile', he made no effort to correct them. And when they pronounced his surname with a silent 'W', like Fenwick, he told himself that must be the right way to say it. These were the sorts of people who bought their clothes at Harvey Nichols, their groceries in the Harrods Food Halls. How could they be wrong?

Jack licked his dry lips. All of that posturing felt so far away now. Like the alluring pastries in the deli window across the street, so close he could walk over and grab one, but impossibly distant to a man who'd lost his wallet as well as his phone.

'Let's go,' Jack said.

And so they went, across the road, back into the alleyway behind the greengrocer's, keeping hidden behind a pair of rancid old wheelie bins. Jack wasn't ready to be an orphan. He wished, beyond anything, that he could call his mum and apologise for all of it. He stared down the street, hoping to see that elusive phone box, hoping to avoid any familiar faces. The fox slipped into one of the bins, emerged forcefully from it like a whack-a-mole, displacing balled-up newspapers and old plastic bottles with the slamming of a lid.

I have something for you, it said.

Jack looked up. 'What?'

In the fox's mouth was an old banana skin. Limp and sadly brown. The fox nosed it towards him enthusiastically. Jack, with an upturned lip, took it from him with all the grace he could muster.

I know you're hungry, said the fox.

Jack thanked the fox and politely encouraged it to find some food for itself. When it had disappeared back into the bin, he flung the banana skin over his shoulder. As the fox rummaged, Jack returned to the pavement, to the window by the front of the greengrocer's, taking refuge in the front porch. It was mercifully quiet, and no one seemed to have spotted him yet. He still pondered trying one of the pubs, asking to use their phone. Which one did Charlotte work in? He imagined they'd be sympathetic, even if their doors weren't open yet. They could pour him a cold pint to calm his nerves. Jack had a clear route across the road, should he wish to take it. And yet, still, he stalled. The whitewashed window behind him felt soothing against his inflamed skin. He pressed the backs of his forearms against it, then turned and did the same with his forehead. Through the semi-transparent fog of the paint, Jack could see inside. He never had asked the fox what state the greengrocer's was in.

The shop was exactly as he'd remembered it. Just emptier. The island in the middle, the shelves across one wall, the counter across the other, from which his dad had fed him sweet, raw peas. All dormant, all covered with dust. And perhaps it was simply the intensity of his hunger, but Jack saw something else for just a second. Dressed tables, tall and flickering candles, windows steaming with the laughter of dinner guests.

Jack pulled his head away. He wiped his forehead, banished the thought from his mind. And as he did so, he spotted something else. A bright green piece of paper, pasted to the window in front of him. Jack took a step forward to peel it from the glass, in order to read it more comprehensively. As he did so, something crunched underfoot. He picked up his dirty trainer, saw the flattened pistachio shells which littered the front step.

'I know where you are,' said Jack, under his breath.

Then he called the fox from the alleyway and crossed back over the road, returning to the woods.

thirty-five

A man sits in a room in a hospital, holding his wife's hand. 'Do you understand, Mister Penwick?' the specialist says, after giving his diagnosis. The man sits there, staring not at the doctor but beyond him, out of the window and into the leaves of a tree on the lawn outside.

'How old is that willow?' Gerry asks, eventually.

They all look out of the window in unison, Hazel through eyes spilling with tears. The specialist is dumbfounded. He shuffles some papers, harrumphs.

'I'm not sure,' he says.

Gerry must know, Hazel thinks. He's only asking because he doesn't want to address the matter at hand. His roundabout way. Her husband is like an encyclopaedia, in which the chapter on humans has been ripped out. He knows about everything, except social interaction. He's always been inadvertently rude, has never once been on time in his life. His old group of anarchist friends, now all scattered or expired, used to call him 'the late, great Gerald Penwick'. But these days, in busy places, Gerry recognises people he doesn't know, and forgets people he's known for years. The 'great' is fading, he'd chuckled recently, with a telltale tremble in his hands. I'm becoming, simply, late.

One man went into the woods. Another came out. This is how Hazel would remember it, though she knew it wasn't quite true. Over the years, that long-haired idealist who'd strolled up to her in that orchard had morphed into a pensioner with a penchant for sleeveless sweaters and marmalade-on-toast. Was Gerry still capable of political convictions? He'd voted Green in the last election, though Hazel thought that might have been just because he liked the colour. And though he'd always been scatter-brained – his half-finished projects visible from the window ranging from the rotting treehouse to the toppling trellis to the greenhouse missing almost all of its panes – Hazel had turned a blind eye to how much he was forgetting, forced herself to forget every time he got something wrong. But each time he left a bath overflowing, or a hob unattended, or their bed in the middle of the night with the intention of going outside and gardening, it became harder and harder to ignore. After that night he'd been found in the forest, they couldn't just brush it off as forgetfulness any more.

'It's just Mother Earth,' he'd said, about the mud, as she scrubbed it from his hands and bare feet, sponged it from the cuffs and hems of his pyjamas. 'There's no problem getting a little dirt on you.'

Only after he'd gone to sleep, after the medics and the police had left, after the sun had started to rise and Charlotte had stopped tossing and turning in the room next door, had Hazel allowed herself to cry.

The more muddled things became over the following months, the more sharply her emotions came into focus. Fear. Love. Frustration, and it wasn't just here. Gerry knew what was happening to him. But didn't knowing only make it worse? He became impatient when he was forgetful, withdrawn when he was left to ponder what came next. She'd never loved him more than she did now. They spent very little time without each other in those first weeks, barely stopped talking in case it left them time to think. They lay in late, had breakfasts in bed, still laughed as if nothing had changed since the mornings when they'd drink coffee from tin mugs in the fold-away bed of the Ship of Theseus. Charlotte, who'd been thinking about uni- versity, suddenly decided to defer. Eventually, she abandoned the idea entirely, got a job at the local pub instead. She took to spending more time with Gerry in the garden, nodding obedi- ently when he told her what to plant, and where. Hazel called Jack, who liked to think he was more on top of things than he was. It was a courtesy call. His response went something like this: I'm sorry. That sounds awful. Dehydration, maybe? Urine infections can make men manic. Right, yes, I see. I'm sorry, I've got so much work on. I can't come back right now. I hope everything's OK. I can't. I'm sorry.

Gerry had been advised to give up work, so he did. He was

always here, but more distant than he'd ever been. Hazel used to find him so easy to understand. But as the months went on, he retreated, became less talkative. Conversations began to go nowhere. Hazel would find traces of her husband more often than the man himself. Muddy footprints, or abandoned nature guides, or Post-it notes with meanings she couldn't discern. Sometimes, they would make her smile: 'do not eat this', on top of a packet of raw bacon, 'no matter how good it tastes'. Sometimes, she'd find ones which veered away from English and into nonsense, and they'd fill her with a very specific kind of despair. She built a new existence around Gerry's quirks, the cupboards he spontaneously reorganised, the rooms he left in a mess in search of childhood books he'd lost decades ago. The worst thing she could have done was to impose her own order on him. After all, on any given day, you might not have guessed that anything had changed. Gerry seemed much the same as his old, unusual self, pottering about in the garden or working on a crossword at the dining table. Then there were the bad days, when Hazel might get a phone call saying there was a man on the bridge in the village who didn't know how he got there, where he lived, or whose was the phone number written on the card inside his wallet. It was hers. He was hers. He didn't leave the house on his own, any more.

Time sinks. And Hazel had found that getting older was like sinking, too, sinking back very slowly into a very large armchair. Comfortable, yes. Settling, sure. But harder to get back up the further down you sank. Was this the end of fun, for Hazel? Was this the end of freedom? It felt far too soon. She'd once dated a greasy-haired, semi-famous rock star whose one-hit wonder was still played on adverts. He now sold holiday homes in the Canary Islands. She used to occasionally go out with the local rambling club, but even that pastime had stumbled and foundered. Her only friend in the village, Bea, was eighty-two years old. She couldn't climb the hill to Mole End any more, so house guests were at an all-time low. Not having anyone to send postcards to used to be a point of pride, because Hazel and Gerry only needed themselves and their children. Now the idea that they only had each other felt like an albatross around her neck. Was it normal, to always feel this lonely? Despite the great noise of nature, Mole End could feel awfully quiet. With every year that went by in this house she'd felt her nerves pulled tighter like metal strings that must eventually snap. Here she'd always be standing, in her kitchen, drinking tea and speaking to no one, wondering if today would be a good day, or yet another bad one.

It was the worst part of her, the part that envied her husband. The part that wished she could forget it all, no matter how momentarily. The part that wished she had the blind faith to step out, barefoot, and get lost in the forest. Thirty years ago, on the Isle of Mull, Hazel had failed to see a sea eagle. In hindsight, that failure felt significant. Hazel wondered if Gerry would remember what he'd told her, about the fishermen in the Shetland Islands. Their belief that as soon as a sea eagle appeared, fish rose to the surface, belly up. Hazel didn't want to be the fish, any more, forever exposing her belly, surrendering herself to be pecked to pieces by a life which pulled her this way and that. She felt as if she'd lived that life in an average-speed check, longing all the while to be racing down a road towards a

343

tunnel, trying to remember the French word for pharmacy. She wished she could sit in that passenger seat again. She wished she could turn to Gerry, her best friend, her only-ever person, and she wished she could say this. Keep driving. The adventure doesn't have to end.

'Do you remember France?' she'd said, broaching the subject.

'Of course.' He'd smiled, with a wistful look in his eye. 'We were hunting for truffles. With the pigs.'

She couldn't spirit Gerry away for one last adventure, no matter how much she wished she could. She couldn't take him away from his medicine, from his doctors, from the routine he needed to stop his brain spiralling out of control. She couldn't leave him. But she couldn't stay, either. She didn't want to be the fish, any more. She wanted to be the eagle.

This idea soon began to take flight, beating its wings against the confines of her mind. And because she couldn't leave him, because she couldn't stay, this would be one journey which Hazel would have to make alone. It became an obsession, in the weeks after she first had the thought. Her quest, her pilgrimage. She secretly took to looking at van rentals on Jack's old computer, at fuel allowances and train timetables, writing down longitudes and latitudes and foreign laws around wild camping in a note-book she kept hidden in the top pocket of her anorak. She didn't need to go missing, so much as find what she had been missing. An adventure. I will see a sea eagle. I will see more than that. I will soar, further than we ever even planned, on flights and on ferries, putting six thousand miles between myself and Mole End. I'll do this, because I need to do it, before our life becomes what it's about to become. Then, I'll come home.

'There's something—' she'd said, early that morning, when she couldn't hold it in any more. 'There's something I have to do.'

Her daughter understood. She wasn't a child any more.

'Get lost,' she'd said, with a smile, before they'd hugged goodbye, dry-eyed and determined as they came to terms with what they were about to do. 'While you still can.'

thirty-six

Jack should have gone straight to the oak tree in the first place. If there was anywhere in these woods his dad might be, it was there. Had Jack been avoiding it? No, he'd got lost. It was embarrassing to not remember where it was. His dad would know exactly where to find it, and exactly what would happen if he didn't. He must have seen that green piece of the paper, the tree removal notice plastered in bold letters across the front of it. He must have known that his beloved oak was about to be chopped down. Was a tree more important than Jack's mother? He imagined his father, chained to the ancient trunk, warding off lumberjacks with enormous axes. He imagined his father, scared and confused, lost in the woods.

This doesn't make sense, the fox was saying, tripping to keep up with Jack as he ploughed his way through the woods. *He won't be there. He can't. He's looking for your mum.*

Jack kept moving, the fox dodging its way in and out of trees behind him.

'There doesn't need to be a logic to it,' Jack said, not looking back, keeping his focus on where he remembered the oak to be. What he didn't say was: nothing my dad does makes sense. That's what makes him my dad.

I'm not talking about logic, the fox said. *I'm talking about—*

'Instinct,' said Jack, cutting the fox off. 'I'm using my instinct. I'm following my nose.'

No, you're not, the fox called after him. *You're following words on a piece of paper.*

'I don't have time to argue.' Jack stopped, but only briefly. 'I never asked you to come with me.'

The fox was quieter after that. Jack didn't have time to feel guilty, either. He pressed on, focused on the tree, on where it would be if one was approaching it from the other side, from the village. It had always stood halfway between civilisation and Mole End.

I think we should go this way, the fox said, quietly. It was pointing its muzzle towards another road, another verge, another cluster of trees.

Jack ignored the fox. He was thinking about Charlotte, about whether she'd have located their mum. She must have been worried, back there in the house on her own. Their argument, the day before, felt like a lifetime ago. The interview was so distant, so unimportant, that Jack almost wondered if it had been just a bad dream.

'We're nearly there,' said Jack, wading through a waist-high sea of ferns. 'Then you'll see.'

You're playing a guessing game. The fox sounded frustrated. *I thought you were starting to understand.*

'The oak is—'

I don't think you know—

'Nearby,' said Jack, forging on. 'Once we're there, everything will be alright.'

We should go back to the village, said the fox, not convinced. *Or the house. Lone foxes—*

'Die alone,' Jack cut the sentence off, hacking his way through a bush. 'I know. You mentioned.'

But it's true, said the fox, its voice small.

Jack wasn't thinking about lone foxes, but about what he'd say to his dad, at the oak. How could you? What were you thinking? We've got enough going on, with Mum missing, without you going missing, too. Part of him was holding out for an apology. A larger part wondered whether it was he who should apologise. This was the kind of thought the fox might tell him to have, so he snuffed it out and kept going. There was no time for radical impracticality. Not until they'd found his father.

Walking was making Jack dizzy. The woods were pressing in on him. It was like his magnetic poles were shifting, up becoming down and down becoming up. The closer he came to the oak, the closer he felt to understanding. In his old world, the world of churn rates and burn rates and returns on investment, Jack had long ago stopped considering where squirrels sleep, why foxes cry at night, how the owl turns its head. In an unexpected twist of fate, he'd ended up out in the wild, and these questions now filled his brain.

'No snap in the flap,' his father had once said.

The strangeness of the phrase, presented without prompting, as they crouched beneath the oak one Sunday afternoon. His dad had been holding a feather aloft in the early morning light, specks of dust and dew bouncing around it as he turned it this way and that. The feather was white, brilliantly so, shot through with streaks of caramel and gold. Fringed like a comb, designed for silent flight. A barn owl's feather. No snap in the flap, he'd said to his young son, as if it were the most obvious thing in the world.

'Their wings make no sound.'

At first, Jack thought it was the shriek of the barn owl which brought him back to reality. After all, he had more or less reached the oak, and the oak was nothing like Jack had remembered it. Were these fences always here? The houses behind them definitely weren't, new in style but already several years old by the faded colour of the brick. It was the best part of two decades since he'd been down here, and the remoteness he'd remembered was nowhere to be seen. The river was brown and shallow, the tree itself smaller and, somehow, sadder. Was that crack there before? Hadn't there been more branches? Jack recognised the whorls in the bark, the way the massive, knotted roots plunged into the earth like the tentacles of a kraken. But he didn't remember the lack of leaves, nor the missing limbs, nor the great cleft two-thirds of the way up the trunk which made the whole thing look like it had been hit by lightning. The rope swing was gone. There was very little canopy left, the tree having seemingly been pollarded some years ago to protect those new houses. Jack could tell, from this angle, that the oak was dead, and had been for some time. The jagged hole in its ancient trunk was dark and anguished, like a mouth gasping for air, like something enormous, screaming for help.

Jack stopped dead. The fox bumped into the backs of his legs, looked around them, then shrunk back again. What was he seeing? Signs of human activity littered the scene. Warning tape, tyre tracks. Things which weren't supposed to be here. Another memory fell from what remained of the canopy. They were hitting Jack more often, with more force. His dad had taken him on a rare trip as a child, driving miles to see the Major Oak, that tree which had sheltered Robin Hood and his Merry Men. But the proud arms of that legendary hiding place had been supported by scaffolding, and they'd both left disappointed, his dad decrying the fact that humans either have to hold everything up or tear everything down, that humans are constitutionally incapable of letting things run their course, that humans are intent upon ensuring that the world suffers death by management. The humans now in front of Jack, the hard-hatted ones flanking the river and surrounding the oak, were planning a swifter execution. The shriek hadn't come from a barn owl. It had been a throatier sound, the roar of the chainsaws in their hands. They'd already taken off most of the oak's remaining branches. Now they were going for its trunk.

'We're too late,' said Jack, unheard over the din of the chainsaws.

More branches came crashing down. Jack thought of himself, falling from that falling branch, a hazy memory of hurting his ankle, a clearer one of being caught and cradled by his dad. All gone now. There was no sign of his father, and no indication that he'd been here in the first place. Between Jack and the oak, the slip and the slop of the water sounded like a thousand pleading mouths plopping open and closed. It was as if the whole river was speaking to him, every fish in the forest coming out of their little damp houses and imploring him to help, to intervene, to run away.

It's not right, said the fox, cowering, staring at the source of the noise.

'I am right,' said Jack, shaking his head. 'I have to be.'

But his dad wasn't here. And if his dad wasn't here, Jack had no idea where his dad might be. He scratched his wrist, tried to brush away the feeling that there were things crawling all over him, not just the sawdust billowing through the air above the clearing and the fox whimpering behind his calves, but wood-lice, spiders and earwigs, a whole menagerie of tiny intruders making beds out of his hair and his armpits and the pockets of his gym shorts. It was as if the forest was eating him alive. Jack took a step back as if in a trance, barely heard the man in the hi-vis jacket forcefully telling him he couldn't be there. The chainsaws were wailing, the fox creeping back, away from the humans, its glowing eyes wide and wary. So cornered, so out in the open. Jack's heartbeat was drumming in his ears, the chainsaws impersonating that old sound of radio tuning, the one he'd thought he was rid of. Was this a panic attack? Was that the rumble of thunder overhead? Jack swallowed, felt the eyes of the workmen upon him. He retreated, turned to the fox. But the fox was backing away from him, too.

'Wait!' shouted Jack.

The fox looked afraid, its eyes darting this way and that.

'Don't you dare!' Jack yelled over the din of the chainsaws, his arm outstretched.

The fox flinched, looked back into the forest.

'Please,' said Jack, half falling, reaching out. 'Don't leave me too.'

Jack wasn't shouting any more. He was whimpering, more so than the fox, anger giving way to anguish. Taking pity, the fox took a step forward, its black paws grazing the ground. Jack stretched his fingers further, reached out to touch its blazing fur. He felt the need to hold it, protected, in his arms.

An ear-splitting crash filled the forest, and a wave of dust rolled over them. The air was cleaved in two. Behind him, above him, the oak was coming down. Jack turned, watched the once-mighty tree topple over the river. By the time he'd regained his senses and turned once more, the fox had already fled.

thirty-seven

A woman dusts off an old hiking rucksack, so huge that it dwarfs her. She carefully fills it with provisions, cross-referenced against a packing list and a carefully plotted itinerary. She studies her route with academic precision, factors in stop-offs, makes enough allowances for going off the beaten track. For the first time in decades, she'll find herself at sea. For the first time ever, she'll be further away than the Alps. She packs her passport. She packs foreign currency, checks for her camera, her notebook, his binoculars. She is putting something off, the only thing she really has to do before that six-thousand-mile journey begins. She has never dreaded anything as much as this one thing.

Hazel knew she needed to talk to Gerry. But how could she tell him she was leaving him behind, at the exact moment that he needed her most? I have to do this, she'd said, to herself, in her head, when she rehearsed the conversation. I have to go now, so I can come back to you. She dreaded him asking her to stay. She dreaded him not understanding that she wanted to leave. Or, not caring. Most of all, she dreaded the days when he wouldn't know her inside out, wouldn't know whether it was what she needed or not.

Hazel delayed the conversation until the last possible moment, early on the morning she was planning to leave. Her rucksack was packed in the hallway. She had a train ticket, a van booked in her name. The sun was barely up, so she knew that her husband would be. She found him in the garden, staring off into the trees.

'Gerry,' she said. The grass was wet underfoot. No problem, in her walking boots, but his slippers must have been soaked through. She stroked the back of his head, the wispy hair which almost seemed to float. 'You should be inside.'

He shushed her, but not forcefully. He simply held up a finger and implored her to listen. For a moment, there was nothing. Fog rolled off the trees, settled on the lawn. The odd chirp in the lingering dimness. The insistent drumming of a woodpecker. Then, in the distance, another noise. A scrape, which started low and then became a shriek. She knew the sound. A barn owl.

'I believe you now,' she said. The words felt heavy, almost unbearable.

Gerry didn't even look at her. 'I told you he was out there,' he said, but not with self-satisfaction. It was more like he was letting her in on a secret.

'Look,' Hazel said, fiddling with the zip on her jacket. 'There's something—'

Gerry did look at her. Behind his dew-speckled glasses, his eyes were amplified. The sepia light of the dawn accentuated the flecks of gold within them. Gerry blinked, enormous eyelids over enormous eyes. Then he furrowed his brow, frowned.

'What is it?' he said. 'You look upset.'

'It's—' Hazel began. 'Well, it's nothing.' She shook her head, took a deep breath. 'OK, it's not nothing.'

Gerry's face softened. 'Tell me,' he said, putting one of his broad, paw-like hands on her arm. 'A problem shared is a problem halved.'

The owl shrieked again, but neither of them were listening. Gerry's eyes were fixed on Hazel, and Hazel was fixed only on what his face looked like at this moment, before she broke his heart. In the reflection of his glasses, her bushy black hair was wire grey. She closed her eyes. Why am I doing this? Why would I, when it hurts this much?

'I'm leaving,' she said. 'Not for good.' She paused, caught her breath. 'But for a while.'

She opened her eyes again. Gerry was still looking at her. It was a moment before he seemed to register what she'd said. Then, without warning, his face broke into a smile.

'An adventure,' he said. 'I thought you'd never ask.'

Her stomach reached a cliff edge, then began to drop.

'Where are we going?' he said.

And, for a moment, Hazel was worried that her heart might literally stop beating. She'd prepared for this. She'd worked up her excuses. But it was different, out here, with him. She brought her careful reasons to mind, found herself unable to look at her husband. She stuttered as she spoke.

'I—'

His hand on her wrist stopped her. He squeezed. She looked up. His smile had lessened, to a knowing smirk. There was a twinkle in those icy blue eyes.

'I'm joking,' he said.

'What?'

'I'd only slow you down,' he said, matter-of-factly. 'And you'd have to do all the driving.' He looked back towards the trees. 'I've probably forgotten which one's the accelerator and which one's the brake.'

Hazel was stunned for a moment. Then, she could only cry through her laughter. Or perhaps she laughed through the tears. Either way, she told Gerry about her adventure, and he told her that he couldn't wait to hear all about it, when she was back. Then he held her as he used to, and she held him, and she felt his soft skin against her cheek and he breathed in deeply the smell of her bushy hair.

She wiped her eyes as he let her go. She smiled. 'Don't forget me,' she said.

Gerry shook his head, stared at something in the trees which only he could see. 'I could never do that.'

thirty-eight

Did you know?
On Alderney, the hedgehogs are blonde.

Gerry lay in the dirt. His head was swimming. His leg was in agony.

And there's a type of shrew that only occurs
on the Isles of Scilly.
The lesser white-toothed shrew, it's called.

His glasses were scraped, filthy. He used two trembling fingers to remove them, then threw them away.

He'd dreamed he was a shrew, sleeping on a beach. When he

woke, he felt beneath him and he found not sand, but mud, twigs, leaves.

There was a beech above him, and a forest floor below. Was he dead? Had he died? If he had, at least he could still move his fingers.

Imagine that.
Heaven, as a forest floor.

Gerry grounded himself, tried to gather himself up.

That same tall tree over that same trickling stream. In the beginnings of that stream, he now lay.

He saw how far he'd fallen, and it was far from a lethal height. But it was high enough to have hurt, high enough that one of his legs was now causing him agony. He shifted, groaned.

He remembered, for no reason he could ascertain, crouching with his son in this very forest and saving a creature tangled in barbed wire. It hadn't been a rabbit. It had lived.

He and his son had hugged, because they'd shared something they couldn't put into words.

His son?
He doesn't have a son.

And even if he does,
they don't hug.

Gerry would have liked to be held now.

Gerry had always striven to be brave, to be solid and sturdy,
to never be in need of a shoulder to cry on. He was the
shoulder. But it would be nice to be comforted, to be told it
was all going to be alright.

The woods could be a frightening place, if you were on your
own. The clouds were drawing in. And the sky sounded like
shrieking, like chainsaws, like a coming storm.

Gerry closed his eyes, tried to imagine a more comforting
forest. One from the books that he and Johnny had once read
to each other.

The books that Johnny had once read to Jack.

He sees toads with motor cars.
He sees mice with well-stocked larders.
He sees a hedgehog, wiping its paws on an apron.
He sees a boy and a bear, its head stuck in a honey pot.
He sees an owl, asleep in an oak with a
squirrel-tail door knocker.

Gerry had always been good with his nose. He smelled the
rain, long before it started to fall.

White clouds above the canopy. He tried his best to look around. There were no books in this clearing. If there were, the water would turn them to pulp.

There was something new, though. A neat black hole, in the ground.

> A rectangular whirlpool.
> A vortex of light and sound.

It was not a black hole, not a rectangle cut from the earth. It was a mobile phone.

Gerry couldn't reach it. He wished he could make a mental note, could force himself to remember that it was there.

Why can't you talk like a normal person? That's what his son had said, aeons ago. Why can't you be proud of me?

Every day, I feel lucky to have you. Every day, I think how much it would hurt, to lose you.

Gerry had never been good at keeping hold of things. He was only thinking in his son's best interests. He'd only wanted to keep him safe.

> An elm. An eclipse.
> A black butterfly. Midnight,
> a fox crossing your path.

Johnny's death had been the nail in the coffin for Gerry's ailing father.

The old man spat venom on his deathbed, told him that the wrong son had died. Gerry blamed the drugs they were pumping into him, or the delusions that came when the world altered your brain.

Funny, because now that Gerry's own brain had changed, all he wanted to do was tell his son that he loved him.

> I am proud.
> I always have been.

Gerry hoped that his son hadn't followed him. This forest wasn't kind to those who usually stuck to the roads.

Foolish. A fool's errand, Gerry saw now, his brain jolted by a short fall from a tall beech tree. His wife had told him where she was going, and it wasn't into a hollow oak to share a nest with a barn owl.

She'd told him to wait, to stay put, but he'd acted like the old Gerry, a man of action, and now he'd ruined everything, for everyone. He hoped he wasn't in trouble. He hoped he hadn't got her into trouble.

He hoped she'd made it further than the oak tree. He hoped she'd seen those sea eagles.

> White-tailed eagles
> are monogamous.
> They roost in pairs,
> on rocky coastlines,
> and in lochs, by the sea.

Gerry knew where Hazel had gone. But he also knew this sensation, this all-consuming, all-confusing haze which was descending on him more often, every day.

Was he a barn owl, or was he a sea eagle? Was he the magpie or the Larsen trap, the earth or the form, the alder or the oak? Or was he something else entirely, something grounded, something returning to the ground?

Was it raining? Or was his brain leaking, the breached lake of time bursting through its dam, the river of his brain finally breaking its banks and flooding the forest, washing him away?

> *What are you?*
> asks a shrew, passing by.
> *Where are you going?*
> says a swallow,
> up on high.

At the very moment when the confusion seemed like it might break him, when his brain felt like it might short-circuit, when the stream or the rain began to soak through to his bones, when he wanted to give up, Gerry saw him.

Two black feet in the mud, forming soft and trepidatious footsteps, a clear path over wet leaves. Gerry didn't mind that he was lying in a puddle. His mind was on the visitor, and the visitor alone.

Gerry couldn't turn, so his mind filled in the blanks. Well-shined black shoes, and a pair of midnight-blue suit trousers which barely creased as he crouched.

Combed hair, and a dry-cleaned coat which the rain wouldn't touch.

There is
no quiet
in the
city.

Johnny loosened his tie and undid his top button. Johnny smiled that same old mischievous smile, put a warm hand on Gerry's cold shoulder.

Johnny told Gerry that if his brother needed saving, he'd save his brother, because that's what brothers do.

Gerry told Johnny: I'm sorry, I miss you, but I know it can't be you, because we only ever talk about you in the past tense any more.

Did they talk about Gerry in the past tense, too?

> The barn owl still shrieks.
> Perhaps Gerry is a tawny, after all.
> Not shrieking, but hooting.
> Who? Who? Who?

'I'm tired, Gerry,' Johnny said, and suddenly the rain touched him.

He'd become not a man, but a boy, with wet hair and scraped knees, and though Gerry said lie down, then, lie here next to me, Johnny was already up on his feet again, splashing about.

> Humans love
> to be lost.

Johnny wanted to climb the alder, to take the boats out on the lake, to read one of their books, to play badger and owl like they used to.

There'll be time for that, Johnny, Gerry wanted to say. But Johnny was insistent, so Gerry made an effort to sit up.

It took a while. His body didn't work like it used to. He slid around in the mud. By the time Gerry was halfway up, his brother had transformed again.

White shirt became white ruff. Black shoes became black paws.

The fox's eyes shine
like coins found.

The fox, which had been nuzzling Gerry's glasses, now stared at him. Gerry understood something in the fox's eyes. Something reassuring. Something calm.

Have you seen my son? Gerry wanted to ask the fox, whose fur was slicked down by the rain. Whose ears twitched, whose eyes glowed. Is he OK?

But for all this water, Gerry's mouth was impossibly dry. So he nodded, instead, and pointed to the discarded phone.

The fox seemed to understand. Then it was gone. And Gerry, lying in his puddle, melted back into the earth.

thirty-nine

'Fox?' shouted Jack, crashing out of a bush, wiping dirty hands on the front of a sweat-smeared T-shirt. 'Fox!'

He'd never learned the fox's name. He'd never asked if the fox even had a name, if that was something animals even do.

Vulpes vulpes, he could imagine his dad saying.

Bloody typical. His mum, tutting. *How could you not ask your friend's name?*

Urgh, his sister might add, rolling her eyes. *Why do humans feel the need to anthropomorphise everything?*

Jack called for the fox because he was afraid to call for his father. Jack called for the fox because he was afraid he wouldn't find his father without the fox. How had he let things get to this point? Why hadn't he called the police, immediately, when his dad had disappeared? Regardless, Jack knew that the problems went back much further than today. He imagined his mother, staring out of a kitchen window, deciding to leave. He remembered himself, sitting at a glass-topped table in a glass-fronted office, ignoring the world behind him. His eyes drawn by bright lights, everything else in the rear-view mirror. Jack swore, loudly, kicked a root which put up more resistance than expected. He swore again, grabbed his toes. He was heading, ostensibly, in the direction of Mole End. But he'd already forgotten where that direction might be. He remembered this being a ten-minute walk as a kid, but that kid had turned into an adult, and that short walk had turned into an arduous trek. Jack didn't want to admit that he was still lost. He didn't want to admit that he was just as directionless as Charlotte seemed to think.

'Where are you?' he said, quietly, as he stood in a clearing and stared up into the canopy, not sure who he was speaking to, this time.

The answer came quickly, in the form of a precise, bracing sensation, as if his cheek had been pierced by an icicle. What was that? Another, on his right arm, then on his left. It was raining. Jack stared up into the darkening sky, closing his eyes as fat globs of rainwater struck his face. He imagined being cleansed, being purged, being melted down and made anew. He reached up a bone-white hand and wiped some thick strands of wet hair out of his eyes. He spat out the water which had pooled between his lips.

April showers, the fox might have said, in its bouncy voice, if it were still here.

'It's June,' Jack might have replied. Unless it was already July. He was losing track of the days.

The rain was getting heavier. The surrounding pines bent and crowded around like distant relatives over an open coffin. Was he the corpse? The only living thing he could make out was high above, a lone kestrel hovering like an enemy drone. Jack wiped his eyes, tried to see around him in a forest which was getting harder to see. He imagined himself as Noah, with the fox returning to help him face a great flood. Was it too late to build an ark? Perhaps he could head back to the fallen oak and climb inside, lash down the branches and batten down the hatches. Perhaps he could hide there.

'Fox!' Jack yelled, again, shielding his eyes from the rain.

The fox didn't appear. Jack almost wished he was back in the city, under the cover of concrete and glass. His body vibrated like a tuning fork as he imagined the varying timbre of bus engines and mopeds zipping by. His hand flexed instinctively at the thought of thick cotton bath towels, made warm by radiators. He really wished he was back at Mole End, lying in his childhood bed with a sleeping fox on his stomach. No weighted blanket, no lavender sleep spray, no valerian root extract could give him that level of comfort. He wished he hadn't lost the fox. He wished he'd found his father. He wished he hadn't wasted so much time.

My little old man and I fell out. How shall we bring this matter about?

Thinking of the fox had lit a kind of warmth within Jack. He tried to harness it, to imagine what the fox would tell him to do. Act on instinct. Follow his nose. Reluctantly, Jack stopped in his tracks, closed his eyes again. He stayed as still as he could, listening to the sky beat against the dry earth beneath

371

him. He breathed in, allowed the scent of the fresh-fallen rain to fill his nostrils. He let the smell wash over him, let the rain wash over him, too. He pictured his own thoughts, clear as rainwater. He opened his eyes.

Forest floor. A fox darts between trees.

It breathes so hard that its mouth foams slightly at the sides, the fox panting and exerting itself and pounding the ground beneath its paws until, somewhere far away from the roar of the human world, it skids to a stop in the dry earth.

Ears quiver. Whiskers hum.

If the fox were an owl, with one ear slightly higher up on its head than the other, it might be able to locate exactly where a sound came from, to hone in on a square inch in a million acres of woodland.

It might be able to hear a mouse turn in its sleep, deep in a tunnel beneath the ground, one of a hundred hollows, one of a thousand creatures tossing or turning, wriggling or crawling in the dry earth.

Or it might be able to pinpoint a single raindrop, glowing round and pregnant with possibility, falling like a bomb and breaking open like an egg on a flat leaf that, until moments before, had been entirely dry.

If one drop falls, another will follow. Soon, the world will be alive with the drumbeat of water, the whole woods suddenly in commotion. Earth will be upturned, bushes flattened, every burrow filled with every manner of body.

The rain will come harder, falling so fast that you'd no longer be able to tell where one raindrop ends, where another begins. A single sheet, and within that sheet, a pattern that any living creature could see.

The fox is a fox. It thrives off the thrum of the forest, and of that which cross-crosses this not-quite-wild. Roads and towns and parked cars and car parks.

A team of tree surgeons packing away their chainsaws. A map-laden rambling club picking their way through the ferns. A miserable dog walker using a stick to flick excrement off the edge of a path.

In the canopy, a squirrel, anxiously leaping from tree to tree. In the mud, a hedgehog, excitedly picking away at the emerging worms.

A father, lying at the foot of a beech tree. A son, calling out for that missing father.

Somewhere between them, the fox. It narrows its eyes, sniffs the air.

Jack was going nowhere, and the fox had somewhere it needed to be. Jack might have opened his ears, but he still refused to listen.

Over the scream of the chainsaws, the fox had picked up a trail leading from the toppling oak. A scent on the wind which had shown the fox how all of this fitted together, and how the fox could fix it.

The fox runs. It runs sniffing and sounding, moving like a beast which hunts by plucking the strings of the earth's magnetic field, seeing every noise, listening to every smell, existing within the great vibration which connects every single thing to everything else. This to that, and everything in between.

This fox was born beneath a tumbledown shed in somebody's back garden. In the city, its life was always in peril, its existence underscored by the thunder of engines and the lightning flash of man-made danger.

Out here, it can feel every stream and every road in this entire forest, can see the way that each one crosses over another, the woods itself an endless network of golden strings.

The vibrations in its whiskers are an orchestra of understanding. Behind its eyes is a symphony of everything.

Now the fox stops again, sniffs again, searches the air. It reaches for a wisp of something with its wrinkling nose, grasps it with quivering ears.

There you are. The fox swishes its tail as if winding itself up, then sets off running again.

The rain, which began as a single drop falling from a great height, has passed through a gentle patter on the surrounding leaves into a solid, pounding torrent.

The fox keeps running, through the rain and the resulting cacophony, through a thousand new threads, across a road and down into a ditch, propelled forward with an electric, euphoric motion which stops only when it sees something twinkling in the wet dirt.

A talisman, a relic of something it has seen before, two pieces of scratched glass attached to a thin wire frame.

The fox treads lightly over a carpet of wet leaves, approaching the spectacles, prodding them with its damp nose, fogging up the lenses with the proximity of its nostrils.

In the glass, its own orange face is reflected like fire. It stands for a moment, mesmerised, hearing only the whisper of the leaves overhead, the breath of the bushes around it.

Then the fox's whiskers tell it of the sound of a body, an ache. It abandons the glasses to investigate.

It finds Jack's father, lying in the mud.

It seems a strange place to rest, on one's back, on the ground, at the base of a beech tree. But then, Jack's dad doesn't seem at rest. He's making a valiant effort to sit up.

The fox can smell the man's pain. It can see something spreading inside his head. It can hear the bruises already blossoming on his injured leg.

The fox looks at the leg, then at the man to whom the leg belongs.

The fox and Jack's father share a simple understanding, contained within two sets of shining eyes. I was looking for someone, thinks the fox. I was looking for you.

The fox's intentions are implicit. I'll tell him you're here.

The father's response is clear. I'm not going anywhere.

He points to a phone, Jack's phone. The fox thanks him, takes it gently in his mouth. The fox runs.

It runs and it runs, between trees, under rain and over puddles, trees, more trees, the water running off its back.

Its face bears a heat-shedding grin. Steam escapes its black lips, more steam rising from its damp coat as it pauses, shakes off water.

The rain falls harder, then harder still. Its drumming on the surface of the previously dry earth makes the entire world pulse with possibility.

The fox's coat is soaked now. It slips and it trips and it tumbles but it never falls, smoking like a blazing firework as it runs through the forest, through the rain, back towards the road.

Is the fox smiling? Can a fox do that? If a fox can find happiness, it has done so in adventure.

And even if this is the end of their adventure, if saving Jack means once again being an outsider, an observer, the fox will fulfil that role gladly.

If the fox must once again exist on the fringes, on the common land between the real world and the unreal, between life and the other thing, then these extra days have been a gift, these present hours in the forest a treasure in themselves.

As the fox nears the road, the very earth seems to rumble beneath it. The fox runs, and it runs, and it runs, and as it does, it realises. This is it. Cold rain on my fur, warm earth beneath my paws.

I exist, thinks the running fox. I live, I've existed, and I am happy to have done so.

The fox climbs the bank, reaches the road and keeps running, straight into the path of an oncoming car.

forty

As he stood in this particular clearing in that wild, old place, as he opened his eyes, Jack didn't see what he'd expected to see. He thought he'd find woods through the trees, bracken through the woods, a hedge through the bracken. A slope which turned into a garden, which might just turn into Mole End. Or, failing that, his father, not lost or frightened after all, welcoming him back with open arms. He found neither of these things. Jack had thought that following his nose would lead him back home. Instead, it had led him further, back into the past, sniffing out a long-diluted memory of a moment which had taken place, years ago, somewhere out here.

'What is it?'

How old could Jack have been? Eight? Nine, at most. He was old enough to have become someone who didn't slept well, someone who woke so early in the morning that the sun hadn't yet come up, someone who roused himself and descended the stairs in his pyjamas while the rest of the world was still asleep. He walked carefully. His ankle had only just healed, although it seemed like something else was beginning to break. The mood at Mole End had been uneasy since his uncle had left. Jack was old enough to pick up on that, too. And yet, still young, young enough that coming downstairs in the dark and hearing a noise like that was enough to send a shiver down his spine. Jack was afraid of this forest. At this shadowy hour, it seemed greedy to get hold of him. And yet, in the purplish light of this particular morning, the woods didn't seem so scary. His father stood on the patio, fully dressed, staring at the black expanse of trees beyond the garden. He was never a good sleeper, either, and neither of them would have slept through this. From between the trees came that noise. A cry which would have been frightening, were Jack's dad not between himself and it.

'I don't know,' Jack's dad had said, pensive, but concerned. 'It sounds like it's hurt.'

It was an unexpected adventure. Jack, in his slippers, and his dad, with an improvised first-aid kit, sneaking over the lawn so as not to worry Jack's mother, plum-coloured light flooding the garden. They didn't need to say much. Their mission was enough. They descended into the undergrowth, keeping their voices low as they searched the forest for the source of the sound. They found it, in time. At first, Jack had thought it might be a rabbit, caught fast in a snare. A keening, a yelping. A flash of white at the end of a flailing tail.

The fox seemed poised in suspended animation, its forepaws

churning the earth as it tried to run, its back legs hovering in the air, one of them red raw, caught in barbed wire. The entire fence rattled and twanged with every kick of the fox's bloodied leg. When it noticed Jack and his dad creeping closer, the fox only kicked harder, began to emit a piercing cry.

'There, there,' Jack's dad said, his voice a comfort blanket. 'It's going to be alright.'

The fox seemed to believe him. It stopped kicking, went limp. It stared up at Jack's dad with eyes as golden as pouring honey, a quivering snarl fixed on its black lips. Jack was scared. His father noticed, patted him on the arm. But when Jack suggested going back to the house, letting someone better equipped sort the creature out, his dad restrained him.

'When we see an animal in pain,' he'd said, firmly, crouching beside the creature. 'We don't just look the other way.'

The fox watched Jack's dad. Seemed to consider biting him. Decided against it. Jack's dad, meanwhile, contemplated the animal, stroked its flank to soothe its stress.

'Scissors,' he said, quietly.

It was only by his outstretched palm that Jack knew he was talking to him. They'd fostered baby birds before, pink and unfortunate things which had fallen, broken, from their nests. But they'd never done anything like this. Jack put on his bravest face, nodded resolutely, took the tiny scissors meant for cutting bandages out of the first-aid bag. He crouched, too, helped hold the fence steady as his dad set to work freeing the fox, gently snipping at the fur that had caught on the wire, holding the fox in place. It wasn't easy. The fox watched them, whining every so often, kicking intermittently. Eventually, after what seemed like an age but was most likely only a moment, the scissors did their magic. The fox, freed, suddenly sprang back to life. Then it scarpered, not sticking around for a bandage, not lingering long enough for a goodbye. Jack found himself cheering. Shedding his usual reserve, his dad was cheering, too. They jumped on the spot, laughing until they cried, Jack collapsing from all the excitement in his father's arms. And as they broke apart, as Jack landed once again on the forest floor and looked towards the trees into which the fox had disappeared, he caught a glimpse of something. The fox was a mother. She slinked into a bush, followed closely by a kit, its fur still downy soft, its ears still little more than candy-floss tufts of blackish-orange fur. The little fox cub was all curiosity. It turned, looked back, locked eyes with Jack. He could picture those eyes, even now, all these years later. They burned like fire.

Jack's own eyes were burning now, his body seized by something purer than a migraine, more profound than a panic attack. It was so long since he'd cried, he wasn't sure he even could. The rain rolled off his forehead, droplets tapping a rhythm against his chin. Jack felt himself wracked by sobs, jerking movements which shook the water from his face, tears intermingled with the rain. He didn't need to realise that his dad wasn't a villain. He didn't need to know that he wasn't one, either. There were no villains in this particular piece. There was nothing so dramatic, and there never had been. Just big things that never really mattered, and little moments that hadn't seemed like moments, the first time around. Saving a fox, yes, but smaller things, too. A half-built treehouse. A rope swing tied to an old oak. Shelling peas together, or wading through a river, side by side. Time spent before sunrise. Sitting together at the dining table, reading a nature guide, or standing on a patio, staring off into the woods. Perhaps that's one thing Jack and his dad still had in common, after all these years. Waking in the small hours, sharing small talk.

Jack dropped to his knees, felt the weight of the rain pushing him to the forest floor. His breath was coming short, the canopy above obscured by a veil of pure water and things unsaid. They all welled up inside him now, those words Jack had never been able to bring to the surface, as well as the ones he'd never heard, and a feeling, one he hadn't been able to shake since he'd left Mole End, since before he'd left the city, since long before even that. A feeling of being out of his depth. Now, as if he were drowning, Jack knelt in the pooling water, pounding the wet earth with his fists. He rocked back on aching knees, kept those muddy fists clenched, pointed his exhausted eyes at the bawling rain and the moody sky above it.

'Dad?' Jack shouted, weighed down by old troubles, choking on liquid air. Over the deluge, he had to strain to be heard. 'Dad!'

It wasn't his father who answered. It was someone else, with a shriek that Jack was getting used to, though he'd never heard it this close in all the years he had lived at Mole End. It had come from behind, and so Jack turned, scraping his knees around in the mud, almost falling over when he saw it perched there above him.

'Jesus Christ,' he said.

Not quite, although there was certainly something biblical about the creature which had settled on a branch at the top of a gentle slope ahead. Its great white wings stretched out cross-like, the branch below pierced by its spear-sharp talons, like stigmata. A barn owl, up close, seems enormous. And with its sheer size, and in the light breaking through the clouds behind it, Jack saw a sheer beauty, a dazzling ripple of white and ochre which seemed to shimmer in spite of the grey fog of rain. The owl tucked its wings into its body, tilted its head only slightly as it watched Jack with ponderous, black eyes. Its face was stark white, like a ghost, like a death mask pinned to the sky. Awful, in the most ancient sense of the word. Awe-inspiring. Every bone in Jack's body rattled with the feeling that he should be afraid. And yet, he wasn't. He felt a memory of his dad between himself and it. Did you know? Three-quarters of barn owls now live in man-made nesting boxes. Did you know? Barn owls carry on their wings more sorrow than a son like him could possibly imagine. The thought occurred to Jack, in his dad's roundabout way: this must be the other quarter. This must be the wild.

'My dad,' Jack said, to the owl. 'Have you seen my dad?'

The owl made no sound. It simply blinked its heavy lids, shook a little water from its wide, white wings, then tucked them against its body. The rain continued to fall, pattering on the mud, drumming on the flat tops of the leaves overhead. Did you know? If an owl has orange eyes, it hunts in the day. This owl, with its black eyes, was out of place, out of sorts. The fox's eyes were orange, and it was still nowhere to be seen.

'A fox,' Jack said, trying his luck. 'Have you seen a fox?'

His dad had also told him that barn owls were an omen of death. That seeing a barn owl before battle used to signal casualties to come; that hearing a barn owl's shriek outside when you were on your sickbed meant you weren't long for this world. Perhaps that's why, when the owl blinked again, when it swivelled its head and raised one vast wing in the direction of the road, Jack moved like that injured fox on being freed from the barbed-wire fence. He didn't stick around to say thank you, didn't linger long enough for a goodbye. He simply swallowed, climbed to his feet, and ran.

forty-one

Summer. A woman steps out of a wonky old house and on to a patio. She sniffs the morning air, listens out for sound which doesn't come. She can't help but smirk, knowing her husband and her daughter are no doubt making themselves scarce. This is her moment, so she cocks her ear and tunes into the dawn chorus instead. Then she steps off the patio and on to the lawn. The prospect of what lies ahead courses through her veins, the whole world spread in front of her like a just-opened book. She doesn't look back. She descends, down the slope, through the hedge, into the bracken and straight into the open arms of the forest. She walks, with walking poles, with walking boots, with her sights set on whatever she's been missing. In five days' time, the sea spray will lash at her face. In ten, she'll find herself high off the ground, far from the human world. She doesn't know what awaits her, in the six thousand miles that lie ahead. She has a suspicion that what she needs won't be found wherever she's heading, but in the act of flight itself.

Hazel walked purposefully in the woods, purposefully not thinking about what she was doing, purposefully putting out of mind what she was leaving behind. And while she was only heading to the bus stop in the village, the first stop of many, it had seemed right to take a roundabout route. She paused to plunge her hands into the cold water of the old river, beneath the old oak. She paused again, to catch her breath and get her bearings, by a tall beech in a small clearing. She trudged on, towards the road, out of the forest, into the village and past her husband's old greengrocer's. It was there that she saw it, stuck to the whitewashed window. A bright green slip of paper. Hazel's mind couldn't have been further from trees, from removal notices, from things scheduled to happen in woods next to villages far from where she soon intended to be.

No sooner had Hazel finished reading the notice than she adjusted her heavy rucksack, slung her walking sticks over her arm, and continued walking, past one pub and over the bridge and towards the bus stop and the bus which would take her to the train station in the next village along. At the bus stop, the same piece of paper. The same beloved tree. No time for tears. She was still trying not to think about it by the time her train pulled into the terminus and she handed over her deposit for the van.

How did Hazel feel, as she fled north in a not-quite-Ship-of-Theseus, as she sailed like a sea eagle towards isles unknown? She was half guilt, half adrenaline. She hooted and hollered like a whooping swan the whole way up to Scotland, got rip-roaring drunk on whisky in a seaside inn. Going back to Mull would have felt too familiar, too safe for the kind of adventure she was seeking. She'd chosen one of the most remote of the Shetland Islands, had taken two days to get there by the time she was welcomed with open arms by the white-bearded birdwatcher she'd been corresponding with. The island itself, little more than a patch of impossible green balancing on an outcrop of fearsome cliffs, a lone farmhouse battered by relentless wind. The salt spray on her face had been a long time coming. In that wind, that spray, Hazel waited. Those Shetland farmers of old would smear their bait with sea-eagle fat to trick fish into going belly up. Hazel was here for the eagles, not the fish, and she wouldn't need to employ such tricks. All she needed was patience. She'd already been waiting for thirty years. What was two more days?

When she first saw them, swooping down on a flock of feasting gulls with brutal purpose, it was as if her soul had left her body. She'd been told there was a nest up the way, had only needed to keep watch on the spot in the sea where the food was. Sea eagles have eyes eight times as powerful as humans', can spot a fish from two miles away. Hazel had her old film camera, her husband's beaten-up binoculars, but she needed neither. They were enormous, as huge and historical as she'd hoped. Eagles so distinctly eagle, they looked like an artist's impression. Those fierce eyes, that proud plumage, an alarmingly yellow beak, a dreadful set of talons. They flew together, these enormous birds, swooping low over the choppy water. They danced an ancient dance. She felt, briefly, for her camera, but stopped, remembering an ibex she'd once seen, aeons ago.

Some things are better kept in your mind's eye. Up here, on the cliff, she'd waited for one sea eagle. She'd been met with two. White-tailed eagles pair-bond for life. They never leave each other's side. To see two of them felt not impossible, but inevitable.

There's a phenomenon, in the avian world, called reverse migration. Misoriented birds sometimes head north when winter comes, flying just as far as they usually would, but in the wrong direction. Hazel had sometimes felt an affinity with those birds, freezing to death in the Arctic based on choices made a thousand miles back. Setting out with noble intentions, but ending up in the exact opposite place to where you're supposed to be. In the past, she'd supposed it was an apt metaphor for her life. But maybe it was a better metaphor for ending up here, bedded down in a van that wasn't hers and wasn't Gerry's, on an inhospitable island somewhere between the Atlantic and the North Sea. For the first time since she'd left, Hazel was struggling to sleep. She turned on the small light in the dingy cabin, placed two crumpled pieces of paper side by side. On one, the next chapter of her journey. Ferry details, plucked from a folder with thousands of miles' worth of map routes. A boat over to Norway, too late for the Northern Lights, but not too late to watch whales and pick her way along fjords. Then south, into Denmark, and east, as they'd always planned, but with her own twist. Enormous things, the entire way. Wolves in Poland, brown bears in Kazakhstan. A six-thousand-mile route of her own making. She hadn't told Charlotte where she was going. She'd only told Gerry. They told each other everything.

The other piece of paper was far simpler, and bright green.

It was made up, mainly, of three words: tree removal notice. The Sellotape with which it had been stuck to the bus-stop noticeboard still clung to its corners. As she looked at it, she didn't feel guilt, nor regret, but something weightier. This was a homesickness, then a lifesickness, a longing which was ticking like a clock inside her head to the tune of a tree which would be removed, nine days after the day she'd left Mole End. Then seven. Then five. Midnight turned three into two, and the roots of the oak penetrated deeper into Hazel's consciousness. It felt like a metaphor. Everything felt like a metaphor. The sea eagles were bigger, in spirit, than anything she'd ever laid eyes on, so big that the sight of them seemed to make up for a life which she'd once hoped would be bigger, too. They were beautiful, but they weren't her family. They were everything she'd hoped for. They were also just birds.

What was going through Hazel's mind, as the ferry to Bergen left without her, as she doubled back, as her van raced south, as she reverse-migrated to the very place she was supposed to have left behind? It wasn't regret. It was fulfilment, tinged with an all-fulfilling sense of purpose. She didn't need to see more than she'd seen. But there was something else she needed to see to, before she made it home. She wasn't angry that she'd cut her journey short, nor was she angry at the prospect of driving right through the night. She was angry at whoever had decided, whoever thought they had the right, whoever could feel it was necessary to tear down the oak tree which had once meant so much to her and her family. She wouldn't start a petition, or complain to the local council. That wasn't her style. Once she was back at the oak, she'd do something dramatic. Something to save it. If she could save something, that would be enough.

Hazel returned the van. She returned to the village, by train, then bus. And though she set out walking for Mole End, back over the bridge and past the greengrocer's where the notice still hung, it was deep into the woods she went, at the precise same break in the bracken from which she'd climbed over a week before. Did she know just how dramatic things were going to get? Had she planned to end up here, instead of there, in her own home, with her own family? All Hazel knew was that she arrived at this old tree, a short distance from Mole End, as the crow flies. And though she could just as easily have carried on walking, have climbed the garden path and explained herself to her son, her husband and a no-doubt-disappointed daughter, have kicked off her affirmative action in the warmth of her own house, that same sense of purpose stopped her. She swayed in the shadow of the oak, staring upwards, feeling fixed, feeling forced.

The clearing was empty, the river eerily quiet. Fences cut through what used to be forest, lights in bedroom windows now visible through the space where the canopy had been cleared. The oak itself was barely an oak at all, any more. More a glorified trunk, a few remaining branches clinging on for dear life. Hazel inspected her surroundings. Neon cordon tape and spray-painted markings foreshadowed the brutality to come. Maybe that's what kept her. Maybe it was madness. The ancient tree had a hollow, two-thirds of the way up, above which tufts of emerald-green foliage from an opportunistic invader were sprouting from a space where branches used to be, cascading down like the wild, unruly hair of a slumbering giant. If Hazel wasn't supposed to be here, then why did she fit into the hollow like a bumblebee into a buttercup?

A short climb preceded a long afternoon, and an even longer night. What on earth was she doing? Hazel convinced herself it was resolution, not hesitation, which had led her into the tree. This resolution: the oak cannot, will not, come down. And yet, in the drey she'd made for herself in the compact confines of the tree, she second-guessed herself. Why was she stalling? Were things still alright, across the river and up the way? She supposed she could have asked, but the battery on the brick phone Charlotte had given her had dwindled days ago. Asking would betray the reality, that she'd abandoned her adventure halfway through. Who would be more disappointed, Charlotte or Gerry? She supposed she'd have to face Jack's judgement, too. The idea that any of them would be relieved to see her return was somehow even worse. Instead, she bedded down in the warm, cramped interior of their oak tree, in a sleeping bag that was even warmer, and even more cramped.

It was a fitful night's sleep, not helped by the shriek in the woods that seemed to come from everywhere, all at once, both outside the oak and within it. Hazel already knew to whom the shriek belonged. She'd found a fringed feather when she'd first climbed inside, right next to a pile of pellets, smooth and shiny and compacted from half-digested fur, gristle and bone. The barn owl. Gerry's barn owl. Hazel's guilt was twofold. She realised that she'd encroached on the owl's home, that it wouldn't return while she stayed put. And as she realised this, her suspicions were confirmed. Gerry hadn't been making things up, all those months ago, when he'd wandered off into the night and told her he was at this very oak, with this very owl. Why hadn't she listened, rather than flying off the handle? Still, her purpose only grew stronger. She was not just saving the oak for Gerry, for all of them, but for the owl, too. If she left, if she allowed the barn owl to return to its home, she knew they'd arrive with their chainsaws the following day. Then there'd be no oak for anyone. Not Hazel. Not Gerry. Not the owl.

She told herself this was her reason for staying, when she didn't leave the oak that night. She told herself the same thing the next morning, when she assessed her situation in the harsh light of day. They arrived early, with their chainsaws, exactly when the notice had said they would. Hazel stayed inside the great tree, unsure and unmoving, seized up like a surprised shrew.

'Stop!' she shouted, in her most commanding voice.

The sound of bewildered men, with churning saws, stopping. The trickle of the river behind them. Hazel liked the idea that the hollow might look like the mouth of a monster, and that the ancient oak might seem to be talking. It almost made her smile, that the booming voice they might expect from an ancient tree-beast was, instead, hers. It had been years since she'd used the same voice to demand they call off a fox hunt, or wielded it as a peaceful weapon of protest through the barrel of a speakerphone.

'Leave the tree alone,' she said.

The tree surgeons didn't know what to do. They exchanged baffled glances.

'This tree is dead,' they said. 'When it falls down, which it will, it might fall on those houses.'

Hazel paused, considered the houses which had sprung up behind her oak in the years since they'd hung the rope swing. 'The tree was here first,' she said.

'I'm sure it was,' said the team leader. 'But it's coming down, with or without us.'

The impasse that followed lasted all day. She told the tree surgeons that nothing deserved to be flattened, just because it wasn't the same as it had been. They told her that dead oaks don't come back to life just because madwomen climb inside them. Hazel ate cold baked beans from her remaining couple of tins, wondered how long one could go without washing until you stunk yourself out of such a confined space. It wasn't like the movies, where tree-huggers are seen off by gun-toting sheriffs bribed by logging companies. The council didn't have the budget for round-the-clock surveillance. At the end of the workday, the workmen left, and Hazel could finally relieve herself in the river. There was a bathroom, up there, at Mole End. She was struggling to remember the point to all this. In the encroaching darkness, she imagined climbing the hill, then climbing into her own bed. She envisaged Jack, prowling the patio like a hungry fox, eyes glowing through a cloud of smoke from that stupid electronic cigarette. Or, worse, Gerry. His face looming accusingly, ghostly as a barn owl, in the window of their bedroom upstairs. I'll be home soon, Gerry. I'm closer than you think.

On Hazel's second night in the oak, she finally began to waver. The liberation of having no phone battery was now replaced with panic. The panic that Charlotte couldn't reach her. The panic that she wouldn't know what was happening with Gerry. What was she doing? Gerry was her person. And yet here she was, leaving him behind, pretending to do something important, play-acting at big things in a space far too small for her. Being cut off from Mole End, from her family, gave the house a gravitational pull. When Hazel finally slept, she dreamed of that mossy brick, that weathered white clapboard. The lattice windows, and the beautiful creatures who'd made their nest behind them. By the time she woke, her mind had been made up for her.

The men with the chainsaws returned early the next day. Hazel shouted herself hoarse, but her heart was no longer in it.

'If I leave, will you just chop it down?' she asked, deflated, from the confines of her oak-hole.

'If we say no,' the tree surgeons shouted back. 'Will you leave?'

The question had been a formality. She stayed put for an hour or two, out of a sense of duty. Then she shook her head and gathered her things. Her thoughts, too, were gathering at pace, and they'd settled on something like this. Not everything is a metaphor. Not everything has to stay the same. If things didn't end, there'd be no enjoyment in them. If rotten oaks were never pulled down, no new trees could be planted in their place. The owl would find a new home. And Hazel would make a new home out of the home she had, up there, at the top of that hill.

And so it was that, ten days after she'd stepped off the lawn of Mole End and into her adventure, Hazel climbed out of a hollow in the side of a tree, after making a decision which should have been difficult but ended up being easy. She hugged the bewildered tree surgeons goodbye, made her way back towards that very same lawn. Above her, around her, thick curtains of rain. Somewhere behind her, the sound of chainsaws. And ahead, at the top of a hill which felt like it stretched on for six thousand miles, the only place she wanted to be.

forty-two

Anyone who saw Jack Penwick stumble from the forest at the side of the road might have assumed he'd been lost in the wild for weeks. His skin was dirt-strewn and dust-caked, all manner of things caught up in his knotted hair, filthy clothes hanging off his frame. He'd been running, which, on slippery and uneven terrain, had proved an effort. When he reached the road, he stopped running, because he'd already seen the fox, and he'd already pieced together what had happened. It took all of his strength to keep moving, to climb the bank and emerge, his eyes wild and wide, his wet hair sprouting outwards. The road had become a flat, slick mirror. Two foxes, one a reflection, neither moving. Jack stepped out, shielding his eyes, squinting, then falling to his bare knees on the hard tarmac. The fox hardly noticed. With each laboured inhalation, its chest barely rose, its breath rasping and ragged. When it saw Jack, it didn't seem to recognise him. Its eyes flickered this way and that, agitated and alarmed, never blinking.

'I've been looking for you,' said Jack, his voice cracking. 'Don't worry,' he said, soothing the frightened animal. 'I'm here now.'

The fox didn't reply. It only whimpered a little, the sort of sound one might expect a fox to make. Jack looked up the empty road, down the road again, if only to avoid looking at the fox. The car which had done this was long gone. Jack could feel water trickling out of his hair, down his face, around eyes which were beginning to sting. He closed them, listened to the rain, tried to imagine he was anywhere but here. Then he forced himself to look down. He placed one hand on the fox's sodden chest, another, gently, beneath its head. The fox flinched at his touch, whined again. Its eyes went to the woods, as if planning to run. It wouldn't get very far. Though its coat was slicked down by the rain, the most prominent colour on the white bib of fur beneath the fox's mouth was a vivid red. Its once-proud, long limbs were filthy and twisted at unnatural angles, its head lolling slightly even as it eyed its escape routes. There was more blood, infusing the rain on the tarmac. Jack used to be squeamish. Now, when he removed his trembling hand from the fox's chest, he couldn't see the colour of his own skin.

'I could have—' Jack began. 'I should have—'

The fox keened in pain, looked up at Jack. He'd have recognised those flaming eyes anywhere. But the fox seemed to be searching for something it couldn't find in Jack's face. Its eyes went back to the woods, to the road, to something else lying upon it. Jack sniffed, wiped his wet cheeks, followed the fox's gaze. On the tarmac, there, a phone with a smashed screen, pooling with rainwater. The fox must have dropped it as it was hit.

'My phone,' Jack said, his voice sounding as if it had come from someone else.

The fox looked up at him again, whined, looked into the woods on the other side of the road.

'My dad?'

The fox made another, more desperate sound.

'He's hurt?' Jack said, peering through the trees, barely processing the information. He'd reverted to a child-like state, snotty-nosed and trembling-lipped. 'You're hurt.'

The fox trembled. It was frightened, but it didn't try to flee. It let Jack hold it. Beneath his palm, the fox's chest was a delicate thing, like a bird's, the heartbeat within sluggish. Jack rubbed his eyes with a bloody hand before placing it back on the fox's chest, counting out the rhythm.

'We'll find a vet,' he said, nodding to himself. 'We'll get you to . . .' Jack peered frantically down the road again. 'An animal hospital.'

Even as Jack said it, he knew there was nowhere to go, no one to flag down. Who'd stop in the pouring rain to help a feral man and a dying fox? Jack looked desperately in either direction, saw nothing but empty road, empty forest, and the rain in between. If only he hadn't isolated himself. If only there were people out here. Jack shook his head, bit into his knuckle to stop himself screaming. Fox blood ran down his chin and into his matted beard.

'This is all my fault,' Jack said. He was crying hard now, so hard he was struggling to get the words out.

The fox whined, a little quieter than before.

'Speak,' Jack said, in a whisper at first. 'Speak. You can speak. I know you can. Please.'

He was sobbing. The fox, meanwhile, had stopped whining altogether. The rain didn't relent, beating the road even harder than before.

'I'm not leaving you here,' Jack said, choking, drowning.

Lone foxes die alone, he thought. He pictured the common, the clearing, everything in between. He wished he'd decided to stay in the forest for ever. He wished he'd never come to the woods in the first place. He wished things had gone differently.

'Goodbyes always come too early . . .' Jack said, willing the fox to continue for him.

The fox wasn't looking at Jack. It stared into the trees, let out a few ragged breaths. It turned back to Jack, but showed no sign of recognition. It stopped wriggling, lay still. The fire in its eyes dwindled, then, eventually, went out. Its eyes closed, but the panting resumed, so Jack stroked the fox's fur until it calmed, until its frail chest stopped rising and falling. It kicked its back legs a few times, as if running off somewhere. Then it settled and stopped moving entirely, lying prone in Jack's arms. Jack knelt in the rain, crying, speaking quietly, though the sound of the downfall drowned out his words. There was no one around to hear him. The creature in his arms was just another fox, on another road.

forty-three

As he lay on the forest floor, the weight of the rainstorm
pressing him, like a fossil, into the earth, Gerry wondered
when he'd been happiest.

He considered his childhood, with Johnny, between
the lake and the alder and the great, wide world.
But how could he have been happiest as a child,
when he didn't have his children?

How could he have been happy, before Hazel?

> You're not in Alderney.
> You're not at the alder.
> Hazel, where were you?

Gerry knew that he'd have found her at the oak, if he'd managed to find the oak.

He knew, also, that oaks die, just as surely as acorns give birth to new life. He knew that the world was arranged in concentric circles, like the cross-section of a tree. That life ends as often as it begins.

If the oak was dead, he wouldn't stop the men with their chainsaws from destroying it. He'd simply rescue his wife and the owl from their nest, and fly them far away.

> Too-whit, too-whoo,
> that's what I'll do.

Gerry closed his eyes, breathed in deeply, and thought of the fox who'd watched him for a while.

He thought of the owl, of its all-suffering shriek and its all-seeing eyes, and he knew a simple fact. The oak was dead. Long live the owl, elsewhere.

Gerry made peace with this fact, just as he made peace with his resting place, a deepening puddle on the floor of his favourite forest.

> A squirrel watches Gerry
> from a branch.
> *Hello*, it says.

Have you lost your way?

Gerry might have been drowning, but he'd had enough of being scared.

'Washed up.' That's how Johnny had described himself. Now Gerry felt washed up, too, lying drenched on his back, staring up at the sky.

The gurgling stream at the base of this beech had fast turned into a torrent. Now Gerry was marooned in the flood.

Soaked in cold water. The rising tide lapped at him, lathered his hair and washed his trousers.

> A crack, at first,
> which became a rift,
> which became an ocean.
> Gerry, drowning in it. His son
> on the shore, too far away
> to see him wave.

In moments like this, Gerry's sense of self returned with a screech.

In moments like this, this sense of Gerry fell with a splash from the canopy, or surfaced from the bottom of the lake, or crawled out of the depths of the puddle, and forced its way back into his skull.

405

His memories were as clear as aquarium glass. Cold water
will do that to you. The shock of a fall, of falling rain, might
jolt you back into yourself.

> Gerry
> and Jack
> wading in a river.

In moments like this, his mind would say: here's what you've
been missing. Or, how could you have missed this?

A gap-toothed boy in waders. Grazed knees dangling from a
greengrocer's countertop.

> Gerry
> and Jack
> shelling peas.

What would Gerry say to his son, if his son were here,
standing over his puddle?

Gerry could say: I'm sorry. For drifting. For ending up just as
distant as my own father had been. For turning you into your
uncle. For hurting you, because I could never help him.

Or, Gerry could say nothing. He could, simply, give his son
a hug.

Gerry
and Jack
rescuing a fox.

Gerry had once hoped his son might inherit the
greengrocer's, but his son had laughed at the idea.
His son had moved away, instead.

Gerry and his son, never to fish together, never to forage
together, never to track murmurations or constellations over
flasks of steaming tea. Never then, and never again.

Would his daughter like to be a grocer? He knew, even when
she helped him in the garden, that Charlotte was only being
kind. Behind those hazel eyes, she had her mother's spirit.

There were worlds within Charlotte, and she couldn't see
them yet. There was so much she needed to see, and he was
only holding her back.

Foxes are born
with blue eyes.
In a matter of time,
they'll be set ablaze.

A shift in the clouds. A shock of cold water. His daughter,
splashing him from a paddling pool.

His newborn son! A bolt from the blue, a spark of lightning across a clear, unclouded sky.

Eyes like a baby animal's, like those of a magpie chick or a fox cub. Looking into those eyes was like stepping through a doorway, into ice-cold air.

Nothing behind him matters.
His world begins anew.

Gerry thought of Johnny, sitting on the end of his nephew's bed, reading from a children's book.

He thought of Johnny, dangling from the alder, playing an animal from that same story. The character, the scene, a whole lifetime before.

Even drenched, even hopeless, the thought brought a smile to Gerry's face. A connection with his brother, built on talking animals.

A connection with his son, built on talking about them.

Humans are
palimpsest people.
Each generation
writing all over
the next one.

Gerry thought: it all repeats itself, it all happens, again and again. And the thought wasn't dreary, but uplifting.

Like concentric circles. Like the blinding fractures in the canopy above him. Like the sun existing, always, above the rain.

Like a fallen tree, which becomes not a dead thing but a cradle of new life, a rotting reservoir of biodiversity, a fallen miracle of microclimates.

A legacy made up of life itself.

Isn't the world wonderful?
Isn't it something?

What would Gerry say to the world, if this was it? What would he say, after all?

He'd say: thanks for having me. He'd say: I hope
I left things better rather than worse. I wish I'd patched things up with my son, seen my daughter thrive like
I know she will.

I wish I'd sold the greengrocer's, finished building the treehouse in the garden, but then, those things never mattered in the first place. Hazel, their life, their little comedies. That's what mattered.

What would he say to Hazel? More or less the same. Thanks for having me. I hope it was as wonderful for you, too. I wouldn't change a minute.

I'll never forget how much I've loved you, thought Gerry, as he lay on the forest floor, forgetting everything else for a moment but Hazel.

> Looking for something?
> Yes. For you.

Gerry stared up at the tree above him as the rain pooled below, and let out a sigh.

He saw things. Patterns, where the forest met the air. Tendrils of white sky split the trees above, like a delta at the mouth of a mighty river, flowing into the ocean.

Things in the trees themselves. People, animals. Boundaries were blurred. And whoever Gerry saw in the trees, be it his son or his brother, his daughter or his wife, the fox or the owl, he thought the same thing.

> I'm here, he thinks.
> I'll catch you if you fall.

forty-four

A woman steps out of a tree and into a forest, then out of a forest and on to a lawn. The slope of the garden has turned the threshold of the woods into a gutter. The woman stands ankle-deep in the sluice of it, staring up at her old house ahead, trying to remember what it was like to lower oneself into a warm bath and watch the steam on the still surface of the water evaporate with one's worries. It has been a strange couple of weeks. Things will undoubtedly get stranger. The haze of a long-abandoned bonfire creeps over the lawn like dry ice. At the edge of the garden, buttercups poke through the grass like city lights on a distant hill. There is a spiderweb between two branches, the raindrops suspended within it sparkling like beads of glass.

The woman shakes some of the rain off of her wiry hair, wipes some of the rain out of her weary eyes. Then she takes a tentative step on to the slippery grass, followed by another, then another. She passes a disused shed, a set of patio furniture, the rotting husk of a half-built treehouse. Halfway up the hill, she stops and observes a lawn which, beneath the rain, has turned black. A large chunk of the grass has been burnt away, this dark patch reduced to a tar-like sludge by the rain. The woman knows she should worry but, just for now, she holds the worry at arm's length. She remains rooted, only because she wants to take one last look at the sky. Gazing upwards, she almost expects a break in the clouds, an optimistic rift of bright blue. There is no such thing. The sky is just as grey, and the rain falls just as hard. Perhaps the break in the clouds is inside, then. The woman thinks of nothing but the clean rainwater washing over her face. Then she thinks of something else. Sea spray. And, above it, sea eagles, wheeling about behind the clouds.

'Mum,' Charlotte says, from the back door, worlds within her voice.

They look at each other. Hazel soaking wet, Charlotte's eyes wide as ever. Hazel crosses the patio, and the rain collecting in the creases of her raincoat doesn't matter to Charlotte, who crushes her mother in a hug which must soak through the warm, clean jumper she's wearing. It's one of Gerry's. Hazel doesn't ask after her husband, yet, nor her son. There will be time.

forty-five

Jack Penwick was a man who took things at face value. On the face of it, not everything was as it had seemed. As he descended the melting escarpment, striking a path back through the dense foliage in pursuit of his missing father, he felt weighed down. Not just by his lank hair and his sodden rucksack, but by revelations which thundered through his brain like a stampede of furry bodies rolling over one another, hooves and claws and paw pads beating out a rhythm inside his head. If foxes were broadly nocturnal, why had his fox only ever woken in the morning and slept at night? Despite their endless conversations, Jack couldn't actually picture how it had formed words, couldn't see its lips moving in his mind's eye. Working things out was Jack's forte. Wasn't it? So if it was, why did nothing make sense?

Jack's heart hurt, his head ached, his ears filled with a

413

scraping sound not dissimilar to that of an old radio, tuning out. What lay ahead of Jack Penwick? In the immediate future, some aggressive-looking brambles that he'd have to tackle as best he could. Beyond that, he had no idea. He couldn't fathom a five-year plan, didn't want to imagine a grand strategy or a great success lurking somewhere beyond these woods. He didn't want to imagine not having a fox to guide him. But animals don't define themselves by what they do for a living. They live by what they eat and where they sleep and the sounds they make after another day when they didn't die, when they had the pure fortune to be alive and to be free in this forest and on this earth. An oak tree wouldn't stoop just because it was condemned. If a fox was doomed, its eyes would blaze until the very last moment.

Something else which didn't make sense. Or, in the greater scheme of things, probably did. Jack's sister was calling. Beneath the raindrops quivering on its surface, beneath the spiderweb of cracks across its screen, his phone was lighting up, vibrating. Jack wiped the rain away and wondered what he might say to Charlotte. What he might ask. No one asks me anything, she'd say, when he eventually did. Then she'd tell him about the money she'd put aside for university, about the girlfriend she hadn't yet introduced to Mum and Dad, about the weight of the guilt which accompanied her desperation to start a new adventure in the city, not to follow in her big brother's footsteps but forge her own path. About the fact that staying put had started to feel like struggling to breathe. The old Jack had thought Charlotte was a coward, for not leaving. Now he knew that not leaving was the bravest thing of all.

'You go,' Jack would say, though he didn't know it yet. 'I'll stay.'

And she might say: about bloody time. Or she might say: I know that you long for a simpler life. There's an empty green-grocer's in the village. You're good at doing accounts. And even if you couldn't always see the magic in Mole End, perhaps you could weave your own there. In a kitchen, among a cluster of dining tables, within a warm place where you can bring people together. What she wouldn't say is: thank you, it means the world to me. She wouldn't need to. They'd both know.

For now, Jack ignored the call, was left with his own frag-mented reflection in the cracked black screen of the phone. His hair was a tangled mess, his beard getting out of hand. His cheeks were smeared with fox blood. No time to think about that. Up ahead was a tall tree, a twisted tree, the same one he'd climbed earlier that day. Jack was still going in circles. He shook his head, raindrops spraying in all directions. He closed his eyes, tried to follow his nose. He was distracted, by a cough. There was a man, lying in the mud. A man who happened to be his father.

Gerry lay a few paces away in the middle of a small clearing, staring up into the sky as if salvation might come from above. Then he turned, with difficulty, and saw his son. He barely seemed surprised. Jack had a thousand things he wanted to say. After all, the language of the woods, of foxes and foraging, of trees and those that dwell within them, was the language of his father, a language he finally felt able to speak. But all of that felt insignificant, right now. Something to be buried, then revisited, when the rain wasn't so heavy and things didn't feel so hard. Instead, Jack crouched in the muddy water, touched Gerry gently on his soaking-wet shoulder.

'Dad.'

Gerry squinted at him. 'I hoped you'd come.'

Jack looked down at his dad's leg, a glimpse of bruised and swelling ankle above his hiking sock. 'You're hurt?'

'I'm OK,' Gerry said, as if he'd been asked a different question. 'How are you?'

'I think I'm better now,' Jack said, as if he'd been asked something else, too. 'Can you stand?'

'I think so.'

A pause.

'I think we should go home,' Jack said.

'I think so, too.'

Gerry seemed pleased, if not a little cold. He was lying in at least an inch of rainwater. Jack knelt there beside him, two men still unable to hold a coherent conversation. Perhaps they didn't need to. Perhaps what needed to be said was said by the leaves in the trees and the rain on the puddles. They listened to these sounds in silence, until Gerry eventually spoke again.

'I'm sorry,' he said.

'No,' said Jack. 'I'm sorry'

'No,' said Gerry. Then he gave up, smiled. 'I know.'

Gerry moved slowly upwards, reaching for his son. But just as Jack moved to put his arms around his father, Gerry shrank back from Jack's chest.

'Jack,' he said, after a while. 'Why are you carrying a dead fox?'

Jack looked down. Admittedly, it must have been a strange

sight. The rucksack which had been slung over his shoulders was now strapped to his front, the fox tucked tightly within it. Its bright orange head poked out from between the zips, its eyes gently closed and its black lips half smiling as if it were simply asleep. He'd promised the fox that he wouldn't leave it. And if he buried the fox at Mole End, it would mean that he never would, that there'd always be some reminder of what they'd shared out here, in the real world. Jack could almost imagine, in a clearing in the woods on the other side of the road, their adventure continuing. A man and a fox would always be climbing on the log stacks, or chasing each other between the trees, or lying on their backs in this very clearing, staring up at the canopy.

'It's a long story,' Jack said. 'I'll tell you when we're home.'

This time, they didn't try to hug. Gerry allowed Jack to hook one arm under his shoulder, to heave him out of the mud and to his feet. He cried out in pain as he put a little weight on his right foot, but he didn't fall. Jack caught him, then secured his arm around his dad's back so that he was shouldering most of the burden. Jack was worried about the journey ahead, but he tried not to show it. He mustered all of his old practicality, focused only on the journey itself. They turned with some difficulty, hobbling out of the clearing, struggling up the escarpment, finally rejoining the road. It was only when they were there, standing on the wet tarmac, that they paused for breath. Jack stared up the slick slope of the road and into the distance, knowing what he'd find at the end of it. Mole End. Beyond that, a far smaller, infinitely more massive life.

Jack's dad leaned into him. Jack smiled slightly, taking his weight. Though they were preparing for a long climb, in the driving rain, with only three legs between them, he knew they would manage it. For the first time in a long time, his dad had remembered his name.

If you have lived, if you have truly existed, I hope you'll be happy to have done so.
The barn owl thinks this, as it perches above a river where an oak once stood,
staring down from up on high at a clearing where a sapling now grows.
The owl sees two women swim in the cold water, and, downstream,
two men, quietly fishing. As it watches, the owl thinks:
they might call me an omen of death.
But I would roll my eyes,
at that, and say:
not today.

acknowledgements

It's a bit unfair that only one name ends up on the cover, because it takes so many people to make a book. Thanks, as ever, to my wily fox of an agent, Millie Hoskins, for always being by my side and guiding my way. And to my wise owl of an editor, Frankie Edwards, who was so instrumental to this novel becoming what it became, that it would be unrecognisable without her.

To my dream team: Patrick Insole, Jessie Goetzinger-Hall, Alara Delfosse, Elise Jackson and Oliver Martin at Headline, and Amy Mitchell and Alex Stephens at United Agents. Whether it's screaming eggs or talking foxes, no idea is too weird for you to run with. And to everyone who helped make *Isaac and the Egg* a success – booksellers, book bloggers and fellow authors and readers who've championed it far and wide – thank you. This book, and whatever comes next, wouldn't exist without you.

I'm thankful that my relationship with my parents is a little less complicated than Jack's. Thank you to my dad for always believing that I could build a life out of doing something I love, and to my mum for giving me the tools with which to do so – and for being such a huge part of turning this particular novel into what it is now. Thanks also to my second family, Lindy and Jeremy Griffith, for your early reading, love and support. Every single one of the fox's mannerisms came from my dog, Gromit. If you can rescue a silly little animal like him, don't hesitate to do it. As for my wife, Nina: you've supported me like no one else, read a hundred versions of this book, and held my hand through all the especially thorny patches. Thank you will never be enough.

Like Jack, I had to inhabit a few different worlds to bring this story to life. One of those was the idealised British countryside of so many childhood books – including, but not limited to, Roald Dahl's *Fantastic Mr Fox*, Alison Uttley's *Little Grey Rabbit*, Kenneth Grahame's *The Wind in the Willows*, Arthur Ransome's *Swallows and Amazons*, Clive King's *Stig of the Dump*, Jill Barklem's *Tales of Brambly Hedge*, Colin Dann's *The Animals of Farthing Wood*, as well as Hugh Lofting's Doctor Dolittle books, the Redwall series by Brian Jacques and – of course – the works of Beatrix Potter and A. A. Milne.

But like Jack, I needed to live in the real world, too. To make his time in the wild believable, as well as to suitably stuff Gerry with knowledge of the natural world, I was lucky to have help from people a lot smarter than me. For research, I read *The Fox Book*, *The Owl Book* and *The Red Squirrel Book* by Jane Russ, *The Complete Fox* by Les Stocker, *The Secret Life of the Owl* by John

Lewis-Stempel, James Lowen's *RSPB Spotlight* on hedgehogs, *The RSPB Pocket Guide to British Birds* by Simon Harrap and a battered old *Reader's Digest* guide to the animals of Britain. I learned so much from both *Foxes Unearthed* and *Losing Eden* by Lucy Jones, and found endless inspiration in the nature writing of Robert Macfarlane and Helen McDonald. Richard Powers's *The Overstory* taught me all about trees and the habitats they create when they die, and it was from Danusha Laméris's poem 'Feeding the Worms' that I learned that earthworms have taste buds on every inch of their bodies.

For more specific research, I was able to lean on a vast number of helpful resources available online, for free. The London Wildlife Trust and the Natural History Museum taught me about the city as its own kind of wild; the Woodland Trust provided crucial forest intel; and I don't need to tell you what I learned from Princeton University's 'Outdoor Action Guide to Animal Tracking'. Sophie Yeo's wonderful *Inkcap* newsletter taught me all about wild boars in the Forest of Dean, and I could envisage Hazel's sea eagle encounter thanks to one episode of the BBC's *Deadly 60*. Isn't the internet great?

Weirdly, the thing with the fox on the common actually happened to me – although, in my case, the fox didn't speak. That strange experience was the spark for this book, so I'd like to thank The Fox Project for their tireless efforts in rescuing and rehabilitating foxes like that one, and to founder Trevor Williams for generously giving his time to talk to me about the plight and peculiarities of the fox, both in London and beyond. You can find out more about the charity's amazing work, and donate, at foxproject.org.uk.

The other world I needed to explore for this book was Gerry's. I knew from the start that I didn't want to diagnose Gerry with a specific condition on the page, both for the story's sake and because I'm far from an expert in anything. But while keeping several possibilities open, I also wanted to give dementia and Alzheimer's the due diligence they deserve. As with my nature research, I was fortunate to receive plenty of help from experts in their field. And, as with my nature research, any errors I've made – or instances where fiction has trumped fact – are purely my own.

The writer and campaigner Wendy Mitchell is a truly inspirational figure. I learned so much from her book *What I Wish People Knew about Dementia*, and from her interview on my friend Pandora Sykes's *Doing It Right* podcast. Other resources which proved invaluable were Age UK's pamphlets on living with dementia, the Alzheimer's Society's 'Dementia Friendly Media and Broadcast Guide', and Marion Renault's article in the *New Yorker*, 'A French Village's Radical Vision of a Good Life with Alzheimer's'.

Most of all, I can't thank Dementia UK enough for taking the time to speak to me and for providing me with vital advice – both on how to depict a diagnosis like Gerry's properly and positively, and on some of the finer medical points of how his condition might manifest on a day-to-day basis. You can learn more about the important work they do at dementiauk.org, and if you're looking for personal advice or specialised support regarding dementia or Alzheimer's, you can call their free helpline on 0800 888 6678.